Messy Little Christmas

Messy Little Christmas

SOFIE DAVES

This is a work of fiction. Names, characters, organizations, places, events, and incidents are either products of the author's imagination or are used fictitiously. Any resemblance to actual persons, living or dead, or actual events is purely coincidental.

Text copyright © 2024 Sofie Daves

All rights reserved.

No part of this publication may be reproduced, stored in a retrieval system, or transmitted in any form or by any means, electronic, mechanical, photocopying, recording or otherwise without the written permission of the publisher and/or author.

ISBN-13: 9798301180583 (paperback)

Cover design by: Sofie Daves

www.SofieDaves.com

Printed in the United States of America

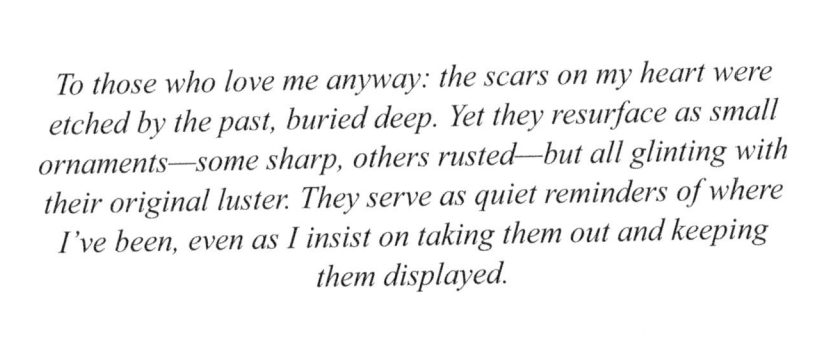

To those who love me anyway: the scars on my heart were etched by the past, buried deep. Yet they resurface as small ornaments—some sharp, others rusted—but all glinting with their original luster. They serve as quiet reminders of where I've been, even as I insist on taking them out and keeping them displayed.

Table of Contents

Chapter 1: Lena.. 1
Chapter 2: Tyler... 24
Chapter 3: Lena.. 50
Chapter 4: Tyler... 71
Chapter 5: Lena.. 86
Chapter 6: Tyler... 104
Chapter 7: Lena.. 119
Chapter 8: Tyler... 137
Chapter 9: Lena.. 150
Chapter 10: Tyler... 169
Chapter 11: Lena.. 189
Chapter 12: Tyler... 212
Chapter 13: Lena.. 231
Chapter 15: Lena.. 265
Chapter 16: Tyler... 280
Chapter 17: Lena.. 295
Chapter 18: Tyler... 314
Chapter 19: Tyler... 328

Chapter 20: Lena 344
About the Author 371
Books By Sofie Daves 373

Chapter 1: Lena

The second I stepped into the church, it was like all the oxygen had been sucked out of the room.

Every head turned, and boom, there it was—that unmistakable "Oh my God, she actually showed up" energy hanging in the air.

My skin prickled like someone had cranked up the judgment thermostat, and I could practically hear the collective thought bubble above their heads: *Here she comes—Miss Walking Disaster.*

To be fair, they weren't wrong.

I mean, it wasn't every day someone ran out on a wedding and then strutted into church like it was no big deal, wearing a green velvet dress that practically screamed, "Yes, I have flaws, but at least I look amazing in them!"

After all, my dress *was* a masterpiece, hugging every curve just right, with a neckline that flirted without being all "Look at me, sinners." The soft fabric swished around my legs as I started walking down the aisle, each step daring someone to say something.

Honestly, I thought it struck a tasteful balance between *sassy but repentant* and *don't hate me because I'm fabulous*.

Whether the congregation would agree, well, that was another story.

The scent of Pine-Sol and incense wafted through the air. Usually comforting, but today? It just reminded me of how far I'd fallen. Like, *hey Lena, remember when you weren't the poster child for bridal meltdowns?*

Still, I kept my chin high. If I'd learned one thing from this whole mess, it was that you shouldn't let whispers and side-eyes get under your skin. Besides, if I was going to be a hot topic, I might as well give them something worth talking about.

The church looked like Christmas threw up—but in the best way. Fresh pine wreaths at the end of every pew, towering columns decked out with white lilies, and poinsettias everywhere. It was like stepping into a festive explosion of holiday cheer. Festive, sure, but not nearly enough to distract me from the fact that every single person here had an opinion about me, and none of them were good.

I squared my shoulders, doing my best impression of someone who totally wasn't about to burst into flames under the weight of all that judgment. *Let them judge*, I told myself. *They can clutch their pearls and whisper all they want—I'm not living my life for them.*

With a deep breath, I stepped into the nave and headed down the center aisle. Dozens of eyes bore into me, their collective disapproval practically palpable. If stares could poke, I'd look like a pincushion.

Somewhere nearby, carolers were rehearsing, their harmonies as cheerful as a Hallmark movie. Too bad it couldn't drown out the rustle of stiff shirts and classy dresses as people leaned in to whisper to each other.

Oh, I knew exactly what they were whispering.

This moment, my first time back in this church, had haunted me for five weeks. Ever since I bolted from my wedding like a runaway train draped in chiffon and poor life choices.

Now that I was back here? Yep, it was just as awful as I'd pictured—like walking into the opening scene of a cringe-inducing soap opera where I was cast as the scandalized lead.

But, if people were going to gossip, I might as well give them a performance worth their subscription to <u>Small-Town Drama Weekly</u>.

I glanced at the pew to my right and locked eyes with Auntie Tessa.

Oh, Auntie Tessa.

She was decked out in full "Ho, Ho, Holy Moly That's A Lot" mode. A red, green, and white patchwork dress, tiny red ornament earrings, and a flashing necklace of multi-colored mini lights that blinked like she was an actual Christmas tree. Her outfit screamed "tis the season!" But her face? It whispered, "You're a colossal disappointment."

The tight lines around her eyes and the downturn of her lips could cut glass. The fake smile she wore was a masterpiece, one I knew all too well—my own "everything's fine" grin had gotten plenty of use over the past five weeks. But Auntie Tessa? She was an Olympic-level judger.

And, she wasn't alone.

By the looks on the other faces scattered throughout the room, my runaway bride moment was still fresh enough to be trending on the town's social grapevine. They were internally gasping in shock and tut-tutting about how I'd brought shame to...what? The institution of matrimony? My family name? The church floor I'd left behind with a heel mark in my mad dash for freedom?

Whatever. The decision to leave my fiancé at the altar was mine, and I'd made it for reasons they wouldn't understand. Reasons I wasn't quite ready to untangle or explain. Not to them at least.

So, I tilted my chin up, smoothed the nonexistent wrinkles in my dress, and thought, *Let them stare. Christmas lights might flash, but drama? Drama sparkles.*

As I passed my parents, I flashed a small, hopeful smile. The kind that said, "Hey, remember how much you love me?" And I prayed they'd skip the guilt-trip express today. The last thing I wanted was to catch that look in their eyes. You know the one. The "we love you, but you've really made a mess of things" look. Classic parent move.

Still, I had one goal: blend in like the world's most awkward chameleon. No fuss. No drama. Just me, here to play my role as sister of the bride, slash maid-of-honor, slash not the accidental headliner of this wedding.

So, I locked my gaze on Mia, who stood up front, glowing like a Disney princess in real life.

There she was with Thomas—tall, handsome, and honestly, annoyingly perfect—standing beside Father Jonas, with the wedding party flanking them like a super-polished bridal army.

The altar looked like it had been yanked out of a Christmas movie: pine wreaths, shiny red and gold ribbons, and these towering gold candle holders with white pillars that flickered dramatically, as if the candles themselves had been cast for the role of *Ambiance*.

My heels clicked against the smooth floor, every step a little louder than I wanted. It was like the floor and my nerves were in cahoots.

At least the rhythm of the sound kept me moving forward, one click closer to Mia and one step farther from the peanut gallery of judgment behind me.

For as long as I can remember, Mia has been obsessed with the idea of a Christmas wedding. Like, *obsessed* obsessed. The kind of obsession where every Hallmark holiday movie becomes a Pinterest board in her brain.

She's always adored the smell of freshly cut evergreen trees, the pine needle scent that clings to the air like a warm hug. Every year, she'd go full Martha Stewart on the house, decorating every inch, trimming the tree, blasting carols, and guzzling hot cocoa like it was a sport.

When we were kids, she used to dream up every detail of her wedding. The dress—princess-style, obviously. The bridesmaids—me as Maid of Honor, because duh. The venue—a toss-up between a church or some fairytale castle.

But one thing was non-negotiable: her wedding would happen during Christmas. And here she was, living her Christmas wedding fantasy.

Mia: 1, Universe: 0.

I kept my eyes locked on her at the end of the aisle, determined not to give the congregation of judgy faces any more fuel for their small-town gossip fire.

Mia looked like a literal angel—glowing, radiant, and all those other clichés people use to describe brides. When she tilted her head toward Thomas, her smile could've powered the string lights wrapped around every tree in town.

But then she spotted me. Her smile faltered, shifting into this awkward, "Hi, I see you, let's not make this a thing" grin.

I'm sure she didn't miss the way the room turned arctic the second I walked in.

But unlike everyone else, Mia actually got it. She actually knew about the mess I'd been wading through these last five weeks. Scratch that—this past year. If anyone had the inside scoop on my life, it was her. We shared practically everything, even when it sucked.

Especially when it sucked.

"You look stunning, Lena," Mia whispered as I finally reached her, her eyes sparkling like someone had swapped them with Christmas ornaments.

Her warm hug was like a weighted blanket for my soul, and I felt the tension in my shoulders melt just a little. This was Mia—my sister, my ride-or-die. She could've scolded me for stealing attention just by existing, but instead, she radiated acceptance and love. Classic Mia.

I hugged her back and kissed her cheek, the way I'd done a million times before. "This is your day, sissy. You are absolutely glowing."

And wow, was she. Her emerald silk dress was pure perfection, clinging in all the right places like it had been designed by someone who truly understood curves. Her Beyoncé-blonde hair was a waterfall of loose waves, cascading down her back like she was starring in a shampoo commercial.

But the real glow came from Thomas—the way she looked at him, the way he looked at her. It was enough to make even my cynical heart feel like a marshmallow in hot cocoa. Despite my own romantic dumpster fire, I was genuinely happy for her.

The wedding planner, Carly, clapped her hands and began corralling us like a festive herd of sheep. "Alright, everyone! Bridesmaids with groomsmen to the vestibule." She pointed down the aisle away from the altar. "I'll signal when it's your turn to strut your stuff."

I walked with the entire wedding party down the center aisle and convened in the front of the church.

As I moved into position, I rounded the nativity scene—because of course, there was one—and suddenly felt like I'd brushed against a live wire. My eyes locked with piercing ice-blue ones, and my heart betrayed me by skipping a beat.

And then, because I'm me, I tripped on some hay and nearly face-planted into the manger. Mary, Joseph, and baby Jesus were about to get a new roommate.

Before I could go full-on Christmas catastrophe, a strong hand grabbed my arm and kept me upright.

"Whoa there," came a deep, smooth voice as I stumbled into the arms of a man who looked like he'd walked off the cover of GQ: Holiday Edition.

"Well, my star in the East!" I quipped, trying to recover both my balance and my dignity. "How's that for divine intervention?"

He didn't laugh, but the corner of his mouth twitched.

Progress.

His strong grip steadied me, and I realized I was still holding on to him like he was my personal shepherd. Mr. Hunky didn't say much, but honestly, with a jawline like that, he didn't need to.

"Well, that's one way to get tangled up in the holiday spirit," I said, brushing off my moment of humiliation and flashing my best I'm-totally-not-embarrassed smile. Then, for extra charm, I added, "Thanks for the catch!"

Looking up from his arms, I gave a playful introduction. "Hi, I'm Lena. Mia's sister. You know, the one who's single-handedly keeping the town gossip mill running."

"Tyler," he replied, all calm and steady, like he hadn't just saved me from an unscheduled nativity face-plant. "Nice to meet you." His hands shifted to my elbows, steadying me like a pro before stepping back. The man was efficient.

It was probably only a couple of seconds that he held me up, but it felt like I'd been locked in his grip for an eternity.

Not that I was complaining. In those few seconds, I managed to notice his dreamy blue eyes, the sharp angles of his jawline, and the unfair perfection of his broad shoulders. Oh, and let's not forget his back muscles. Yes, my hands had definitely copped a feel.

"You all right?" he asked, one brow arched in mild amusement, clearly wondering if I could stay vertical on my own.

"Yep," I said, nodding with exaggerated enthusiasm. "It's a Christmas miracle!"

That earned me the tiniest grin—a flash of white teeth and just enough charm to make my brain short-circuit. And then, like he had a switch, he went back to serious, nodding toward Carly, who was explaining something about the lineup.

Meanwhile, my inner monologue was on overdrive. *Holy Mary, mother of Joseph, this man is a five-course meal. I might need a confessional booth after this.*

He offered me his arm, and I placed my hand in the crook of his elbow, trying not to notice how solid he felt. Spoiler alert: I noticed.

As we turned toward the other couples in line, I realized Mia had seriously undersold her fiancé's best man.

This guy? He wasn't just handsome. He was Greek statue meets lumberjack meets jawline sent from heaven. Six-one or six-two of pure, unfair attractiveness. His dark hair was styled back, though a few rebellious strands fell over his brow. And those ice-blue eyes? They practically drilled into my soul. Don't get me started on his scent. It was woodsy with a touch of holy-crap-what-is-that-magic? He had no right to smell so good.

"Thanks for the support," I said, giving his bicep a small squeeze because, well, it was right there, and I was weak. "I wouldn't want to fall on my face in front of all these people."

But Tyler? He didn't even flinch. His focus was locked on Carly, who was rattling off rehearsal details like she was auditioning for a role in Wedding Planner: The Musical.

Meanwhile, I stood there, trying to act like a normal adult and not someone already secretly doodling his name in hearts all over my mental notebook like a lovesick seventh grader.

I tried to focus on Carly, really I did. But let's be honest—my attention was split between her overly enthusiastic breakdown of aisle logistics and the tall drink of brooding perfection standing next to me.

Tyler's scent—some ridiculous combination of woods, spice, and pure male arrogance—wrapped around me like a blanket I didn't ask for but definitely wasn't giving back. It was distracting, to say the least. And okay, maybe it ticked me off a little that he didn't seem to be struggling with the same hyper-awareness about me.

Carly finally waved us forward, instructing Tyler and me to practice walking down the aisle. Oh, the irony.

I pressed lightly on his arm, a silent "let's do this," and immediately felt the muscles under my fingers tense.

Oh boy. That jolt of electricity? Definitely not from the church's Christmas lights.

He glanced down at me, and for a split second, I thought I saw something flicker in those glacier-blue eyes. Interest? Maybe even a little curiosity? My heart did an embarrassing leap before I shoved it back into place.

As we walked together in slow, measured steps, I stole a few glances his way.

That scowl. The grumpy, brooding charm. The kind of face that said, "I don't care," but in the hottest way possible. And yet, he was laser-focused on the aisle ahead, like this was an Olympic sport and he was gunning for gold.

By the time we reached the altar, I was back to square one—standing next to Mia, trying to look like a person who wasn't internally spiraling. I fixed my gaze on my hands, doing my best to drown out the not-so-helpful voices in my head.

Half the people in this church had watched me walk down the aisle before. And then? They'd watched me run right back out.

Weddings were supposed to be about new beginnings, but all I could think was, *Here we go again. Round two of "Lena vs. Public Humiliation."*

Honestly, the irony was almost funny. Almost.

When the rehearsal wrapped up, I pulled Mia in close, trying to channel all the supportive big sister vibes I could muster. "Sorry I was a little late tonight," I said, my voice soft but sincere.

She shook her head, her blonde waves bouncing like a Pantene commercial. "Everything's fine," she said, smiling like she'd already forgotten about it.

Of course, everything was fine. Mia could charm a brick wall into painting itself.

"You and Thomas are perfect for each other, sissy," I whispered, squeezing her hand. "You're a gorgeous couple."

Mia lit up like a Christmas tree, and I felt that all-too-familiar pang of guilt. While she was radiating happiness, I was over here mentally writing the sequel to *How to Humiliate Yourself at a Wedding, Vol. 1: My Own.*

Focus, Lena. This is about Mia, not the brooding, jawline-for-days best man standing ten feet away.

"Can you believe the decorations?" she gushed, practically bouncing on her heels. "Father Jonas was so sweet! He asked what I wanted, and then he covered the church in thousands of poinsettias and lilies!"

Before I could reply, Carly swooped in like a wedding planner superhero. "That was such a time-saver for me," she chimed in, glancing between us like she was expecting applause. "It let me focus on making the rehearsal and reception even more amazing!"

I bit back a laugh. Carly's enthusiasm deserved its own reality show. But Mia had totally worked her magic on Father Jonas. She probably fluttered her lashes at him, and the next thing you know, the church looked like the set of *It's a Wonderful Life*.

"Hey, the rehearsal's done!" Carly said, already halfway out the door. "I'll talk to Father Jonas and then let everyone know about the rehearsal dinner!" And just like that, she was gone, a blur of efficiency in heels.

Thomas appeared then, stepping around Mia with his arms wide open. "Hey, my new sis!" he said, pulling me into a hug. "Thanks for being part of our big day."

I leaned into the hug, smirking up at him. "Well, I checked my schedule," I quipped, pretending to jot notes on an invisible planner. "And shockingly, I've got nowhere else to be."

Thomas chuckled. But for a split second, I saw it. The flicker of something heavier in his eyes. Guilt? Disappointment? Yeah, probably both.

Five weeks wasn't long enough to erase the train wreck that was my wedding day, and Thomas had been tight with Marco. I knew he was still pissed at me for leaving his buddy at the altar.

If I could go back, maybe I'd handle things differently. Or maybe I wouldn't. Either way, there was no time machine, and today wasn't about me.

When we broke apart, Mia wrapped her arms around both of us, pulling us into a three-way hug. "You two are my family," she said, her voice catching just a little. "You're my people."

I squeezed her back, swallowing the lump in my throat. "Always, Mia. You know I'm here—for both of you."

"All right, everyone!" Carly's voice rang out like a PA announcement, and we turned to see her addressing the crowd. "The rehearsal's done! Thomas and Mia invite you all to The Cliff Club for dinner. See you there!"

Mia turned to me, her eyes sparkling. "Can you help Tyler bring the big framed picture and the photo posters to the restaurant?"

"Sure thing," I said, snapping into a mock salute. "Mission accepted."

I didn't dare glance in Tyler's direction just yet. If I was lucky, maybe I could carry the frame and my dignity to the car. But knowing my track record, I wasn't holding my breath.

Thomas grabbed Mia's hand from behind, and she spun toward him, giggling like a lovestruck teenager in a rom-com. He pulled her into his arms, and they fit together so perfectly it was like the universe custom-ordered them as a matched set. Then, of course, they went straight into a kiss—a long, slow, we're-the-only-people-in-this-room kind of kiss.

"Ahem!" I said, my fake throat-clearing echoing in the holy acoustics of the church. "Just a reminder, folks: this is a place of worship. And, uh, you're not married yet. So let's save the tongues of angels for after the vows, huh?"

A smattering of laughter rippled through the room, but Mia just waved me off with a grin, completely unbothered.

Then Mom swooped in, her hug as warm as her mom-voice. "You okay, honey?" she asked, her tone laced with that same concerned undertone she's been using ever since *The Great Wedding Debacle* five weeks ago.

I plastered on a smile, quick and breezy—at least, I hoped it looked breezy. "Oh, yeah! Just, you know, big weekend for Mia and all."

Mom nodded, her hands gently brushing at my wrists like she was sweeping away invisible lint—or possibly my defenses. Her eyes stayed on me, searching for cracks in my "totally fine" façade.

I tugged at the edge of my sleeve, a habit she'd always said made me look small. Maybe that was what I wanted tonight: to shrink down, blend into the background like one of those poinsettias. Just another decorative touch no one noticed.

Our gazes drifted to Mia, now gliding toward the doors with Thomas like she was starring in the finale of a Hallmark movie. She was laughing, glowing, and practically floating in her emerald-green dress, which, by the way, should be illegal for someone to look that good in.

I swallowed the lump in my throat, a bitter mix of pride and envy that went down like a jagged pill. Mia's life was picture-perfect. Mine? More like a puzzle with half the pieces missing.

"We'll see you at the rehearsal dinner, sweetheart," Mom said, squeezing my shoulder in that way she did when she was trying to reassure me—or herself.

I wanted to shake off her sympathy, but instead, I just stood there, rooted like one of the wise men statues.

With a sigh that felt about three hours long, Mom turned to join Dad and Thomas's parents as they made their way out. And just like that, I was standing at the altar, staring down at the pews where my failed fairytale had unraveled not so long ago.

A weird, bitter ache settled low in my stomach, the kind you get when you realize your life is more of a cautionary tale than a love story.

As the last of the guests trickled out, it was just me and Tyler left in the church. Just us, standing in front of rows of empty pews and the now-vacant altar.

Real cozy, right? Except not.

Tyler had already grabbed the photo posters and the big framed picture Mia wanted and stacked them like they weighed nothing. His biceps flexed as he lifted the whole setup off the easel like it was a piece of printer paper. (Was it hot in here, or was I just mad at him? Jury's still out.)

Then he turned to me, his face as unreadable as a contract I'd never bothered to skim.

"You look miserable," he said, deadpan.

"Wow, thanks," I shot back, slapping on the kind of smile you save for relatives who insult your outfit at Thanksgiving. "Exactly the vibe I was going for."

One of his eyebrows did this slow, unimpressed raise, like he couldn't decide if he should laugh or walk away. Then he turned his attention to the church, his gaze sweeping over the place like he was sizing it up for demolition.

I crossed my arms, the heat crawling up my neck. "You're just a peppermint stick of holiday cheer, aren't you?"

Tyler turned back to me, his face unreadable, like I was one of those Magic Eye puzzles he had no interest in solving.

"I've got the photos Mia wanted. I'll take them to the rehearsal dinner," he said, his voice cool and detached. "You just need to bring the easel."

And just like that, he turned and started walking toward the exit.

Seriously? I stared at his back, my teeth practically grinding into dust. The guy acted like I'd insulted his mom or run over his childhood pet.

"Do you have a problem with me?" I called after him, my voice sharp enough to cut wrapping paper. "You're like… ice in a snow cone."

He stopped and turned, his expression neutral, but his eyes? Total frostbite.

"You don't need ice cubes in a snow cone," I added, waving my hand. "Okay, dumb example. The point is, ever since my whole run-in with the nativity scene, you've been acting like I kicked a puppy or something. If I did say or do something to offend you, just tell me so I can apologize and we can move on."

For a second, I thought maybe he'd thaw a little, but nope. His face stayed locked in "serious business" mode.

"I don't have a problem, Lena," he said, his voice steady and infuriatingly calm. "I'm here for Thomas and Mia. That's who we're all here for."

Ouch. That one stung. Mostly because he was right. This wasn't about me, and he'd just thrown it in my face like a bucket of ice water.

I opened my mouth, but for once, nothing came out. No snark, no clever comeback, not even a passive-aggressive dig. Nada.

And just like that, he turned and walked out, leaving me standing there, fuming.

I glared at his retreating back, my frustration boiling over. Sure, he was tall, broad, and annoyingly good-looking in that tailored suit, but did he have to act like I was some kind of inconvenient fly buzzing around this perfect little weekend?

Oh, I had a problem all right. And its name was Tyler.

Chapter 2: Tyler

The rehearsal dinner was...fine.

As far as awkward gatherings in dimly lit rooms filled with people, most of whom you're pretending to like, can go.

The steak was decent, the wine was flowing, and, thankfully, Lena wasn't directly in my line of sight. Because, let's face it, she was already camping out rent-free in my brain.

I swear, since the second she walked into that church, all I could think about was her. With that wavy, brown hair doing that perfect, effortless thing women claim only happens when they're not trying. And those sultry brown eyes that could probably unlock classified government secrets if they stared long enough.

But here's the thing. Lena? She's a walking red flag, a Category Five disaster waiting to happen. And the last thing I needed was for Hurricane Lena to crash-land in my life. Nope. Not today, Satan.

She was seated next to Mia, laughing and looking...yeah, okay, gorgeous.

Meanwhile, I was placed on the other side of Thomas, who was leaning in like a nervous prom date grilling me about the bachelor party.

"Everything's set for tomorrow night," I told him, jabbing my steak like it owed me money. "Stuey and Mac fly in first thing, and the rest of the guys will meet us at the club."

I kept it vague because, one, the whole thing was supposed to be a surprise, and two, my focus was split between not spilling the beans and not looking at Lena.

I was dropping the ball on the second part like it was a bad pass in the fourth quarter.

"So, no hints about where we're going?" Thomas asked, eyebrow cocked, looking like he thought I might sell him to pirates. "Do I need to bring a stack of singles? Update my will?"

I smirked and wiped my mouth with my napkin, which felt very civilized considering the chaos going on in my head. "Relax, dude. We're giving you a night to remember—without doing anything that'll require an alibi."

"That's not as comforting as you think it is," he muttered, shaking his head but laughing anyway.

I could hear Lena's laughter over and around Thomas's big head. Every time she spoke, my focus wavered like I was a moth drawn to a flame. A really annoying, tempting flame. I had to keep forcing my attention back to Thomas and the guys, reminding myself that Lena wasn't my problem.

The rest of the dinner passed with the usual jokes and banter among the groomsmen. We were all in on the harmless plan. Renting a limo, bar hopping, nothing wild. But messing with Thomas by letting him imagine the worst? That was half the fun.

The other half? Not thinking about Lena. Which, apparently, was a losing battle.

Joking around with the guys didn't do a damn thing to keep my mind off her. She was like a virus. I'd try to shake her off, but every time I looked up, there she was. Laughing, smiling, her eyes sparkling like she was trying to put a spell on me.

And her hair. Don't even get me started on that wavy mess that looked like it had been crafted by some kind of sorceress. Each strand seemed to fall perfectly into place, with just the right amount of tousled chaos that made me want to run my hands through and never stop.

I was stealing quick glances her way, pretending to be all cool and disinterested, but damn, she was frustratingly vivacious and annoyingly attractive. And the worst part? She was everything I didn't want or need right now.

But it didn't matter what I told myself. It was like my brain was a malfunctioning GPS, and no matter how hard I tried to focus, I kept getting rerouted right back to her. Her presence was like a damn siren song, pulling me in when I was supposed to be keeping my distance.

I had a job to do. Best man, remember? My duty was to Thomas and Mia. Not to get distracted by the bride's sister, who was clearly on a mission to derail my sanity.

When the dinner wrapped up, I hung back at the bar like some kind of sad, underachieving philosopher, watching the room spin around me.

Holiday decorations were everywhere—twinkling lights, fake holly garlands, and Winter Wonderland playing in the background. A picture-perfect nightmare. The kind of thing I'd ignore if I had any sense left in my head.

But instead? I just thought about Lena.

At dinner, she had been sitting on the other side of her sister, but when Mia turned to talk to Thomas, Lena looked like she wanted to be anywhere but there. She was tracing the rim of her champagne glass, lost in her own thoughts like she was trying to block the world out.

Something about that hit me harder than I'd care to admit.

I took a slow sip of whiskey, hoping it would drown the feeling. It didn't. It never did.

She had this quiet magnetism, like a tractor beam pulling my attention every time I tried to look away.

I needed to keep my distance. I needed to not think about her. But there I was, hoping, praying, wishing that we'd run into each other again. Just so I could act like I didn't give a damn.

Yeah, because that always works.

Get a grip, idiot. I tried to remind myself again that I was here for Thomas and Mia. Not for some fleeting, stupid attraction to Mia's sister. But that didn't stop my brain from betraying me.

Another sip of whiskey. I set the glass down, tapping my finger on the condensation.

Thomas had told me about Lena. The runaway bride.

Apparently, she'd left her fiancé standing at the altar, leaving everyone—including him—stunned. Thomas had even spoken to the guy afterward. Guy was just as clueless as everyone else.

I don't even remember my first reaction when I heard the story. Probably didn't care much since I hadn't met her yet. I wasn't the kind of guy who needed to get involved in other people's drama, and honestly, women like her were just easier to keep at arm's length.

But now? Now I was stuck here, thinking about her like a dummy.

I sighed and drank a long swig of my whiskey. The night was over, but I knew it was going to drag on, thanks to this mental tango with Lena that would stick with me the whole damn time.

When Lena walked into the church today, it was like a wrecking ball to my system. All eyes were on her, and I swear the floor tilted just a bit beneath me.

She made her way down the aisle, and I couldn't pull my gaze away. She had this vibe. Confidence, strength, the kind that shouldn't be as damn sexy as it was.

I wasn't the only one noticing her. A few people turned their heads, covering their mouths like they were trying to hide what they were thinking. Yeah, I could guess what they were whispering. "Look at her, poor thing. Or maybe she's just flat-out nuts for bailing on her fiancé at the altar like that."

I knew the rumors. Everyone had warned me about her: Thomas, his family, my family. She was the runaway bride, the one who just bailed and left everyone in her emotional dust.

But here's the thing. I couldn't stop looking at her. Something about her pulled me in, and no matter how hard I tried, I couldn't stop wanting to know more.

But I had to be smart. I'd finally started getting my shit together. A good job, a new house, and hell, I didn't need anyone asking me "Are you okay?" every five minutes.

The last thing I needed was drama. And Lena? She was wrapped in drama, as much as she was wrapped in that body-hugging green dress.

"Get it together, Tyler," I muttered under my breath, glancing at the wall of liquor behind the bar. A holiday crush on Thomas's sister-in-law? That was the kind of complication I didn't need.

She was still picking up the pieces of her own wrecked wedding. I could see the storm brewing behind those big brown eyes of hers. She had "hot mess" written all over her, and I'd had more than my fair share of that already.

Another sip of whiskey, and I was lost in my own damn head again. Then, *tap*.

I turned, expecting someone who'd probably just dropped their napkin or needed directions to the bathroom, but no. It was Lena.

Of course it was. She was standing behind me with this small, slightly mischievous smile, like she knew she had me exactly where she wanted me.

"Mind if I join you?" she asked, all sweetness and charm, like I wasn't already mentally throwing a tantrum inside.

The thoughts in my head? Oh, they were screaming, "No. I was just about to leave. I mind, I'm done here. There are like, fifty other empty barstools, why don't you pick one of those?"

But instead of saying any of that, my mouth went rogue. "Sure," I heard myself say, motioning to the empty seat beside me. The words left my mouth before I could stop them.

Instant regret. The second she sat down, I wanted to pull the invite back, tell her I wasn't in the mood, that I needed some peace. But nope, too late for that. She was already sitting next to me.

Her scent—some sweet, floral thing mixed with a deeper, warmer something that made my pulse race—invaded my space. Great, now my senses were betraying me too.

I squeezed the glass a little tighter, mentally repeating the mantra, I'm here for Thomas and Mia, over and over again like it was going to work. I wasn't here for whatever drama Lena might bring into my life. I wasn't.

But when she looked at me with those big, curious eyes of hers, my brain kind of short-circuited. "Add whatever the lady wants to my tab, will you?" I asked the bartender before I could talk myself out of it.

The bartender, this older guy with a silver mustache and that look, the one that said he knew exactly what the hell I was doing, nodded at me like he was silently trying to talk me out of this stupid decision. *But what the hell did he know?* I wasn't about to listen to anyone today.

Lena didn't waste any time. "I'll have what he's drinking. Thank you."

I tried not to blink too hard. She didn't even ask what I was drinking, like whiskey was her go-to too. It was like she was one step ahead of me. Damn it.

The bartender handed her the glass, and she raised it. I tapped mine against hers, mostly to keep from doing something ridiculous like actually thinking about this situation.

"Cheers!" she said, her voice light and easy, like she'd just dropped a match on a stack of dynamite. My skin practically caught fire, but I managed to keep it together. Barely.

"Cheers," I muttered back, probably sounding way less smooth than I'd hoped.

We both took a sip. My head wasn't much clearer, but at least the whiskey helped drown out a few of those stupid thoughts.

My drink felt hotter than usual as it slid down my throat, warming me in a way that I wished would do more than just burn a hole through my insides. But, hey, it helped me focus. Focus on the drink. Focus on anything but the damn attraction I couldn't seem to shake. Lena. Of course it had to be her.

She took a long gulp of her own drink and set the glass down with a little too much emphasis. "Ohhh! I needed that!" she said, exhaling like she'd just run a marathon.

I tried not to let my mind wander to how that might sound in a different context.

Then she did this weird thing where she looked over her shoulder, like she was checking to see if her family had magically reappeared or if someone was spying on us. *What was she looking for? What the hell did it matter?*

Her hair brushed over her shoulder, and damn, the curve of her neck was right there in front of me. I could practically feel the heat from her skin just looking at it. Hell, I even wondered what it would feel like to press my lips there. Just a little trail of kisses, maybe, right up to her ear and back down.

I jerked my gaze away, because, really, I'd had enough of that kind of thought, especially tonight. But then she turned back, eyes locking with mine, and I was screwed. She was looking at me like she knew exactly what was going on inside my head.

"Statistics show that forty-five percent of people who listen to true crime podcasts also like hanging out at bars alone at night," she said, all matter-of-fact like she was reading from some weird study. Then, as if that wasn't enough, she added with a grin, "And among that forty-five percent, eighty percent drink whiskey on the rocks."

Okay, so she was trying to break the ice with a weird, made-up piece of trivia. Funny, I guess? But all I could think about was that stupid neck of hers again. What was the right response to this? Do I smile? Laugh? Tell her she was full of shit?

I just sat there, frozen, like an idiot. Watching her smile with those eyes that were just a little too inviting. God help me, she was magnetic. And as much as I wanted to run the hell out of there, part of me couldn't look away. She was... captivating. I hated it, but there it was.

"You okay?" Lena's voice broke through my thoughts, soft and uncertain.

I took another sip, pretending like I wasn't spiraling in my own damn thoughts. "I'm fine." My words came out too fast, like I was trying to convince myself more than her.

But Lena... she wasn't buying it. She was most likely someone who never did. "You haven't seemed fine since I almost took out the Holy Family."

Well, she wasn't wrong. That whole nativity thing was like a bad accident waiting to happen. "It was concerning to watch you almost single handedly ruin Christmas." I couldn't help the sarcasm that slipped out. It was easier to joke than deal with the real crap I was feeling.

She gave me that damn wink. "Just part of my charm."

"Charming," I muttered, taking another swig of whiskey, feeling the burn. Anything to dull the heat in my chest from how much she was screwing with my head. "Luckily for the congregation, baby Jesus was safe and sound."

I could feel her eyes still on me, but I didn't want to look. Didn't want to give her an opening, because I knew exactly how it went.

It started with small talk and a few drinks, and next thing you knew, you were knee-deep in some mess you couldn't get out of. I'd been there before, and trust me, I didn't need another wreckage in my life.

Then she hit me with a question that actually made me pause. "Just wondering, how long into the wedding reception could one go before bailing without offending the entire room?"

I snorted. "The same thought crossed my mind. But you're the maid of honor and I'm the best man. We'll be stuck there until the very end."

Her smirk didn't quite make it to her eyes. Guess I wasn't the only one dragging my feet through this whole thing.

I raised my glass again, hoping the liquor would help me focus on anything other than the damn pull she had on me. But no. I could feel her watching, waiting for me to say something. To give her an opening.

But I knew better. You reached out to someone, and next thing you knew, their baggage was in your lap like a pile of dirty laundry. And I didn't need to go down that road again. Been there, done that. Jumped into relationships too damn soon, only to realize I wasn't even close to being ready. And let's just say, that kind of mess doesn't clean itself up.

"You don't have to pretend to be fine, you know," she said quietly, her voice a little softer than I was used to.

Her words settled over me, pressing close like I could almost feel them. They hovered in the air, too close, too real. Like they had the power to crack through the wall I'd spent years building.

I gripped my glass tighter, trying to steady myself, but it wasn't working. "Yeah, well," I said, keeping my voice even, "you don't have to pretend you care, either."

Maybe it was harsh. Maybe it wasn't. But it was the only way I could keep the clutter from spilling over.

What's your angle, Lena? I glanced her way, trying to figure out what she was really after. *Did Mia tell you my life story, or are you just naturally good at sensing the train wrecks in people's lives?* Nah, I couldn't picture Mia and Thomas spilling my guts to anyone, let alone to her.

But there was something about Lena that felt... familiar. Like I'd seen that look before. The way she tried to keep it together but there was a crack in her armor.

Maybe it was the way she spoke, like she was hiding something heavy. Or maybe we were both just a couple of people who'd been through shit and were trying not to let it show. Either way, I knew one thing: I wasn't about to let myself get sucked into whatever this was.

"Yeah, well. The pretending gets easier the more you do it," I muttered, trying to shut it all down.

There was a long, quiet pause before she shifted uncomfortably in her seat. She raised her glass to her lips and took another long drink, like she was hoping it'd give her some kind of courage.

"I want to tell you something," she said, her voice dropping low and serious. "Something about me."

Well, that was a curveball I didn't see coming. My heart skipped, but somehow my mouth decided to jump the gun before my brain could catch up.

"I already know," I blurted. *Smooth, Tyler. Real smooth.* I was surprised my voice didn't crack, but thank you, whiskey, for numbing the edges enough to make me forget to hide that I'm a total dumbass. Not.

Her eyes flickered like I'd said something she'd already suspected. It wasn't shock I saw there. Just recognition. Like I'd just tipped my hand, and now she knew I knew something. She took a deep breath and locked eyes with me, like she was bracing for impact.

"I'm engaged," she said, her voice so quiet I could barely hear it over the background noise of the bar.

The world stopped for a solid second. Engaged? Wait, hold up. She was still *engaged*? But she was here, drinking whiskey, telling me this. *What the hell?*

I must've had something resembling a dumbfounded look on my face because she seemed to pick up on it. But why was she telling me this? I ran through the interactions we'd had since meeting her this afternoon, trying to find some logic, but all I got was confusion. *What the hell was going on here?*

"We're just standing up for Thomas and Mia at their wedding and walking down the aisle together," I said, trying to sound all detached and indifferent, like I didn't give a damn about whatever personal drama she was about to drop. But the way my voice came out—soft, too quiet, like it was trying to hold onto something I didn't want to admit—kind of betrayed me.

She took another deep breath, like she was gearing up for something big, then took a sip of her drink. I wasn't sure if she was buying my whole "I don't care" act, but I kept my eyes on my glass, spinning it, stalling.

"His name is Marco," she said, eyes locked on the bar. "And I... five weeks ago... I left him at the altar."

Yeah, I already knew that. But it still hit me like a sledgehammer to the chest.

I wasn't about to let it show, so I just kept circling my finger along the rim of my glass, because silence was all I could offer at the moment.

"Well, I suppose that means we're not engaged anymore, seeing as, well..." She shifted in her seat like she was uncomfortable, her gaze wandering up to the ceiling like she was trying to talk herself through it.

I stayed quiet, unsure what to say, because what the hell do you say to that? The whole thing was a damn mess, and I wasn't about to step into that minefield.

"Marco and I haven't spoken since our wedding day. So, yeah. I should assume we're not engaged anymore. I don't know why I started off saying that in the first place."

I shrugged, trying to keep the distance between us. "Well, it's not like you owe me any explanations." I took a sip of my drink, hoping the bitterness of it would settle the storm that was brewing in my head.

She followed suit, lifting her glass, and I couldn't help but wonder why I was still sitting here, still listening.

"Like I said, we're just walking down the aisle together."

She raised an eyebrow, like she was actually trying to bait me. "I guess I just imagined your foulness towards me in the church, then?"

Her tone had a bite to it, and I felt that sting, but I didn't want to admit it. Hell, I wasn't even sure why I was getting worked up over it. I felt bad, but I wasn't about to apologize for my attitude. After all, I hadn't done anything wrong, right?

Still, I knew I had to be careful. I had to keep my distance. No matter how much she pulled me in with those eyes, or her complicated situation. I couldn't allow myself to fall for any of it.

It was damn near impossible to pretend I wasn't feeling the pull of her presence. My brain kept screaming "Run!" But my ass was still planted on this barstool, trying to hold onto some shred of dignity. And let me tell you, that was a battle I was losing.

"Look," I started, the words coming out smoother than I felt. "This weekend is about Thomas and Mia, right?" I glanced at her, and to my relief, she nodded along like she was keeping up.

"Saturday, we show up. We walk down the aisle together, stand up for my best friend and your sister. Simple." I ticked off the points in my head, keeping my focus on anything but the way her hair fell over her shoulder or the way she twisted that empty glass like it was giving her some kind of therapy.

"Then we do one dance at the reception. That's it. We've done our jobs. Everyone's happy." I leaned back a little, feeling like I had it all figured out. *Yeah, right. If I didn't say another word, maybe I could make this whole thing a clean, no-mess operation.*

The bartender approached, pointed at Lena's empty glass and asked, "Another?"

She turned her gaze on me, and my brain short-circuited. It was like she wasn't just looking at me. She was seeing right through me. Like she knew the twisted thoughts in my head, all the things I'd like to do if we were somewhere else, somewhere I could just let go of my guard for five goddamn seconds.

But then, reality slapped me in the face. She was trouble. Big, messy, complicated trouble. And I had enough of that in my life, thanks. Thomas had given me the lowdown on her fiancé situation, and I wasn't about to add that drama to my already-overflowing plate.

I needed to get out of this. I needed to keep my life in one solid direction. No detours. No distractions.

She turned back to the bartender and said, "Yes, I'll have another one." Then she turned to me, her eyes bright with curiosity. "Another one for you too?"

And that was it. My brain started screaming "Danger!" and "Don't do it!" and "This is exactly how your life goes off the rails!" But instead of walking away, my stupid mouth decided to open.

"I just don't want any drama in my life," I said, the words coming out before I could stop them.

Fuck. As soon as they left my mouth, I wanted to swallow them back down. *What the hell was I doing?*

The look on her face? Oh, it was a masterpiece of surprise and rage, like a cocktail I didn't want to drink but was too polite to refuse.

She scoffed at me, like I'd just told her she had spinach in her teeth, and after a dramatic pause, turned to the bartender.

"Never mind," she muttered, as if she were about to have a meltdown but decided to save it for later.

And let me tell you, I saw that immediate shift. Her expression morphed from mildly annoyed to full-on I'm-about-to-set-you-on-fire mode. It was so intense, I half-expected to feel her rage burn a hole through my shirt.

She shot up from her stool like she was about to launch into some epic rant, but instead, she reached into her purse and pulled out a twenty-dollar bill.

"Seems to me you're the type who always gets what you want," she snapped, slamming the bill down on the bar like it was some kind of holy offering. "Well, you're in luck. I'm outta here."

She took a few angry steps toward the door, then stopped dead in her tracks. She spun on her heel and gave me one last look, hand on her hip, full-on diva mode.

"Fair warning," she said, voice dripping with sarcasm and warning, "Don't be a jerk to me at the wedding on Saturday. The last thing you want is me, pissed."

With that, she spun again, her heels clicking like a ticking time bomb, and stormed out.

I sat there for a second, half-amused, half-scared shitless. Yeah, this was going great. Definitely going to keep my distance. Or, you know, at least try to.

I should've been relieved. Seriously. I'd dodged a bullet here, avoided a Category Five Lena storm about to wreck my life, but instead, I sat there, feeling like a total jackass.

What the hell was I thinking? My brain must've gone on vacation while my mouth just decided to play loose and wild with whatever came out. I wasn't some unfeeling robot, but damn, I already knew what it was like getting caught up in the kind of mess that came with the likes of her.

It wasn't all me though. The whiskey had a hand in it. And maybe I wasn't as immune to Lena's charm as I'd like to think.

I left three twenties on the bar like I was paying off a debt and rushed out of there, my heart hammering in my chest like it was trying to make a run for it.

As soon as I stepped outside, I saw her. She was by her car, back turned, about to open the door and drive away upset because of some asshole thing I said. Yeah, that wasn't happening. Not on my watch.

I jogged over to her. "Lena, wait," I called, my voice practically pleading. I was trying to sound steady, like I had a grip on the situation. But who was I kidding? I sounded like I was begging for forgiveness. And maybe I was.

She spun around and—damn it—her eyes were glassy. But it wasn't the kind of tear-filled look that made me want to pull her into my arms. No. This was fury. Pure, unfiltered, blazing rage.

"What do you want, Tyler?" she snapped, her voice sharp and cutting through the night air. "I'm not interested in your judgment or your pity."

My stomach dropped, but I stepped forward anyway, probably walking straight into a trap.

"Hey," I said, voice soft but firm. "I'm sorry. I didn't mean to hurt you. I just…"

What? What the hell was I supposed to say? I wanted to make this right, but I already knew that the more I tried, the deeper the hole I'd dig.

Before I could even finish that sentence—because let's be real, I had no idea what I was going to say anyway—she yanked me toward her. And then, bam!

Her lips were on mine, crashing against me with a hunger that nearly knocked the wind out of my chest.

It was messy. Raw. And all kinds of hot. The kind of kiss that made every other thought in your head disappear.

I couldn't breathe, couldn't think, couldn't remember my own damn name. Just her lips, her heat, the way her tongue moved with mine like she had something to prove. Like we were both drowning in whatever the hell this was.

I wrapped my arms around her, pulling her closer. My hands roamed to her waist, feeling the curve of her body against mine. Perfect fit. Way too perfect.

She moaned softly into my mouth, her fingers threading through my hair, tugging me closer like she didn't want any space between us. For a second, it felt like the parking lot disappeared. Like there was nothing else but her and me.

And then, just like that, the kiss ended. Her lips left mine, and we both pulled back, gasping for air like we'd been holding our breath for years.

She stared at me with wide eyes, chest heaving. "I... I should go," she whispered, voice raw, the kind of hoarse that made my pulse spike again.

I nodded. Couldn't trust my voice right then. Couldn't even trust my thoughts. My mind was still playing catch-up, trying to figure out how the hell we got here, what that kiss meant. But there was no way in hell I could ask her to stay, not when my whole body was screaming to pull her back.

She gave me a look, like she was waiting for me to say something. But I couldn't. The words wouldn't come.

With one last lingering gaze, she slid into her car and drove off, leaving me standing there in the cold. Heart hammering in my chest like it was about to explode.

And I knew. Damn it, I knew. She was trouble wrapped in a firecracker of a woman with a past that was as complicated as mine.

Even so, I couldn't shake the feeling that the second she walked into that church she'd made herself a permanent resident in my thoughts.

She was everything I didn't need in my life. But somehow I couldn't shake the feeling that she wasn't going anywhere.

Chapter 3: Lena

My heart was doing somersaults as I replayed the kiss with Tyler over and over in my head. I swear, it was like my mind was stuck on repeat, running the whole scene on loop, like some sort of romantic blooper reel.

Just moments before that kiss, I was ready to throw a full-on tantrum in the bar. Drama? Seriously? *Drama?* Yeah, Tyler, you're one to talk.

But the thing is, as much as I wanted to strangle him in that moment, I also couldn't deny that I had been thinking about kissing him since... well, pretty much since the first time I tripped over that ridiculous nativity scene at the church.

He had that whole brooding, grumpy, I-hate-my-life-but-also-want-you-to-kiss-me vibe going on. Plus, those eyes. Those searing ice-blue eyes that practically scorched me where I stood.

When we finally kissed? Well, it was like the universe paused. Like the world hit the brakes and said, "Hey, Lena, let's forget about all that 'I'm-slightly-mad-at-this-guy' business."

I didn't feel angry anymore. I didn't feel anything but the heat of his lips against mine, and let me tell you, it was exactly what I had been wanting for far too long.

I wanted to kiss him again. Right now. Like, literally right now. But I wasn't about to make that mistake again, so I shoved those thoughts aside. Sort of.

I was walking up to the restaurant where Mia and I were meeting for breakfast—just a quick pow-wow before the wedding madness and tonight's bachelorette party. Of course, I had to be early. Because, well, I'm Lena, and I always need the prime seat. Outdoor patio, here I come.

The sun was just rising, casting a golden glow over everything making the world around me look like it was straight out of a cheesy romantic movie. It was a Northern California December morning. Crisp, clear, and ridiculously perfect. I took a deep breath of that fresh air, and for a moment it felt like the world was just... right. If only I could stop thinking about that damn kiss.

The waitress bounced over to me, her ponytail swishing behind her like she was auditioning for some cheerleading reality show or something. "Can I get a drink started for you while you wait?" she chirped while practically glowing.

"Yeah, I'll have a bottle of the Brut," I said, pointing to the menu like I was some kind of wine connoisseur. "And a small glass of orange juice on ice."

She nodded, clearly impressed by my sophistication, and sashayed away.

As I sat there, waiting for my sister to grace me with her presence, my mind somehow managed to wander back to Tyler.

Specifically, to the way his solid muscular bicep felt under my hand as he escorted me down the aisle yesterday. *Mmm, yeah.* Can you really blame me for wondering what the rest of him was like under that shirt? I mean, the guy's got a body that could kill… well, probably not literally, but you get the point.

Then last night at the rehearsal dinner I accidentally overheard him talking to Thomas about the bachelor party, and let me just say—his voice? Deep. Sexy. Like velvet wrapped in gravel. I could've listened to that man talk about the weather and still felt things. But then my eavesdropping took a turn.

The guys were all yammering on about wanting to do a fishing trip up to the family cabin, and Tyler casually dropped, "Mia can come too, if you want. She can invite a girlfriend. So she doesn't get bored."

Okay, fine. Totally reasonable. But then Thomas—aka Thomas, that bastard—had to go and make it weird. "Yeah, it just won't be her sister. Lena would be Mia's first choice, but it's better to let all those circumstances around her just round themselves out."

What. The. Hell. *Circumstances around me?* What the hell does that even mean? I mean, Marco and I are done. The guy's out of the picture. There's nothing left to round out. *Ugh*!

And who did Thomas think he was, talking about me behind my back like I was some kind of problem to be solved? Like I was the social equivalent of a bad rash that needed ointment. Oh, you bet your ass after this wedding, and after the honeymoon, I was definitely giving Thomas a piece of my mind.

But first, I needed this drink to calm down my rage spiral.

"Hey, sis!" Mia's voice yanked me out of my Tyler-induced brain fog. She swooped in behind me and planted a big kiss on my cheek. "I need some yum yum juice to start my last day as a single woman."

"Thanks for not saying 'spinster,'" I quipped, raising an eyebrow. "You're not an insensitive jerk!" I flashed her a grin, knowing she was being extra careful with her words. Especially considering I was the older sister with no marriage material on the horizon.

She slid into the seat across from me, with the kind of smile that could light up a room glued to her face. "Have you ordered drinks yet?"

"You know I did," I replied, feeling smug. "I just got here myself, but I'm a pro. Ordering drinks was the first thing I did."

The waitress showed up with champagne flutes, our bottle of bubbly, and a small carafe of orange juice.

"I'll pour," I said, giving the waitress a polite but firm wave to back off, making it obvious that the champagne was my domain.

I poured half a glass into Mia's flute and a full glass for myself. As I placed the champagne bottle back in its icy home, Mia filled the other half of her flute with orange juice, then handed me the carafe. I topped off my glass with a little splash of OJ, just enough to make it a mimosa and not a crime.

"Drunk," Mia teased, shaking her head at my "generous" pour.

"Lightweight," I shot back, pointing at her flute, which was practically all orange juice. "You're over here drinking breakfast, while I'm enjoying brunch."

She laughed at me, and we clinked glasses. We started talking about wedding stuff. Final plans, bridesmaid duties, last-minute to-dos that Carly would have to juggle because Mia wanted everything to be perfect.

And trust me, with Mia as the bride, perfection was a requirement. She had her iPad out, swiping like she was hunting for Pokémon, checking over every single detail like it was a matter of national security.

"Oh, I almost forgot!" She snapped her fingers, all excited. "Let me call the lead string musician. I want to surprise Thomas with Skid Row's 'I'll Remember You.' He'll love it!"

She pulled out her phone and turned away to make the call, her whole face lighting up with that wedding-planner-crazy energy. Honestly, the girl was relentless. But in the best way.

While Mia was busy making wedding magic happen on her phone, my brain kept wandering back to Tyler.

I mean, how could it not? That kiss—*oh, that kiss*—was like fireworks. A giant boom, chemistry that still had me feeling hot under the collar.

Was he thinking about it too? Or was I just a little footnote in his day, the one who kissed him and then bolted? Was he regretting it? Or was he as drawn to me as I was to him? Ugh. Why did I even care?

I downed my second mimosa like it was water, nibbling on my breakfast—well, more like devouring it while Mia daintily nibbled like some sort of delicate bird. Whatever. Not that it was anyone's business.

My thoughts drifted back to tonight's bachelorette party. I wondered if I could find a way to slip away from the chaos and get some alone time with Tyler. Maybe I could "accidentally" bump into him?

Oh, I'd come up with something. Because honestly? I wanted another kiss. No, scratch that. I needed it. And I may or may not have been picturing what was under his shirt the entire time I sipped my drink. Sue me.

"So, then the pigs arrive and we'll send the balloons off at noon," Mia said, interrupting my absolutely inappropriate thoughts. I didn't even realize she'd finished her call and was back to wedding planning.

"I hope so," I replied, trying to sound casual. "That sounds as though it's exactly how you planned it."

Nailed it.

Mia raised an eyebrow, clearly unimpressed with my level of enthusiasm. "What the heck? Where is your mind right now?"

I shrugged, a little too quickly. "Oh, you know, just... pigs, balloons. Stuff." And Tyler's lips. *Wait, did I say that out loud?*

I froze for a second, my brain scrambling to catch up with what Mia was asking. What was she talking about? I couldn't even remember the last five minutes of conversation, so I just blurted out, "We're not... not exactly. But I think there's something... wait, what were you asking me about?"

Mia's eyes narrowed, that knowing little sister look flashing across her face. "Oh my god, Lena. I knew it. Can't you keep your high school boy libido in check for just one weekend?" She paused, dramatically lowering her voice like I was a teenager caught sneaking out past curfew. "Did you and Tyler hook up last night?!"

I swear, she was about two seconds away from pulling out her phone and making a viral Instagram story of my humiliation.

She downed her mimosa like it was water and slid her empty glass toward me like I was some sort of magic bartender. "Make me one of yours and give yourself a refill. Buckle up. Because I'm about to give you a talking-to that you are not going to like. And only champagne and a little gentle sisterly nudging might allow you to actually listen to what I have to say."

She was completely serious. Oh, I could already feel my face heating up. "Mia, seriously. You're making me sound like some sort of... of... horny teenager."

She gave me a look. You know, the kind that says "Don't make me drag this out of you, because I will."

Ugh, fine. She wasn't wrong. But the last thing I needed was a talking-to about my inability to control myself around a guy I couldn't seem to get out of my head.

"Sissy," I started, kicking myself for always resorting to that loving nickname when I felt guilty. You know, because it wasn't enough that I was practically drowning in my own mess of a life. We should add some extra guilt on top. "You know I've been through a lot this past month. And even before my wedding..."

Mia was silent, just sitting there with that quiet patience of hers while I poured two full glasses of champagne. A generous splash of OJ into each, because I wasn't a total monster.

"Mia, it was just a kiss," I said, finally breaking the silence. But it came out sounding like a confession. Weak, even to me. "You make it sound like I set his house on fire or something."

I handed her her glass, and she just looked at me. No words, just that tight, disapproving mouth that said everything without her even having to open her mouth.

With a full mimosa in each of our hands, Mia began what was sure to be the most condescending sisterly lecture ever.

"Lena," she started, and I swear, when she said my name like that, I could already feel the dread in my gut. That's the voice she used when she was about to hit me with something serious. "You have been through a lot. And I hope I've been a good sister to you, supporting you whenever you've needed me."

"You have," I reassured her. Though at this point, I was starting to feel like she was about to lecture me about how I should have been a better everything and less of a hot mess. "And I want you to know that I appreciate you."

"I know you do," she said, with this understanding in her voice that made me wonder if she had secretly been plotting her next move. "But…"

There it was. The *but*. I could practically feel the "here it comes" on the tip of her tongue.

"Thomas and I have been together for eight years. And I've been waiting to marry him for the last three years, since he proposed to me," she continued, eyes soft with nostalgia like she was about to launch into some lovey-dovey romantic monologue.

"Yes, sissy, I know your history," I said, because, duh. "Thomas wanted to focus on his NFL career, travel with the team during the season, and you—bless your saintly patience—went ahead and built your career as a nurse while waiting for the wedding bells."

Mia took a deep breath, clearly preparing herself for the real heart-to-heart. "I've been so patient, and he was well worth the wait. Because tomorrow, I'll be marrying the man of my dreams, and I couldn't be happier."

She looked at me then, all dreamy-eyed and content, like she was about to ascend to some wedding-day heaven, and I couldn't help but want to be part of her happiness.

I wanted to be happy for her, damn it.

"I know you love me. And I know you want the best for me and Thomas," she said, taking a sip of her drink, clearly swallowing down whatever hesitation was left in her. I could see it: she had something big to say, and it wasn't going to be easy to hear.

Another *but* was coming too. And it wasn't going to be a small one.

"There's something I need to tell you."

My heart did a little tap dance in my chest, like, "Oh great, here we go." I brought my drink to my lips, trying to look casual, but let's be real. Casual wasn't happening. I took a long sip of my mimosa to buy some time, waiting for Mia to keep going.

"Tyler is off-limits," she said, dead serious, like that little sentence was all the explanation I needed.

I blinked. "Okay..." My voice trailed off, but inside, I was like, *Wait, what?* What the hell does Tyler being off-limits have to do with anything? I mean, I wasn't asking for an invitation to his bedroom or anything (yet), but this felt... off. So, I asked, "Why?"

Mia sighed like she was about to drop some heavy family news. I braced myself for impact. She looked at me like she was breaking bad news about a beloved pet. "Thomas's and Tyler's families are so close, Lena. They've been friends since preschool. They're like brothers."

I nodded, still not fully processing. "Well, Thomas is a great guy. So that means Tyler must be a good guy, too, right?"

She nodded, but the way she was looking at me made it clear we were not on the same page. "He is. Tyler's great too," she said. The *but* was coming eventually.

"Tyler and Thomas played football together in high school and went similar routes to the NFL. Tyler signed with the Falcons after U of I and had a solid career for four years. He had a rough go when he stopped playing, but last year he got a job as a sports analyst on ESPN. He's been rebuilding his life."

I was still stuck on one thing: Tyler's off-limits. What the hell was that about? I needed this to make sense, so I kept pushing. "Okay, that's all good. But, like, how does this affect me?"

Mia didn't answer directly. Instead, she put the pieces together for me, but it was like listening to someone read a manual in another language. "And because of that, our families are concerned about him being the best man and you being my maid of honor. They think you need time to heal, Lena. Figure things out."

Ouch.

I felt a little pang in my chest, but I tried to shove it down. I smiled. Fake, of course. "Yeah, okay," I said, trying to sound nonchalant. "Well, I can always count on you to make me feel like a walking disaster."

Mia sighed. I knew it was because she still hadn't gotten to the part I wouldn't like. She shook her head, her voice soft. "It's Christmas time. This is supposed to be a time for family. And you just go and… I mean, the family is just now starting to forget about what happened at your wedding."

And there it was.

I flushed, but it wasn't the cute, flirty kind of flush. No, this was more like the shit, here comes the shame kind.

"Of course you'd bring that up," I said, trying to keep the sting out of my voice, but failing miserably. "I'm not exactly the perfect daughter, right? Nothing I do is the right choice lately, so I don't know why I'd start now."

Mia looked at me like she wanted to say something comforting, but she didn't. Instead, she pressed her lips together in that way she did when she was choosing her words carefully. "You could try, Lena," she said softly, like she was saying the most simple thing in the world. "You really could."

The words hit me hard. Like a punch wrapped in velvet.

I opened my mouth, but nothing came out. My chest felt tight, like there was something pressing against my ribs. Here we were, sitting across from each other like we always had, and yet… I felt like we were oceans apart.

There were walls between us now. Ones neither of us could knock down.

We just sat there. Me holding my mimosa like it was my life raft and her staring into space. Both of us pretending to be okay.

But I wasn't. And Mia wasn't either. We both knew it.

Christmas music floated in the background. Some version of *Have Yourself a Merry Little Christmas* that sounded way too cheerful, almost like it was mocking me.

"Just... stop it in its tracks, okay?" Mia's voice softened, but I could hear the edge beneath it. "It's Christmas. It's my wedding. Please don't make this harder for everyone than it already is."

And just like that, the warmth of the holiday faded away, replaced by this chill that crawled up my spine. I felt like a damn stranger in my own life.

It was Christmas. Mia was getting married. And here I was, standing on the outside looking in.

Why was it so easy for her to have her life all together? Why did she get to live the dream while I was over here, still licking my wounds from my own disastrous wedding day?

"I understand," I said, but the lie slipped out so smoothly that I almost believed it myself, even though I didn't understand a damn thing.

I needed time to think. My head was spinning with anger, dismay, disappointment, and—what was that last one? Oh, right. Confusion. Like, was it really such a crime for me to have a little harmless fun with a hot guy? Was that such a big deal that the whole damn family had already had meetings about it? Was I a ticking time bomb now just because I had a kiss with Tyler?

Apparently, Mia wasn't done. "Lena, I'm begging you. Please don't get involved with Tyler. I don't want to see you get hurt again."

Her words hit me like a brick, and for a moment, I couldn't breathe. Yeah, I didn't want to get hurt either, but after everything I'd been through the last few months, I was starting to think maybe the only way out was to take a risk. And now Mia was asking me to shut that down? To put my heart in a box and just pretend everything was fine?

"Everyone thinks it would be best if you two didn't get involved," she added, her eyes all soft and full of concern, like she was some angel trying to save me from myself.

I wanted to scream. To lash out. To tell her that I wasn't some broken little toy she could just put on a shelf and pretend was fixed. But instead, I felt this wave of anger roll through me, like fire in my veins. It was this mix of frustration and hurt that I couldn't shake off, even if I tried.

"Great. So now everyone gets to decide what's best for me?" I snapped, a little too loudly. "Do I need a permission slip to breathe now, too?"

Mia flinched, but I didn't care. The truth was, I was tired of being told what to do, tired of being treated like I couldn't make my own decisions.

The way Mia looked at me, all soft and sympathetic, like I was some sad puppy who needed a nap, almost made me gag. I was a grown woman, not a charity case. I didn't need anyone to swoop in and make decisions for me. Especially her.

I tried to keep my cool. "Mia, I appreciate the concern," I said, my voice smooth and calm, though it was taking all my strength not to throw the nearest object at her. "But none of this is making any sense to me. You started off talking about how you've waited forever to marry Thomas. That the guys are basically brothers and their families are close. You tell me Tyler's a good guy, but then tell me to stay away from him? All this is starting to make me think you're not being entirely honest with me. Am I wrong?"

Mia's eyes softened, like she was about to break the news that I'd just won a trip to Hawaii but it was raining. "I'm sorry, Lena. The last thing I want to do is upset you."

Oh, she had no idea what upset was.

I stared at her, letting the tension simmer. "You're not being honest with me," I repeated, my voice low, controlled. "You're not just worried about me getting hurt, are you?"

The guilt was written all over her face. It wasn't even subtle. I could practically hear the words in her head.

And then it hit me, like a lightning bolt to the brain. I finished her thought for her. "What you're not telling me is that everyone thinks I'm the problem. That he's the one who needs to be protected from me. Is that what this is all about?!"

Mia's face flickered with surprise, but she quickly masked it with that damn defensive look I knew too well. "Lena, that's not fair," she said, practically sputtering. "I'm just looking out for everyone's best interests."

"Really?" I shot back, sarcasm dripping from every word. "Because it sure feels like you've thrown me under the bus before helping everyone else pile on. You know the reasons I didn't marry Marco, but it sounds like you're agreeing with everyone that I'm 'fickle' and a 'maneater.'"

Her face fell. For a second, I saw guilt flash in her eyes, but then she slapped on a smile that was so fake I could smell it from here.

"They all think I just left Marco at the altar for fun," I sneered. "Like I just had a change of heart in the middle of the ceremony. Like it was totally out of nowhere. Guess what? It's my M.O. now, right? I change my mind faster than I change my clothes. Watch out, guys! Lena's back and she's a threat to every man within a five-mile radius."

Mia's lips tightened, and she shook her head dismissively. "Lena, you're being ridiculous."

Oh, now I was ridiculous? I shook my head, trying to keep my composure, but the hurt crept in like a nasty little troll. "You know what, Mia? You, Thomas, your families—tell them all to shove it. You can keep your opinions. And you? I think you're just scared that if Tyler and I get together, it'll ruin your perfect little wedding day."

Mia snapped then, her voice low and menacing. "That's enough, Lena. You don't know what you're talking about."

I sat up straighter, my heart pounding in my chest. I wasn't done. Not by a long shot. "No, Mia. I don't know," I said, my voice trembling now. "But one thing I do know is that I'm not going to let you control who I fall in love with."

"Love?!" Mia almost spat the word. She leaned in close, and her voice dropped to that deadly tone, the kind that only came before a full-on sisterly showdown. "Can you even hear yourself talking? Maybe you should look at your track record before you start throwing around the L-word."

She grabbed her napkin and dabbed her lips, then set it down with the most dramatic flourish I'd ever seen, before standing up.

"Love?!" she repeated, voice rising now. "No one's trying to control who you fall in love with. We're all just trying to prevent the next poor soul from getting their heart crushed. And, yes, by the way, I really hope that poor soul isn't Thomas' best friend."

I opened my mouth, ready to tell her that she had no idea, that it wasn't that simple. But before I could get a word out, Mia had already turned on her heel and walked off, leaving me with my jaw hanging open.

Nice. Just… nice.

Chapter 4: Tyler

"See?" Thomas said, pointing back and forth between Stuey and Mac like he was some kind of Sherlock Holmes with a way-too-vivid imagination. "Right there. Those looks you're giving each other. They're telling me you're all up to no good, and I need to be concerned that your bachelor party plans are gonna get me in trouble tonight."

Yeah, I got it. He was nervous. His wedding was tomorrow, and this bachelor party was basically his last free night before he was legally bound to his one-and-only. But the guy was acting like he was about to get abducted by aliens.

Stuey and Mac exchanged those "We're up to something that'll give Thomas a coronary" glances, their eyes practically twinkling with mischief.

"C'mon. What's the plan, guys?" Thomas asked, trying to act casual but his nervous energy was practically buzzing. The guy's got nothing to worry about, but his anxiety was giving me second-hand stress.

Mac plopped back onto the couch like he was sinking into a pool of marshmallows. "Hey, throw me another one, would'ja?" he asked, holding out an empty bottle like it was a sacrificial offering.

I had what was supposed to be my beer in hand, already popped open, and walked over to him, passing him the bottle.

"Thanks for the door-to-door service," Mac grinned at me, like I was the personal bartender he'd always dreamed of. "I love you, man."

"I love you too, asshole. Next time, get your own drink," I snorted, rolling my eyes. "Anyone else want one while I'm up?" I asked, just to keep things rolling.

"I mean it, guys," Thomas interjected, cutting through the chatter like a knife through butter. "If your plans for tonight involve strippers or prostitutes, I'm telling you right now that they need to be changed. I'm marrying the most incredible woman tomorrow, and there's no reason she should be questioning my honor after tonight."

"You don't trust us?" Stuey and Mac spoke at the exact same time. Not creepy at all.

Stuey smirked, putting his feet up on the coffee table and cracking open another beer. "What are you saying? Do you think your friends would steer you wrong?"

"As a matter of fact, yes," Thomas answered, walking over and kicking Stuey's feet off the table. They landed with a thud. "While I think you guys have good intentions, you have a history of really bad ideas. So, again. What are the plans for tonight?"

Mac paused, pretending to think. "Let's see... Nope. Still don't plan on telling you!"

Thomas stood up like a frustrated father trying to keep his kids in line. He started pacing around, his eyes darting between all of us like he was watching for the first sign of trouble.

I knew what he was worried about. His wedding was tomorrow. I knew he wasn't concerned about getting cold feet. He was scared that his wedding could somehow turn into a shitshow.

He'd seen it happen before. His buddy's fiancée, his soon-to-be sister-in-law, left him at the altar just a month ago. I was sure Thomas wasn't worried that Mia would bail on him. But after that, everything probably felt a little too close to the edge.

As much as I wanted to keep things fun and light for Thomas, I couldn't help but feel a little twinge of annoyance at Stuey and Mac, dragging this out and making him more anxious than he needed to be.

Look, I was all for a good bachelor party. Hell, I was down for a bachelor party to remember. But tonight was supposed to be a celebration, not a free-for-all. And with everything that'd happened with his friend, I just didn't want to see Thomas freak out more than he already was.

Thomas and I went way back. We'd been through a lot, and the guy was basically a brother to me. I was the one who was supposed to keep his mind off the wedding stress. I was the one who was supposed to make sure everything went smoothly for him tonight.

But instead, Stuey and Mac were just pushing his buttons for fun.

"I mean it, guys," Thomas continued, his voice firm. "No antics. Nothing that's gonna break the law or land me with a tattoo on my face." He stood right in front of Stuey and Mac like he was some kind of human barricade, clearly hoping for a more straightforward answer.

I headed back to the kitchen to grab myself another beer and recycle the empty one. I'd had enough of their back-and-forth.

But all I could think about as I cracked open the new bottle was Lena. I couldn't shake her.

Her lips on mine were like an electric jolt to the system. I was still buzzing from it. No idea why she was stuck in my head, but she was.

I mean, the fact that she walked out on her fiancé at the altar only five weeks ago should've been a red flag the size of a football field. Instead, I couldn't stop thinking about her and *that kiss*. The way she made me feel like I was the only guy in the world. It was way too real. And I wanted more.

"Hey, you gotta be straight with me, dude," Thomas said, clapping me on the back. He looked at me, like he needed me to reassure him that tonight was not going to turn into some kind of bachelor party horror movie. "Things aren't gonna get out of control tonight, are they?"

I gave him a grin, trying to calm his nerves, but inside I was still a little jittery from the thought of Lena. "Just know that I've got your back. I won't let you do anything that's gonna get you arrested or put you in some compromising position."

That seemed to do the trick. Thomas relaxed a bit, giving me a nod of appreciation. He knew I was playing the guy code here. No spoilers. I wouldn't be spilling the beans. But I'd also make sure nothing went off the rails.

Still, my mind kept drifting back to Lena. And the fact that, despite the mess she'd been through, I really, really wanted to kiss her again.

I watched Stuey and Mac on the couch, wrestling over the remote like they were five years old instead of thirty. Their laughter rang out, and I couldn't help but shake my head.

Stuey looked like a grown man, but half the time he acted like a damn toddler. Mac wasn't much better. Still, it was hard not to smile at their antics.

God, it felt like a lifetime ago that I was carefree like them. Just a guy hanging out with his friends, not a care in the world. Football games, the cheers of the crowd, the thrill of the game... I'd give anything to feel that again.

But then *she* popped into my head, as she always did, uninvited.

Carrie.

I wasn't even trying to think about her. But you never get to pick what stuck in your brain.

Carrie's face. Her long, golden hair, always swaying in the stands as she cheered for me. She was the one person who never judged me, never made me feel like I had to be anything I wasn't. And now? All I had left were memories, and that phantom feeling of her hand in mine.

Sometimes, when I'd be walking alone, I'd imagine it. Her fingers squeezing mine, her palm warm and real. And for a split second, it was like she never left. But that was just my messed-up mind playing tricks on me. She was gone, and no matter how many times I tried to hold on to her, she wasn't coming back.

I broke out of my thoughts just in time to hear Thomas ask, "You ready for tonight?" His eyes lit up with that gleam only a guy about to get married could have. It was the kind of excited I didn't think I'd ever feel again. Hell, I'd never felt it the way he did. Not after Carrie.

I forced a smile and shrugged. "Yeah, dude. Let's do this." My voice came out flatter than a pancake, even to me. And yeah, I knew it.

Thomas squinted at me, his gaze flicking over my face like he could see through all the bullshit. "You good, man? You seem distracted."

The weight of Thomas's stare hit me like a linebacker. He could tell something was up, even if he couldn't quite put his finger on it.

Maybe it was the way my brain was doing gymnastics over Lena's kiss. The kiss that came out of nowhere and left me spinning. Or maybe it was because I felt like an emotional piñata and Thomas was about to take another swing.

I didn't want to hold onto the secret anymore. Hell, I didn't even know what I was doing with it. So, before my brain could hit the brakes, my mouth took over. "Lena and I kissed."

The words hit the air like a Hail Mary interception. Thomas's face went from neutral to something between disappointed coach and pissed-off brother. His eyes narrowed, and his jaw tightened. "What did I tell you, Ty?" he groaned. "She's trouble."

I threw my hands up, already on the defensive. "It just happened, alright? I didn't plan it. One second we were talking, and the next—bam!—it was happening."

Thomas rolled his eyes like I'd just fumbled a game-winning play. "You know better. I told you about her and her ex. She's got baggage, man. You don't need to hitch a ride on that train."

"Yeah, I know," I snapped, my frustration bubbling over. "But you're not listening. It wasn't just some random thing. Well, okay maybe it was. But, now she's stuck in my head, and I can't shake it."

His expression softened a fraction, but his tone stayed firm. "I'm just saying, think about it. Five weeks ago, she left her fiancé at the altar. That's not exactly ancient history. And you—after everything you've been through—do you really need this kind of complication?"

I rubbed the back of my neck, trying to keep the irritation in check. "You're acting like I'm some clueless rookie who doesn't know what he's doing. Give me a little credit, man."

"I'm not saying that," Thomas shot back, his hands up in mock surrender. "But you've been through enough, Ty. Don't add to the pile if you don't have to."

Of course, he was right. He usually was. I'd spent the last three years carrying a weight I couldn't put down, living in the shadow of grief and guilt.

But there was something about Lena that didn't let me stay numb. She wasn't Carrie. God, I already knew that. Lena was messy and complicated and had her own set of scars. But she made me finally feel something.

And that scared the hell out of me.

I sighed, trying to rein in the chaos in my head. "Fine. I'll think about it. But can we focus on you tonight? This is your weekend, not my soap opera."

Thomas studied me for a moment before nodding. "All right. But be careful. Don't get yourself into something you can't handle."

His words sliced through me, sharper than I wanted to admit. He was right. I didn't need more heartbreak. But as much as I hated to admit it, that kiss? It was like waking up after years of sleepwalking, and I wasn't sure I could go back to pretending I didn't feel anything.

As we exchanged a bro shoulder tap, I felt that familiar knot in my chest tighten. No matter how much I wanted to take his advice, my mind kept circling back to Lena. To the fire she'd ignited. To the question that wouldn't leave me alone.

Was I ready for all of this? Not just the bachelor party, but the whole messy, tangled thing with her? She had baggage. I had ghosts. And somewhere in between, there was a spark I hadn't felt in years.

The limo arrived, and the guys were already hyped for the bachelor party. Thomas was looking a little more uneasy than the rest of us. Poor guy had no idea what was coming. But he didn't have anything to worry about.

We pulled up to The Cadillac, the first stop on what I was already calling "The Bachelor Party Gauntlet."

Deeter—because of course it was Deeter—immediately handed Thomas a beer and told him he had to chug it while doing push-ups on the bar. Classic Deeter logic: combine drinking with physical exertion and pretend it was fun.

To his credit, Thomas, always the good sport, dropped down like this was his Olympic event. I stood there, arms crossed, already predicting the moment he'd start questioning every choice that had led him to this.

He powered through it, the crowd went wild like we'd just witnessed an historic athletic feat, and I gave him a solid slap on the back as he got up. "One down! Six more to go!" I said, smirking.

Thomas laughed, shaking his head as he brushed imaginary dirt off his hands. "Yeah, man, thanks for this 'once-in-a-lifetime experience.' Truly unforgettable."

I watched as he started to loosen up, realizing that tonight wasn't going to be some insane bachelor-party-gone-wrong scenario. It was just a series of scavenger-hunt-style tasks paired with bar hopping. Harmless fun.

But me? I wasn't here for the push-ups or the scavenger hunts. No, I was here to play wingman, make sure no one ended up arrested, and quietly enjoy the chaos from a safe, sarcastic distance.

Around bar number six, my phone buzzed. I pulled it out, and there it was. A text from Lena.

Lena: Come meet me.

Just three words. But holy hell, they hit like a freight train. My heart jumped and I felt that stupid little flicker of hope. The one I kept telling myself to snuff out.

A part of me—the rational part that had been listening to Thomas all night—told me to ignore it.

Thomas had been crystal clear, hadn't he? Lena was a mess. Not in a bad way, just in a not-ready-for-anything-real way.

And me? I had my own Everest of baggage. Survivor's guilt that felt like it came with a lifetime warranty.

So, naturally, I did the responsible thing. I ignored it.

Yup, that's right. I was a grown man with fully functioning adult instincts. I didn't need to go chasing after someone who came with more red flags than a referee's pocket.

Sure, she was sharp as hell, could verbally spar like a heavyweight, and, okay, yeah, she was insanely gorgeous. And sure, she might've lit a fuse inside me that I thought had burned out years ago.

But nope. Not doing it.

It was the right call. *Focus on Thomas, focus on the party.* This was his night, and I was here to celebrate him, not get tangled up in Lena chaos.

We hit the next bar, and I kept up the act. Laughing at the guys' over-the-top antics, tossing out snarky commentary, and egging Thomas on as he powered through another ridiculous challenge.

On the surface, I was having a great time, enjoying the bedlam of it all. In a sense, it was all easy and controlled—because it had nothing to do with feelings.

But deep down, a voice in the back of my head was already calling me out. *Dude, you're lying to yourself.*

Because no matter how many shots or jokes or distractions I threw at myself, the truth stayed there. Like a bruise I couldn't stop poking.

By the time we piled back into the limo, heading to Thomas's place to crash, I was wiped out. Physically, at least. Mentally? I felt like someone had plugged me into an outlet and cranked the voltage.

I pulled out my phone, and my stomach twisted when I saw that Lena hadn't texted back. Of course not. Why would she? She was probably smarter than I gave her credit for. Smart enough to steer clear of a guy carrying as much emotional baggage as I was.

Lena. Her text. Her smile. The way she'd looked at me like I wasn't just some broken-down relic of a guy trying to keep it together.

She made me feel.

And that was the problem, wasn't it? Feeling wasn't part of the plan. I'd spent the last three years mastering the art of not feeling. Of keeping everything locked up tight.

And now here I was, unraveling because of one sassy, infuriating, gorgeous woman who somehow managed to short-circuit my brain with three damn words.

Come meet me.

Chapter 5: Lena

Okay, here we go. Let's do this thing.

Mia's wedding day had arrived and I was one hundred percent, all the way in the party mindset. So I kept reminding myself.

"Mia, honey, you're absolutely radiant!" My mom's voice burst through the door like it was a parade float, loud enough to rattle the house. "I can't believe you're getting married today! Feels like I was just helping you with your first school dance!"

I bet she even added a little dramatic flourish for effect. Classic mom.

Mia giggled, probably because she didn't want to offend our mother's very real emotional breakdown happening in real-time. But I could tell it was sincere. She was just glowing today, like she was made of pure sunshine or something.

Meanwhile, I was over here clutching my half-finished cup of mimosa, trying not to projectile vomit from the pressure of being everyone's emotional support animal today.

I glanced at myself in the mirror. Smoothing my hair like it was going to solve anything. The last thing I needed right now was a panic attack, so I tried to just breathe and ignore the fact that my mom was hugging Mia for what felt like an eternity.

Then, like she just remembered I was in the room, Mom turned to me with her big, sparkly eyes. "And Lena, sweetheart! You're going to be stunning! I just know it. What's the plan for your hair? Have you decided on makeup? You need to get dressed!"

Oh, she was going for the 'I'm the most supportive mother ever' vibe. Adorable, if not a little misplaced.

I forced a smile so tight that my face might have actually cracked. "I wanted to make sure Mia shines before I start getting ready."

"Oh, honey, you'll shine too!" Mom's hand fluttered like she was brushing off a speck of lint, but it was actually more like a pat on the back for being the backup bride. "You're my beautiful girls. I can't believe how grown up you both are! It's all so magical."

Magic. Yeah. If by magic she meant everything was exactly what I'd been told it was supposed to be, then sure, it was magical.

But for me? Right now, not so much. More like an awkward, invisible specter in my sister's wedding party.

Mom kept talking about how "perfect" everything was, which, fine, I got it. But I was standing here, trapped between my sister's perfection and my own general dissatisfaction with my life, feeling like the only thing "perfect" here was how perfectly misplaced I felt.

I mentally checked out of the conversation while watching my mom smooth out Mia's dress like she was about to send her off to the prom. "Just wait until you see the church! Father Jacob went all out for you," she continued, her voice as high-pitched as a Disney character. "More flowers, more everything! It's all so perfect! Just like you deserve."

I forced a smile because that was what people did at weddings, right? Especially when they were desperately trying not to scream internally. "Mm-hmm. Perfect. Magical."

Whatever.

It was when I started shifting my weight between my feet that my brain decided it was time to remind me that I wasn't feeling so 'magical about any of this. The words that just slipped out of my mouth didn't even feel like they belonged to me.

"I should go get dressed," I said, trying for normal but sounding like I was announcing that I was about to be cremated. "Don't want to hold things up!"

Mia and Mom both looked at me like I'd just announced I was running away to join the circus. They looked like they thought I was about to bail on my own sister's wedding.

"Oh, don't be silly!" Mom's voice went up another octave, trying to hold it all together. "You're my daughters, and I want to see you both dolled up."

I swallowed hard, forcing myself to not snap back with a snarky, "Yeah, well, I was dolled up at my own wedding, remember?" But instead, I smiled. A fake one. "Sure, Mom. I'll go get dressed."

I tried to blend into the wallpaper, but of course, they were both too caught up in their own world to notice. My exit was practically a whisper. I couldn't even tell you how much I just wanted to crawl into a hole and disappear right now.

But instead, I slipped out of the bridal boudoir and into the adjoining room.

I closed the door, leaning against it, my breath coming out in a heavy sigh. I needed a moment. A real one. One where I didn't have to wear one of those forced smiles that everyone thought I was so good at.

My phone buzzed in my hand, and I immediately felt a twang of hope.

The disappointment hit me harder than I expected though when I saw there was still nothing from Tyler. That little "Come meet me" text I sent last night still had no response.

Seriously? Why couldn't I just get a simple text back? Maybe I was a glutton for punishment, but I thought maybe he'd be just as into this thing as I was.

I tossed the phone on the bench and slid out of my clothes, throwing on the bridesmaid dress as if it was going to magically fix everything. It didn't.

The fabric felt tight around my chest, but I squeezed it harder, like I could force all the frustration and disappointment out.

It didn't work. No matter how much I yanked at the seams, I couldn't get rid of that gnawing feeling.

***

The heavy church doors swung open, and my heart started to thump like I was running a marathon, not walking down the aisle.

Seriously, who even invented this tradition? Whoever it was, clearly never had to do it in front of a bunch of strangers. Well, today they weren't all strangers, half of them were actually my family. But my sister's wedding day felt like an open mic night for all my insecurities.

I shifted my weight as I waited my turn to walk down the aisle. First bridesmaid. Second and third. Now me. *Here we go!*

I tried to focus on the music. The string quartet was doing their thing, and the violins were trying their best to calm me down, but nope. Still felt like I might spontaneously combust.

Then there he was. Tyler.

The man who had the audacity to be standing at the altar next to the groom, looking like he was born in a tuxedo, without even having the decency to look at me. I swear to God, if there was a spotlight on him, it would've had angelic music playing over it.

But, whatever. His face looked like a cold, hard wall of stone.

Great, here we were. Me, feeling like I might choke on my own feelings, and him? Blank as a Sunday morning.

I mean, what the hell? After everything that happened between us, this was how we were doing it? No reaction? Nothing? Fine. I mean, it's not like I was dying to see him look at me with any emotion. Nope, totally fine.

I forced a smile. A big, stupid smile. For Mia, for the guests, for the fact that I was trying my damn hardest to keep it together. Smile, Lena. You can do this. Smile. No big deal. It was just your sister's wedding, and it was just Tyler acting like you weren't standing ten feet away from him. Deep breath.

By the time I reached the altar, I was practically sweating with frustration. I thought maybe he'd at least flinch or acknowledge me. But nope. Nada.

My heart sank like an anchor, and suddenly, I wasn't sure if I was supposed to laugh or cry.

When the ceremony finally wrapped up, I had a tiny sliver of hope when Tyler stepped forward and offered me his arm.

Oh, good. He was going to speak now, maybe apologize for his ghosting me and for being a complete jerk...right?

Wrong.

Not even a glance. I tried to ignore the ache in my chest as we walked, my heart picking up speed for the wrong reasons. But he just stared straight ahead like he couldn't be bothered to notice I was there. I tried, but I couldn't stop the snarky little comment from escaping: "Guess you're not talking to me."

I swear, if I didn't know better, I'd say my words went in one ear and out the other. He didn't even bat an eyelash. *Great, Tyler. I get it. Just keep being your hot, brooding, emotionally unavailable self.*

As we stepped into the vestibule, the air was suddenly flooded with hugs and congratulations, everyone spilling out like a bottle of champagne shaken too much. Thomas and Tyler did their bro thing, and Mia—bless her heart—whisked me into a hug like nothing was wrong.

"Oh my gosh, Lena, I'm married!" Mia squealed, practically bouncing off the floor. "Isn't it just perfect?"

"Yeah, it's beautiful," I said, matching her energy as best I could. Which was a huge swing from one end of the spectrum to the other. Honestly, my insides were ready to start a riot.

I held on a little longer than I should've, hoping that maybe the way I clung to her would distract me from the fact that my brain kept flashing to Tyler, standing there like a statue, making me feel invisible.

I barely even noticed the photographer rounding us up for group photos until I was shoved into place beside Mia, plastering another fake smile on my face.

Tyler was right there, stoic as ever. How did he do that? Be so unaffected?

My stomach twisted as the photographer snapped endless pictures, my patience eroding by the second.

Tyler stood chatting it up with Thomas and the groomsmen, while I just stood there, pretending like my soul wasn't withering in the corner.

I watched him from across the room, laughing at something Thomas said, like everything was fine. Like I didn't matter.

And that, right there? That hurt more than I cared to admit.

***

Dinner was over, the plates cleared, and the clinking of glasses filled the room like some kind of symphony. The party had settled into a rhythm, champagne glasses in hand, murmurs of conversation blending into a soft buzz.

Meanwhile, I was about to have a heart attack from the anticipation of being up next.

I looked around the room, the soft glow of the candles making everything feel cozy, almost magical. The twinkling lights strung up everywhere made it feel like a scene from a Christmas movie.

And then there was Mia. My little sister, all glowing and giddy, laughing at something Thomas whispered into her ear. She looked like she was living a fairytale, and I just… well, I felt like I was at the edges of it all, looking in. A part of it, but not quite a part of it.

I took a quick sip of my drink, trying to shake off the weirdness, but before I could talk myself out of it, the DJ piped up: "Alright ladies and gentlemen, now it's time to hear from Lena, Mia's sister and the maid-of-honor!"

Cue the clinking of silverware. Everyone's eyes were on me. Great. Just what I needed. I could feel them all looking at me like, "Hey, wasn't this supposed to be *your* moment once upon a time?"

But I squared my shoulders, shook off the weird vibes, and stood up.

Mia shot me this quick little smile—one of those "you've got this" sister smiles—and I could tell she was already hyped.

I didn't want to let her down, so I decided right then that I was going to do this with style. And by "style," I meant the kind that was just a little bit too much.

Grabbing my glass, I cleared my throat and tapped it, all eyes now fully on me. I glanced down at some invisible notes in my hand, ones I wouldn't follow anyway. No, this was always going to be off-the-cuff, just like the best speeches are, right?

I flashed a smile at Mia, giving her a little wink, and then I leaned into the mic.

"Alright, first things first," I said, taking a deep breath. "Hi, everyone. For the half of this room I may not have met yet, I'm Lena, Mia's slightly older, marginally wiser, and let's be honest, more entertaining sister. As the maid of honor, it's my job to stand up here, give a speech, and pretend I'm not secretly hoping that the open bar stays open forever."

A few chuckles bounced around the room, and I could see Mia's face light up. Her eyes practically sparkled. The crowd was with me.

"Now, when I was told to make this speech, I did what any self-respecting, procrastinating millennial would do. I Googled 'how to give a great maid of honor speech.' And let me tell you, the Internet is full of bad advice. Apparently, I'm supposed to say something heartfelt, avoid embarrassing stories, and keep it short. So naturally, I ignored all of that."

Laughter rippled through the crowd. Mia rolled her eyes like she always did when I made silly statements.

"Let me take you back to when we were kids," I continued. "Before Mia and I moved to our own rooms, we originally shared a bedroom. Which, let me tell you, is not as adorable as sitcoms would have you believe."

"One summer, we decided we wanted bunk beds. You know, because we thought they'd be fun. So the first night, Mia got the top bunk because she was 'braver.' Cut to about two in the morning, when I'm deep in REM cycle and suddenly *WHAM!* Mia rolls off the top bunk and lands directly on me. No warning. No apology. Just a human meteor straight to my spleen. I screamed, she cried. Mom and Dad came in explaining to her that 'gravity is not optional.'"

"The moral of the story back then? Bunk beds are a terrible idea. But the moral of the story tonight? Love is kind of like those bunk beds."

I paused for effect, shaking my head. "Stay with me, people. Sometimes, you're going to fall. You're going to roll right out of the cozy spot you thought was safe, and it's going to hurt. But if you're lucky, you've got someone there to break your fall. Or, in Mia's case, someone to scream at you until Dad comes in with ice packs."

That got a good laugh. Mia grinned at me, her whole body relaxing, and I could feel the room warming up to the story.

"And Thomas? You're that someone for Mia. You've shown each other, and all of us, what it means to truly love someone. To lift them up when they need it, catch them when they fall, and always, always keep their heart safe." I waved my hand in the air dramatically. "Well, I've sure got some things to figure out."

The laughter that followed that remark felt real this time. Like a release. And honestly? I didn't care that it was at my expense because I needed it.

"But seriously," I added, letting my tone shift. I looked right at Mia and Thomas. "You two give us hope. You show us that love can work out. That if we stick around long enough, we can make it happen. And, let's be honest, you make the rest of us believe that maybe we can get it right."

I raised my glass, and the crowd responded with a round of applause. Mia's eyes were a little glossy as I hugged her fiercely. She was happy, so so happy, and that made all of this worth it.

As the DJ grabbed the mic from me, Tyler took his place.

I caught Thomas giving me this half warning, half plea look, but I didn't have time to care. I already spoke. What trouble could I cause now? Besides, I was currently bracing my heartstrings for whatever Tyler was about to say.

Tyler stepped up to the mic and tapped it like he was making sure it wasn't one of those budget ones that would squeal like a dying cat. Then looked out at the crowd with a *Why am I doing this?* expression.

The room hushed, all eyes on him. "Good evening, everyone," he started, his voice low and dry. "I'm Tyler. As most of you know, I've been Thomas's best friend since preschool. And let me just say, if you think *this* is a long-term commitment, try holding onto the same best friend for almost three decades. That's the real endurance test."

Cue the collective "aww" from the room. I almost rolled my eyes, but, hey, self-control.

"All right. Let's see. Where to begin..." he leaned casually against the podium. "First, I'd like to apologize in advance. I don't do public speaking. My last speech was a halftime pep talk, and it mostly consisted of me yelling, 'Don't suck!' I won't tell you whether it worked that time. But maybe it'll work this time."

Chuckles from the crowd.

Tyler cleared his throat and kept going, his face set in that perpetual look of mild annoyance that somehow made him even hotter. "Thomas. My best friend. My brother from another mother. A man who, despite knowing me for so long, still hasn't figured out that cargo shorts are a crime against humanity. But you're a good guy. And Mia..." He paused, glancing at her. "You're the best thing that ever happened to him. No offense, Fantasy Football League Championship 2017."

The crowd cracked up, while Thomas grabbed his hands at his heart like he'd been pained and yelled, "My QB's were terrible!"

Mia smiled, and Tyler leaned into his next bit. "Look, I could stand here and give you the usual clichés. 'Marriage is a journey,' 'communication is key,' blah, blah, blah. How would I know? But honestly? I think marriage might be a lot like a football game." He gestured with his glass, already regretting this analogy. "Sometimes you're on offense, sometimes defense. Occasionally, someone throws a flag, and you have no idea what you did wrong. And don't even get me started on overtime."

People laughed, which only encouraged him. "But the best teams? They stick together. They don't give up, even when the score looks bad. They put in the work. And that's what you two are. MVPs of this whole love thing. Plus, Mia, let's face it, you're the real star player here. Thomas is just lucky to be on your team."

Thomas pretended to groan, and Tyler smirked, looking like he was enjoying himself. "All right, let's wrap this up before someone tackles me off this stage. Thomas, you're a lucky guy. And Mia, you're a saint. Seriously, you married Thomas. Saint status unlocked. Here's to both of you. May your love be as strong as Mia's patience and as enduring as Thomas's terrible taste in music."

He raised his glass and added, almost as an afterthought, "Also, if you ever need marriage advice... well, I'm basically a walking Wikipedia of useful analogies. You're welcome in advance."

Everyone roared with laughter, and Tyler sat down, looking a mix of proud and relieved, like a guy who just survived his first roller coaster. I swear, he might've been grumpy 99% of the time, but in that moment? He put on a show and nailed it.

The DJ called for the couple's first dance and soon the wedding party was called out to join them. Suddenly, I was being dragged onto the dance floor by Tyler. No words. Just a hand extended, and I took it. My pulse instantly racing.

We swayed. I tried not to notice the way his hand felt on my waist, or the heat of him next to me. I forced myself to focus on the dance, but I couldn't help it. I looked up at him, searching for a hint of... something.

"Are you planning on ignoring me forever?" I whispered before I could stop myself.

He didn't look at me. "It's complicated, Lena," he muttered, his voice low and tight.

I scoffed. "Complicated? You didn't seem to think so the other night."

He didn't answer. His eyes flicked away. Great. Just great.

"Maybe we should stay out of each other's way," I said, my voice a little too calm for how I felt.

He nodded, barely glancing at me. "That's what's best."

And just like that, the dance was over. I felt the distance between us widen, and he walked away, leaving me standing there, all the unasked questions swirling in my chest. But I had no choice. I had to keep going, keep pretending like it didn't tear me apart.

So I did what any good sister would do.

I stayed, I smiled, I danced, and I made it through the rest of the night. Only to realize later that, for all the smiles, the night had somehow left me feeling more alone than ever.

Chapter 6: Tyler

The morning after the wedding. What a disaster.

Thomas's wedding? A roaring success. Me? A train wreck with a hangover for cargo. But hey, it wasn't about me today, right?

It was about the fact that Lena was standing just a few feet away, laughing with her sister, and I was using every ounce of willpower not to haul her into some quiet corner and ask her what the hell we were doing.

Seriously, what were we doing?

Her laugh? That laugh should've come with a warning label. Dangerous. The kind of dangerous where you knew full well it was bad for you, but you leaned into it anyway. It was soft, like cotton candy, but it stuck with you long after it should've dissolved. And the worst part? It cut through the room like it was designed to target my willpower. Damn her.

Meanwhile, Mia and Thomas were still doing their farewell lap. Hugging everyone, being disgustingly adorable. While I pretended to be deeply fascinated by the view out the window.

I wasn't.

They were heading off to their dream honeymoon. Thomas? Living the life. Me? I was stuck replaying the way Lena's eyes had flicked to mine last night, like she was testing the water. And I was drowning the second she looked.

I shoved my hands deeper into my pockets, hoping I looked casual and not like a man teetering on the edge of unraveling. But keeping my distance from her? Impossible. It was like trying to hold back the tide with a paper umbrella.

All I could think about was last night on the dance floor. The tension between us was thicker than a defensive line on fourth and goal. That conversation we'd started but hadn't finished? Yeah, it was still hanging there, laughing in my face.

What I really wanted was to pull her aside, get close, and say... something. Anything. Maybe something smooth and profound. Or maybe just, "Hey, you're driving me nuts." But of course, I went with my usual approach. Silent, brooding, and completely useless.

Thomas's mom gave him one of those full-on mom hugs, the kind that said, *I'll miss you, but stay safe and call me when you land.*

Meanwhile, I stood there, trying to act normal—like I wasn't quietly dying inside. "Have the greatest honeymoon ever, you hear me?" I told him, slapping on a grin so fake it could've come from a discount Halloween store. But hey, I was making an effort. Gold star for me.

"Yeah, yeah," Thomas said, chuckling as he clapped me on the back hard enough to make me stumble. "With Mia by my side, that's an easy ask."

Lena hugged Mia, and then her eyes found me. Just for a second, maybe two. But long enough for my chest to tighten like someone had sucker-punched me with a brick.

Perfect. Just perfect. Another reminder that I was absolutely, undeniably screwed.

When the newlyweds finally made their big escape, the room turned into chaos. People scattered like ants at a picnic. Some heading for the kitchen to help, others flopping in front of the TV, probably gearing up for a food coma.

And me? I ended up in the kitchen, recruited—no, *roped*—into arranging crackers on a charcuterie board like I was auditioning for the role of world's grumpiest butler. At least it gave me something to do, though. Distracting myself with cheese arrangements was apparently my new coping mechanism.

But then came the sound that changed everything.

Mom. I didn't need to see her to know it was her. The faint squeal of panic that came from the other room? Yeah, I'd recognize the sound of her voice anywhere. And my stomach twisted, because I knew something was coming.

Nope. Please God. Not today. Not my mom.

"Mom?" I called, voice cracking, already heading toward the living room without even thinking.

And there she was, my mom crumpled on the floor, in the hallway, eyes wide and confused.

Panic ripped through my chest like a linebacker on a blitz. My breath came too fast, too shallow, like I'd forgotten how lungs were supposed to work.

I dropped to my knees beside her, my hands trembling as I tried to hold her arm without making things worse. "Someone call 911!"

My voice cracked. Real smooth, Tyler.

I was unraveling. Completely losing it. She looked so damn fragile, and the thought of losing her? It wasn't just scary, it was unbearable. I couldn't lose her too. Not her. Not now. Not after everything.

And then, like a beacon cutting through the fog, Lena's voice rang out. Calm. Steady. Somehow both gentle and firm, like she'd been trained for this exact moment.

She was on the phone with 911, rattling off details like she'd done it a hundred times. Her eyes flicked to mine, locking me in place with a gaze that said, *"Get your shit together."*

I tried. God, I tried. But my hands were still shaking, my chest still tight.

Then, out of nowhere, her hand reached for mine. Warm, steady, grounding. Like she was pulling me back from the edge of the cliff I was teetering on. For a second, I just held on, clinging to her like she was the only solid thing in a world gone sideways.

Her voice softened as she turned to my mom. "Lorraine, it's okay. I'm right here. The ambulance is coming, and they're going to take care of you."

Mom blinked slowly, her eyes flitting between Lena and me. But she couldn't focus. The sight gutted me.

"They think it's a stroke," Lena said, her voice low but certain. "They advised giving her some aspirin if we have some."

My brain locked up. Aspirin. Stroke. Mom. The words swirled together in a storm I couldn't navigate. I was frozen, paralyzed by the sight of the strongest woman I'd ever known reduced to this fragile version of herself.

"Mom!" Lena's voice sliced through the haze, sharp but controlled. "Charla, we need aspirin, please!"

It was like she already knew what to do, moving with this quiet confidence that was as baffling as it was reassuring. Charla appeared with the pills, and Lena helped me prop Mom up just enough to take them, her touch steadying both of us.

And me? I was barely holding on by a thread.

The sound of the ambulance siren cut through the air like a slap, jolting me back to reality. Watching them load Mom onto the stretcher felt surreal, like a scene from someone else's nightmare. Lena stayed right there, her hand wrapped around Mom's until the very last second.

As the ambulance pulled away, I stood there, rooted to the spot, staring after it like it had stolen everything I cared about.

Then Lena's voice cut through again, calm and unshaken. "Tyler, you're going to the hospital. Do you want me to drive you?"

I nodded, my throat too tight to speak. "Yeah... yeah, thanks."

She didn't push. Didn't say anything else. Just squeezed my shoulder and led me to her car like it was the most natural thing in the world.

The drive was a blur, the streets flying past without me registering a single one. All I could see was Mom's face. Pale, confused, fragile. The image played on an endless loop in my head, a cruel highlight reel I couldn't shut off.

Then Lena spoke, her voice breaking through the chaos like a lifeline. "My grandmother had a stroke once," she said, steady but soft. "It was terrifying. One moment she was fine, and the next... she wasn't."

She glanced at me, her hands firm on the wheel. "We called 911 and gave her an aspirin, just like we did for your mom. They told us later it probably saved her life. She fully recovered."

Fully recovered. The words hit me like a defibrillator, jolting a spark of hope into my chest. "Fully?" I croaked, my voice barely audible.

She nodded, her confidence unwavering. "Fully. We did everything right, Tyler. Fast action. That's what matters."

I swallowed hard, the lump in my throat refusing to budge. I wanted to believe her. Hell, I needed to believe her. But the fear was still there, coiling tighter around my chest with every breath.

When we pulled into the hospital parking lot, my legs felt like lead. But I forced myself to move. Get out of the car and walk into the hospital. Because not showing up for Mom wasn't an option.

Hospitals smelled like failure and lemon-scented denial, and they hit you with fluorescent lights so aggressive they could interrogate your soul.

At the desk, I tried to speak, but the words got stuck, tangled in the knot of fear and guilt and desperation lodged in my throat. And then there was Lena, stepping up beside me, ready to do what I couldn't.

"Hello…" she began, her voice all smooth confidence as she squinted at the clerk's name tag. "…Gina. This is Lorraine Soto's son. She's being brought in by ambulance, and we'd like to get in to see her."

Gina nodded and started clacking away at her keyboard, like she was auditioning for Fastest Typist Alive. "Do you have her ID or insurance info?"

Lena turned to me, her eyebrows raised in question. I stared back at her, probably looking like a deer caught in headlights, except more useless and somehow less photogenic.

"Tyler, why don't you grab a seat? I'll handle this," she said, her voice soft but firm. The kind of voice you'd use to coax a feral cat into trusting you.

I didn't argue. Hell, I couldn't argue. My legs moved on autopilot, and before I knew it, I was planted in one of those hard plastic chairs that seemed custom-designed to add insult to injury.

Time dragged on, each second feeling like an hour. My hands fidgeted in my lap, clenching and unclenching as I tried not to let the storm inside my head spill out.

Finally, Lena sat down beside me. She wasn't frazzled, wasn't even remotely ruffled. "They've got her info in the system," she said, her voice like a calm sea. "Your dad can update anything later if needed."

I nodded but kept my gaze fixed on the floor, as if the cheap tile had suddenly become the most fascinating thing in the universe. My chest felt tight, like someone had wrapped it in barbed wire.

"You want me to go pick up your dad?" she asked gently. "Or I could drop you off first—"

"No." The word shot out of me like a reflex. I cleared my throat, trying to sound less like a human panic attack. "No. Can you just…stay? I don't know how long this'll take, but…" My voice cracked, and I hated it. Hated feeling this raw, this exposed.

Her hand landed on my arm, grounding me in a way I hadn't realized I needed. "Of course I'll stay. Whatever you need."

I nodded again, swallowing hard. Gratitude burned in my throat, but I couldn't force the words out. Instead, I broke the silence with a confession I hadn't planned. "She's not just my mom, you know. She's…everything. My best friend. She's the one who keeps it all together." My voice faltered. "I'm not ready to lose her."

"You're not going to lose her," Lena said, her tone soft but firm, like iron wrapped in velvet. "Not today. She's strong, Tyler. And she's got you."

Her conviction hit me like a life raft in a storm. For a moment, I let myself believe her, let her words chip away at the icy fear that had wrapped itself around my chest.

"She's a fighter," Lena added, her hand still on my arm. "And you? You're exactly what she needs right now."

I let out a bitter laugh. "I froze, Lena. I didn't know what to do. Some hero, huh?"

She tilted her head, her gaze soft but unwavering. "You were there. That's what matters. Sometimes just showing up is enough."

Her words burrowed into me, settling in the cracks of my self-doubt. I exhaled, the breath shaky but real. "Thanks," I muttered. "For everything."

She just smiled, leaning back in her chair like it was no big deal. But to me? It was everything.

Then, like fate had impeccable comic timing, a nurse called out, "Family of Lorraine Soto?"

"That's me," I said, already on my feet, my voice steady for the first time in what felt like hours.

The nurse gestured for me to follow. Lena was right behind me, her presence solid and unwavering, like a shadow that refused to leave.

Walking down that hall felt like marching into a battlefield, every step heavier than the last. My brain served up its greatest hits: every possible worst-case scenario, remixed with guilt and a side of dread.

When we reached the room, I braced myself, but nothing could've prepared me for the sight of my mom. Lorraine Soto, the strongest woman I knew, looked…small.

The hospital bed dwarfed her. Wires and monitors surrounded her, and her skin was pale, her hair unkempt. She never did unkempt.

"Mom," I whispered, the word catching in my throat.

Lena didn't say anything. She just stood beside me, close enough that her shoulder brushed against mine. Her silence spoke louder than words, and for once, I was grateful.

The nurse broke the stillness. "Her vitals are stable. The doctor will be in shortly to explain more."

I nodded, my gaze never leaving my mom. I gripped the bed rail like it was the only thing keeping me from falling apart.

"You're going to be okay," I said, more to myself than to her. Because if I said it enough, maybe it would be true.

Lena slid her hand over mine, her touch warm and steady. I didn't look at her, but I felt it. Her hand was saying what I couldn't quite believe yet. You're not alone in this.

And then the doctor strolled in, clipboard in hand, with the kind of expression that's supposed to calm you down but only made my blood pressure spike. "I'm Dr. Voss," she said, professional but not cold.

I shot out my hand for a quick shake. "Tyler Soto. Thanks for helping my mom. Please tell me she's okay."

Dr. Voss dove into the spiel. Mild stroke. Optimistic prognosis. No apparent serious damage. Consciousness soon.

Blah, blah, blah. It should've felt like good news, but my brain was stuck on the word *stroke*. Like, how the hell did we even get here?

Still, a wave of relief slammed into me. It wasn't over. Not yet.

I dropped into the chair beside Mom's bed, my knees threatening to give out completely. Lena sat next to me, her silence somehow louder than my thoughts. She didn't try to fill the space with words, and I could've hugged her for it. Except, you know, personal boundaries and all.

When the doctor left, I leaned forward, my forehead brushing the edge of Mom's bed. My hand closed around hers, so frail it made my chest ache. "You've got this, Mom," I muttered. "You're the toughest person I know."

The past two days played on a loop in my head, and there was Lena in all of it, like some unexpected constant. The woman who made me roll my eyes so hard I almost saw my brain was also the one who somehow kept me tethered to reality.

And then it hit me: I'd judged her all wrong. Sure, Lena was chaos wrapped in charm, but there was something deeper. Something I hadn't let myself see. Maybe it was time to stop writing her off as a walking tornado.

Before I could spiral further, Mom's fingers twitched. My head snapped up, eyes locked on her hand. "Mom?" I whispered, my voice cracking.

Her eyelids fluttered, just a little, and my breath caught in my throat. Relief, hope, fear—it all crashed over me, and for the first time in what felt like forever, I let myself believe she was going to fight her way back and something might go as I wanted.

Either way, I'd be right here, whether I deserved to be or not.

Chapter 7: Lena

Confusion flickered across Lorraine's face, or maybe it was distress—hard to tell when someone's fresh out of a medical emergency.

The second I locked eyes with her, my stomach did a little flop. I felt the moment thud into place like the awkward silence after you realize you've been waving at someone who wasn't actually waving back.

The sterile stress of the hospital room provided a symphonic backdrop of beeps and hums as Lorraine's eyes fluttered open. Groggy and disoriented. She looked around like she'd just been invited to a party she wasn't entirely sure she wanted to attend.

Tyler leaned in close, his tone all gentle but matter-of-fact. "Mom, you're in the hospital. You had a stroke." His hand cradled hers like it might shatter if he held it too tight.

I recognized this about Tyler's demeanor: rock-solid on the outside, all stormy seas underneath. I could practically feel the tremor in his voice, even though he was holding it together like the broody hero in a melodrama.

Lorraine's lips moved, but the sounds were more abstract art than conversation. Tyler didn't flinch. He just nodded like she'd said something profound and encouraged her to keep going. "It's okay, Mom. Just keep talking. I'm here."

When her gaze slid to me, her brow crinkled. Ah, yes, the universal look of "Who the hell are you, and why are you in my personal space?"

I gave her my warmest "don't mind me, I'm harmless" smile. A classic Lena move—part charm, part defense mechanism.

Tyler caught my eye. For half a second, his usual guard dropped, replaced by something that looked suspiciously like gratitude. Then he was back to Lorraine, telling her, "Lena's the one who called 911. She got us here in time."

Oh, sure, Tyler. Tell her that now, when she's too out of it to remember I was here. But Lorraine's face softened, and her lips moved again, forming something that sounded like it could be "thank you." Barely.

"Of course," I said, swallowing the lump in my throat that came out of nowhere. I touched her hand, mine landing just beside Tyler's like it belonged there. "You're going to be okay. We've got you."

Before I could get all Florence Nightingale in a fluffy sweater, the door swung open, and Nurse Sunshine waltzed in.

"Hi, I'm Tara!" she chirped, clipboard in hand. She gave Lorraine the once-over and then aimed her bright smile at us. "She's looking good! Stable and in great hands."

"Great hands" might've been a under-selling it, given they were Tyler's and his grip on her looked like he was worried she'd float away. But I wasn't about correcting her.

Tara rattled off the plan: rest, therapy, rinse, repeat. Tyler asked a few questions in that gravelly voice of his, the kind that would make you want to spill your darkest secrets or agree to whatever he asked. He finally unclenched a bit when Tara said Lorraine was doing well.

After Nurse Tara left, Tyler exhaled like he'd never done so before. Lorraine was already drifting off again, and the room settled into a quiet that was punctuated by the rhythmic beep of machines.

I stood to grab a cup of water and plopped it in Tyler's hand like I was some sort of hydration fairy. "Drink," I commanded, sitting back down. Our shoulders brushed, which shouldn't have made my heart do a little jig, but it did.

"I'm glad we got her here in time," I said, voice soft. It felt like the right thing to say, even though the whole situation had my emotions playing hopscotch.

"Yeah." He took a sip, then paused. "You were cool under pressure. Thanks for that." His words carried a weight, like he wasn't just thanking me for the ambulance call.

I shrugged, trying to downplay it because emotional sincerity is not my comfort zone. "Just doing my civic duty. Also, family's a big deal, and it's clear your mom's your whole world."

He nodded, looking at her like she was the only thing keeping him tethered to the ground. "She is. And yeah, about us… avoiding each other's been… tricky."

I smirked, going for levity because the tension between us was about to strangle me. "Tricky? Please. We've been circling each other like two pimple-faced middle schoolers at a dance."

That earned a chuckle, low and warm. "More like fate's playing a really long game of chicken."

I snorted. "Or the universe needs new hobbies."

We fell into silence again, the kind that wasn't uncomfortable but wasn't easy, either. Tyler had his baggage, and I had mine. And maybe we were both trying to figure out if the weight of it all was too much—or just enough to keep us grounded.

"I don't know why," he said after some time, while his mom slept. His voice was heavy, like it carried the weight of the world and maybe a side of fries. "But I'm drawn to you. And no matter how hard we try, we keep finding ourselves together. I don't know if I want to keep fighting it. Because it's been a long time since I've felt the way you're making me feel, Lena."

So... this was a pickle. Sitting in a hospital room, surrounded by the faint beeping of machines, the smell of antiseptic, and Tyler Soto—the human equivalent of a broody thundercloud—telling me I made him feel things. Things he apparently hadn't felt in a long time.

Let me tell you, my sass-tastic brain didn't know whether to swoon, smirk, or sprint for the hills.

Cue internal monologue. *Danger, Lena Sheridan. This man is gravelly-voiced kryptonite. Proceed with caution.*

My heart fluttered like it was auditioning for a musical, and I almost said, "Same here, buddy," before doing a pas de bourrée. Instead, I channeled all the self-restraint I didn't use when buying clearance candles at Target.

"Me too, Tyler. But we can't just...ignore reality. I mean, your family doesn't like me, my family definitely doesn't want me stirring up more drama, and, oh yeah, timing? Not exactly stellar."

"All right…" he said, the resignation in his voice doing terrible, sinful things to me. His eyes locked onto mine like he was trying to solve a mystery. Or undress me with his mind. Possibly both.

And there I was, biting my lip like some clichéd romance heroine who hadn't learned a single lesson from her ill-fated love life. Torn between wanting to keep things simple (*Ha! Simple? Who am I kidding?*) and giving in to this insane connection we had.

The worst part? Tyler wasn't just attractive in a "grumpy lumberjack" way. No, he had layers. Tragic, broody, emotionally-constipated layers.

He carried pain like it was an accessory, the kind of heartbreak you could feel in the way he spoke, looked, even stood. And yeah, I was completely wondering what it'd take to make him smile—like, full-blown, teeth-baring smile, not whatever half-hearted smirks I'd managed to pull so far.

As Lorraine's breathing deepened, Tyler's hand brushed mine. Just a small, accidental touch, but it might as well have been a lightning strike.

I didn't move away. Nope, I stayed there like an idiot who wanted to feel that spark again.

He leaned in, and everything in me froze. *Holy crap, was this actually happening? Here?* My lips parted a little because, let's be honest, I was 100% here for this kiss.

But of course, because the universe had a sick sense of humor, footsteps clomped into the room.

Tyler's dad, Emmitt, walked in. The timing was so perfect that I half-expected him to say, "Did I interrupt something?"

"Tyler, son, how are you doing?" Emmitt's voice was warm and fatherly, pulling Tyler out of whatever moment we were about to have.

He stood up, practically snapped to attention like a kid caught sneaking cookies.

Emmitt gave me a polite nod, his eyes lingering just long enough to say, "I see you, and I know you're trouble." Great.

Another adult who thought I was a walking bad decision. Add him to the list.

"Why don't you take a break?" Emmitt suggested after hugging Tyler. "I'll stay with your mom tonight. You've been here all day. You should get some rest and come back fresh tomorrow."

Tyler glanced my way, his jaw tightening. "I could…use some air." His voice was rough, like he wanted to say something else but couldn't figure out how.

I jumped in, putting on my best nonchalant voice. "You stay here with your family. I've got errands to run anyway." Total lie, by the way. My only errand was not kissing Tyler Soto. "Your mom needs you, and I don't want to make things more…"

I was going to say "complicated".

He looked at me, and for a second, I thought he might argue. Instead, he nodded, his hands flexing like he wanted to reach out but didn't dare.

"Okay," he said, barely above a whisper.

Emmitt cleared his throat, reminding us he was still there, watching. "Lena," he said with a nod that somehow managed to pack a lifetime of disapproval into one syllable. Then he left the room, saying something about coffee, leaving Tyler and me alone again.

Tyler glanced at his mom, then back at me, and the room suddenly felt too small. Too hot. Too...everything.

"Your mom needs you," I said softly, trying not to let my voice shake. "And so does your dad. I'll check in with you later."

As soon as the door clicked shut, Tyler pulled me into his arms, his lips crushing mine in a hungry kiss. I melted into him, my hands sliding up his strong back, relishing the feel of his muscular body against mine. His hands tangled in my hair, tilting my head for a deeper kiss. I could taste the hunger and desperation in his mouth, a hunger I shared.

"God, Lena, I've wanted to do that for so long," he murmured against my lips, his breath hot on my skin.

"Me too," I whispered back, my body buzzing with desire. "But we can't... not here."

Tyler groaned, his hands sliding down to my waist, pulling me tightly against him. "I know, but it's so damn hard to stop."

I shivered at his words, my lips aching for him. "I want it too, but we have to be smart about this. We've already caused enough waves. Let's not make things worse." I gently pushed him away, my body protesting the loss of his touch.

With one last lingering look, I turned and left the hospital room, my body humming with anticipation and desire.

***

The hospital doors whooshed shut behind me, and the crisp autumn air smacked me in the face like a reality check I hadn't asked for.

I found a bench, plopped myself down, and exhaled the kind of deep breath that comes after a day of dodging emotional landmines. My brain was doing its best impression of a blender, mixing Tyler's kiss, his broody eyes, and his ridiculous ability to make me feel like a human sparkler.

And then, a buttery voice seemed to slide into my chest from under my skin.

"Lena, I thought that was you."

Oh, good. Just when I thought the universe might cut me some slack, Marco made a surprise appearance.

Of course, he looked like a walking cologne ad—dark eyes, his perfect chin doing it's whole chiseled but tormented thing.

"Marco," I said, turning slowly because if I spun too fast, I might throw up from sheer emotional whiplash. "What are you doing here? Shouldn't you be off charming a room full of unsuspecting strangers?"

He ignored the jab, stepping closer with his trademark I'm-so-dreamy-it-hurts smile. "Visiting a friend. What about you?" His voice was as smooth as ever, but there was an edge—like he was trying too hard to sound casual.

I shrugged, trying to keep my face neutral. "Same. Hospitals are apparently the new coffee shops."

His eyes flicked over me, lingering a second too long, and it made my skin prickle in a way I wasn't ready to unpack. "You look gorgeous, Lena. It's been a while."

Oh, here we go. That half-flirty, half-guilty tone he used when he wanted to sound noble but still remind me he was super available.

"Yeah, well, you know what they say. Running away from your own wedding does wonders for the complexion."

His smirk faltered, replaced by something darker. "Funny. I don't remember laughing about it."

Yikes. Okay. So, we're skipping past polite small talk and diving headfirst into awkward truths hour. Cool. Cool, cool, cool.

"Look, Marco," I started, forcing a sigh. "I know I hurt you, but—"

"But nothing," he interrupted, his voice sharp enough to cut glass. "You didn't just hurt me, Lena. You destroyed me. Do you have any idea what it was like standing there while you turned and ran the other way? While everyone whispered and stared?"

Oof. Direct hit. My shoulders sagged under the weight of his words, but I refused to let him see me crumble. "I wasn't in the right place, Marco. We weren't in the right place. And deep down, you know that."

His eyes flashed, and for a second, he looked like he wanted to argue. But then he just laughed—bitter and low. "That's such a Lena thing to say. You just couldn't handle the pressure, so you ran. Left me to pick up the pieces while you, what? Found yourself?"

"Okay, you know what?" I stood up, jabbing a finger in his direction. "You don't get to throw the I'm-the-victim card around like it's a gold medal. You pressured me into things I wasn't ready for, Marco. You knew I was struggling, and instead of being there for me, you acted like your charm could solve everything!"

His face softened, just a little, and I hated how much it hurt to see that crack in his armor. "I tried, Lena. I really tried to be what you needed."

"Yeah? Well, maybe what I needed was someone who could listen without making it about themselves."

The words hung in the air between us, heavy and raw. For a moment, neither of us spoke. Then Marco sighed, running a hand through his perfectly tousled hair.

"I've missed you," he admitted quietly, his voice stripped of its usual bravado. "I shouldn't say it, but it's true."

My chest tightened, the familiar pull of his presence mixing with the knowledge of all the ways we'd failed each other. "Marco..."

"I know," he said quickly, holding up a hand. "I know it's complicated. I know I shouldn't want you back. But seeing you here..." He trailed off, his eyes locking with mine in a way that made my breath hitch.

I shook my head, stepping back before the heat between us could suffocate me. "We can't just pick up where we left off, Marco. You know that."

He nodded, though his jaw tightened. "I just... I had to say it."

I swallowed the lump in my throat, forcing myself to look him in the eye. "I hope you're happy, Marco. I really do. But I'm not the person you remember. And I'm not sure I ever was."

But then, Marco and his lips crashed into mine like a bad rom-com scene—except instead of swooning, I froze. It wasn't sweet or tender. It was aggressive, like he thought sheer determination could rewrite the last five weeks. Spoiler alert: it couldn't.

"God, I've missed this," he murmured, his voice dripping with nostalgia. "I've missed you, Lena. Your taste, your touch... Querida, let's get out of here."

That was a hard no. My brain went from "what just happened?" to "absolutely not" faster than a toddler with scissors.

His grip on my arm tightened, his hand warm but uncomfortably firm. Suddenly, this wasn't just Marco being Marco—it was something darker, something desperate.

"Marco, let go of me," I said, summoning every ounce of calm I didn't feel. My voice was steady, but my insides were screaming abort mission.

His eyes narrowed, a flash of anger mixing with hurt. "You can't just walk away, Lena," he hissed, his breath way too close for comfort. "Not after this. We had something real. My entire family flew out to watch us get married. You don't get to erase that with a kiss."

Oh, the irony. As if I was the one erasing things. I yanked my arm, but his grip only tightened, the tension in his jaw matching the pressure in his fingers.

"Marco," I warned, my sass cranking up to compensate for the panic creeping in, "this is not a Nicholas Sparks movie, okay? Let go before this turns into something way less romantic and way more 'Dateline.'"

And then, like a hero summoned by sheer willpower—or maybe the universe deciding I deserved a break—Tyler appeared.

"Hey," Tyler called, striding toward us like a grumpy superhero in jeans and a scowl. "Hands off."

The relief that washed over me was instant, though I'd never admit it. Tyler didn't do knight in shining armor vibes—he was more like grump in a sarcastic T-shirt. But right now, I'd take it.

Marco's head snapped up, his expression souring at the sight of Tyler. "This doesn't concern you, dude," Marco growled, his grip still iron-tight. "She's my fiancé. We're having a private conversation."

"Yeah, well, here's the thing," Tyler said, closing the distance between them with a calm that was somehow scarier than yelling. "She's not your fiancé anymore, and that's not how private conversations work. Let. Her. Go."

Marco didn't move. Instead, his free hand balled into a fist. "What do you know about us, asshole?" he spat, swinging wildly at Tyler.

I barely had time to gasp before Tyler ducked with infuriating ease, like he'd seen the punch coming five minutes ago. Then, in one smooth motion, he delivered a left hook that landed with a satisfying crack. Marco stumbled back, his hold on me breaking as he hit the ground in a dazed heap.

For a second, all I could do was stare at Tyler. He turned to face me, his shoulders squared and his jaw clenched, radiating protectiveness and irritation in equal measure.

"Are you okay?" he asked, his voice softer than I expected but still carrying that signature I'm-too-cool-to-care-but-I-totally-do vibe.

I blinked, trying to process what just happened. "Define 'okay,'" I said, finally finding my voice. "Because if you mean 'Did I survive watching my ex get decked by a guy who probably eats sarcasm for breakfast?' then yes. Totally okay."

Tyler's lips twitched, almost like he was fighting a smirk. "Good. Now let's get out of here before he gets up and tries something stupider."

"Stupider than thinking he could win me back with a surprise kiss and a guilt trip?" I quipped, already following him.

"Hey, he's consistent," Tyler muttered, glancing over his shoulder to make sure Marco was still down.

I looked back too. I was relieved to see him sitting up, but happy he was still on the ground.

I couldn't help but grin as I fell into step beside Tyler.

Marco might have been a storm I was still learning to weather, but Tyler? He was the eye of it—calm, steady, and just unpredictable enough to keep me on my toes.

Chapter 8: Tyler

I gripped Lena's hand like it was a lifeline as we walked to her car, her small fingers weaving through mine. She was shaking, just a little, but enough for me to feel it.

Her eyes darted around like she was searching for ghosts or answers I couldn't give her.

I knew that damn ex of hers—Marco, I think—had rattled her. I could see it in the way she carried herself, like she was still in that confrontation with him, trying to outrun it.

I hated it. I hated that she was hurting, and all I wanted to do was get her away from that hospital, away from the mess that was her past, and wrap her up in some kind of calm.

"I'm getting you out of here," I said, my voice low but firm. She didn't need to be stuck in this emotional tornado. "Let's get you home, where the past can just... stay there."

She nodded, her eyes meeting mine briefly before she looked away. Her hair—damn, it looked perfect even in a storm—fell over her shoulder, like she was trying to hide from something. Probably the same thing I was trying to avoid: the fact that Marco had torn open old wounds. But she was tough. I knew she'd tell me she was fine.

"I'm okay, Tyler. Really," she said, and I could hear the bullshit in her tone. She was strong, but nobody's that strong. "I just need some time to process."

Processing—sure, let's go with that. I didn't buy it. But I nodded anyway, squeezing her hand as we reached her car.

I opened the passenger door for her, like I was some kind of gentleman—when really, I was just trying to stop myself from thinking about how she might need me in ways I wasn't ready to handle.

"Do you want to talk about it?" I asked, settling into the driver's seat. I didn't want to push her. She may not be the "talk-it-out" type. So, I gave her the space. But that didn't stop me from wanting to do something to make this better for her.

She hesitated, her fingers toying with the hem of her dress. "I... I don't know, Tyler. It's just... seeing Marco again brought back so many memories. I thought I'd moved on, but I guess I never really dealt with the pain."

I reached over and grabbed her hand, giving it a squeeze. A small move, but it was all I had to offer. I didn't know how to fix her, but I sure as hell wasn't going to let her face this alone.

"You don't have to go through this alone, Lena," I said, keeping my voice low and steady. "I'm here. Whatever you need."

She gave me a soft smile, and damn if it didn't punch me right in the chest. It wasn't one of those bright, I'm-fine-now smiles. It was the thank-you-for-being-here kind of smile. The kind that made me want to drop every wall I'd ever built.

We drove in silence after that, but it wasn't uncomfortable. It was... peaceful in a way. Like we both needed that space to figure out what the hell just happened between us and what was coming next.

When we finally pulled up to her apartment, I turned to her, my eyes locking with hers. "Come on, let's get you inside. Once we're settled, let me know if you want me to stay, leave, or, you know... go on a wild goose chase for whatever it is you need."

She unbuckled her seatbelt and stepped out of the car. I couldn't help but notice how unsteady she looked. Was it because of Marco, or was it because of... us?

Without thinking, I wrapped my arm around her waist, pulling her close. She leaned into me, her body fitting against mine like it was supposed to. I was pretty sure I was doing the whole being-a-good-guy thing for the wrong reasons, but honestly? It didn't feel wrong.

"Thanks, Tyler," she whispered, her breath warm against my neck. "I don't know what I'd do without you right now."

I felt this odd sense of pride at hearing her say that—probably a stupid one. But hell, I wasn't going to analyze it. I was too busy trying not to focus on how much she felt like home, even though we weren't anything to each other at the moment.

We made our way up to her apartment, taking the stairs like a couple of misfits who didn't really know where they were going, but who were, for whatever reason, together.

The silence between us was thick, but not awkward. Like it was earlier, in my mom's hospital room. It was like we were both holding our breath, waiting for the other to say something that would break whatever this weird connection was. I couldn't help but feel the weight of it as we reached her door.

I followed her inside and closed the door behind me, the soft click almost too loud in the quiet room. She turned to face me, and I swear to God, her eyes were holding back a storm.

"I'm glad you're here," she said, barely above a whisper.

I was so close to her now, the air between us thick and charged. "I'm not going anywhere, Lena. Not unless you want me to."

"I want you here, Tyler," she said, taking a step toward me, a slow, deliberate movement that made my chest tighten. "I want you, but..."

But? Seriously? Was she going to pull back now? Because I had so many questions—like why the hell I could feel everything when she was near?

"But?" I asked, my voice suddenly rough. I wasn't going to let her drop the but and walk away. No way. Not now.

"But everyone thinks you should steer clear of me," she said, her eyes shimmering with something like fear or regret. "And I'm afraid to act on this attraction I have for you because I know my emotions are all over the place, and I've still got a lot to figure out. But I don't want to fight it anymore. I want you, and I want to feel alive again."

Her words hit me like a sucker punch. Hell, maybe they were a sucker punch. But before I could overthink it, I cupped her face in my hands. My thumbs brushed over her skin, soft and warm.

"You don't have to be afraid with me, Lena. I'll go at your pace. I'll make sure you feel safe," I said, my voice low, the promise heavy between us.

And then I kissed her. Not because I had to. But because everything in me screamed that it was the only thing that made sense right then.

Her lips were soft and warm, and she tasted like the sweetest temptation.

I kissed her gently at first, savoring the feel of her mouth against mine, then slowly deepened the kiss, exploring her with a building passion.

Lena responded eagerly, her hands threading through my hair, pulling me closer.

I could feel her body pressing against mine, her breasts crushed against my chest, and the hard points of her nipples straining against her shirt. My hands roamed over her back, tracing the curves of her spine, and I could feel her shivering in response.

She pulled her t-shirt up and over her head, dropping it to the floor. This was her way of telling me what her pace was.

I worked on the clasps of her bra. "This thing is like Fort Knox," I complained. "I'm about to rip it from your body."

Breaking the kiss, I trailed my lips along her jawline, nipping and sucking gently as I made my way to her neck, down her bare shoulders. I could feel her pulse throbbing beneath my lips, and I wanted to leave my mark, to brand her as mine.

"I want to be with you," she whispered, her hands tugging at my shirt, trying to get it off me. "I want to feel you, to forget everything but this moment."

I quickly shrugged off my shirt, revealing my toned torso, and then reached for the buttons of my jeans, undoing them with shaky fingers.

"Tyler, please..." she breathed, her voice a mixture of need and surrender.

I smiled against her skin, my hands sliding down to cup her firm ass, pulling her against my growing erection. "Please what? Tell me what you want."

My heart hammered in my chest as I stepped back, my eyes never leaving hers. She pulled me towards the bedroom, our lips never parting, the kiss deepening as we stumbled into the room.

Before we got through the door, my hands were already working on the buttons of her jeans, eager to feel her naked skin against mine.

Her jeans slid to the floor, revealing her lace panties.

Her body was a work of art, with her perky breasts straining against the lace, and her flat stomach leading down to the V of her panties. I couldn't wait to taste her, to explore every inch of her with my mouth and hands.

Lena's eyes widened as I stepped out of my jeans, now completely naked, my cock strained towards her, hard and ready. "Oh, Tyler..." she breathed, her eyes flicking between my face and my erection.

Her playful laugh made me even harder. "Hmmm. I think I might enjoy that," she said, moving her mouth to my ear and taking my lobe between her teeth.

I took her hands and placed them on my chest, guiding them down my body, encouraging her to explore. "Grab me. I want to feel your hands on me."

She didn't hesitate at all, her fingers sure as they traced my abs, then firmly wrapped her hand around my shaft, her touch slow at first but growing bolder as she stroked me.

"Fuck, that feels good," I groaned, my head falling back as pleasure coursed through me. I wanted to show her how good it could be, to give her what she wanted.

I guided her hand, teaching her the rhythm I liked, showing her how to pleasure me. Her strokes grew more confident, and I could feel her getting into it, her eyes glued to my cock as she stroked me.

"You're so beautiful," I said, my voice thick with desire. "You'd better stop or else you'll make me come too fast."

Her eyes sparkled with a mix of excitement and uncertainty. I wanted to show her how amazing it could be, to pleasure her and know the sounds she made when she orgasmed.

I pushed her back onto the bed, following her down, my body covering hers, my hands reaching behind her to find she'd already unhooked her bra. Her breasts spilled free, full and perfect, with dark pink nipples that were already hard and begging to be sucked.

I lowered my head, taking a nipple into my mouth, swirling my tongue around the taut peak as I sucked and nibbled gently.

Lena arched her back, her hands tangling in my hair, holding me to her as I lavished attention on her breasts.

"Oh God, Tyler," she moaned, her hips lifting off the bed, grinding against me. "That feels so good."

I moved to her other breast, giving it the same attention, my hand sliding down her body, teasing the waistband of her panties. I could feel her heat through the thin fabric.

"Here, I have something for you." She shimmied out from underneath me and opened a drawer of her nightstand, pulling out a square package. She closed the drawer and handed me the condom.

I kissed her deeply, while I opened the package and rolled the condom over my hard cock.

She groaned with delight as I slid my hand down her body, finding her wetness again.

I positioned myself at her entrance, my cock throbbing with the need to be inside her.

"Are you sure, Lena?" I asked, my voice thick with desire. "I want to make this right for you."

She nodded, her hands gripping my shoulders. "Please stop talking, Tyler. Yes. I want you, all of you."

I thrust forward, penetrating her tight heat, our eyes locking as I filled her. She was so wet and warm, gripping me like a vice. I paused, letting her adjust to my size, then slowly began to move, pulling almost all the way out before sliding back in.

Lena moaned, her head tossing back as I set a slow, steady rhythm, my hips rolling as I filled her again and again. I leaned down, capturing her mouth in a passionate kiss as I picked up the pace, sliding in and out of her with increasing urgency.

"Fuck, you feel so good," I growled into her mouth, my hands gripping her hips, holding her in place as I pounded into her. "I can't hold on much longer."

"Yes, harder," she begged, her nails digging into my back, urging me on. "I want to feel you come."

Her words sent me over the edge, and I thrust into her one last time, jerking as I emptied myself into the condom. Into her. My orgasm ripping through me as I collapsed onto her, our sweat-slick bodies pressed together and our hearts pounding in unison.

We laid there, entangled in each other, our breathing slowly returning to normal.

I kissed her forehead, my hand stroking her hair, and felt a sense of peace wash over me.

"That was incredible," Lena whispered, her fingers tracing patterns on my back. "I feel so close to you."

For a second I thought this might be a strange sentiment to share, being that we'd only met four days ago. A statement like that was usually guarded and reserved for when a relationship had progressed well into the commitment stage.

But, for some reason, hearing Lena say it didn't feel wrong. I smiled and nuzzled her neck, whispering, "I'm here. And there can be more of it where that came from."

She giggled, her body shifting beneath me, sending a delicious friction between our sensitive parts. "I can't wait to see what else you have in store for me, Mr. Soto."

"Oh, I've got plenty of ideas," I said, my hand sliding down to cup her ass, giving it a playful squeeze. "But first, I think we should get cleaned up. That is, if you can tear yourself away from the bed."

She laughed, her eyes sparkling with mischief. "I think I can manage that. Especially if it means getting to see that hard body of yours in the shower."

I stood up, offering her my hand, and pulled her up into my arms, her naked body pressing against mine. "Then let's get after it. I promise to make it worth your while."

Chapter 9: Lena

We were lost in each other. Our encounter with Marco seemed to ignite our passion like wildfire.

We'd arrived at my apartment, our bodies yearning for each other. As we stepped inside, the cool air-conditioned breeze caressed my skin, sending shivers down my spine.

Tyler's muscular arms wrapped around me, pulling me close, and I could feel his heart racing against mine. His touch sent a jolt of desire through my body, and I knew in that moment that resisting this attraction was futile.

"I need you, Lena," he'd whispered, his breath warm on my neck.

I turned to face him, my hands resting on his chest, feeling the steady rise and fall beneath my palms.

His eyes, a mesmerizing shade of ice blue, held mine captive, and I saw a reflection of my own longing mirrored in their depths.

Without hesitation, I led him to my bedroom, our lips meeting in a feverish kiss as we crossed the threshold.

The world melted away as we explored each other, our hands eagerly removing the barriers of clothing that separated us. Tyler's fingers traced my curves, igniting a trail of fire along my skin.

I let out a soft moan, encouraging him to continue his sensual assault.

As he laid me down on the bed, his gaze never left mine, and I felt a surge of power knowing that I could affect him so deeply. Tyler's lips trailed kisses down my neck, sending shivers of pleasure through my body. His hands roamed freely, mapping every inch of my skin, and I surrendered to the overwhelming sensations.

Our passion escalated, and soon we were entwined, our bodies moving in perfect harmony. Tyler's touch was both gentle and fierce, his desire for me evident in every stroke.

I clung to him, matching his rhythm, our hearts beating as one. The tension built within me, a coiled spring ready to release, and when Tyler whispered my name in that moment of ecstasy, I shattered. My body trembled as waves of pleasure washed over me, leaving me breathless and utterly satisfied.

In the aftermath of our shower encounter and then this third one again in my bed, we laid entangled in the sheets, our hearts still racing. Tyler's fingers caressed my bare skin, and I felt a sense of peace.

Okay, so, here's the thing: I knew what had just happened between us wasn't just some wham-bam-thank-you-ma'am type of situation. No, this was something different.

We'd somehow managed to fall asleep in this cozy, fuzzy bubble of shared pain, like two broken puzzle pieces that fit together, but neither of us was quite ready to admit it.

The sun crept through the blinds, and I swear it was the most annoying thing in the world, especially since it meant we'd have to face the fact that our little slice of imperfect happiness was about to be over.

I stretched and tried to ignore the ache in my body from the night before, and from the weird, deep connection that was hanging in the air.

Then Tyler—grumpy, always-guarded, emotionally-broken Tyler—leaned over and kissed me.

It wasn't anything wild or passionate, but it was enough to make me feel like I'd just been punched in the chest in the best possible way. His eyes said all the things he wasn't saying with his mouth. The "I-don't-know-what-to-do-with-you-but-I-don't-want-you-to-leave" look that gets a girl right in the feels.

"I'm going to go see my mom," he said, his voice rough. It sounded like he was carrying the weight of the world, which, let's be real, he probably was.

I bit my lip and asked, "Do you want to go alone?" Because, honestly, that's what I was expecting. Grumpy Tyler wasn't the "let's-lean-on-each-other" type, but then again, here we were, in a tangled mess of blankets and... well, whatever this was between us.

But then he surprised me. "Are you able to come with me?" he asked, his voice soft but steady. I swear, it was like he'd just dropped a bombshell, and I didn't know whether to run for cover or stay and try to fix him. Something in the way he said it made my heart do this weird, happy thing—and I think it might've actually cracked a little.

I nodded, because, hell, who was I kidding? I wasn't going to turn him down. Besides, his sincerity? It was lethal. It made me feel like maybe I wasn't the only one who needed someone to lean on.

And honestly? That was the first time in a long time I didn't have to search for the words to express what was going on in my head. I was exactly where I needed to be.

***

So, here I was, sitting in a hospital room, trying to look like I had everything together—like I wasn't completely out of my depth here.

But the truth? I felt like a deer caught in headlights, except the headlights were Lorraine's eyes, which were laser-focused on me like I was the last cookie at a buffet, and she was just waiting to devour me.

It was kind of funny, in a "well, this is my life now" way, how the woman lying in a hospital bed had all the power.

Me? I was fully capable of getting up and walking out. But that's not what I was doing. I was stuck, pinned in place by the sheer weight of Lorraine's unblinking stare.

Tyler had bolted a few minutes ago for coffee—probably to escape the awkwardness of this whole "new girl in his life" situation. So, I was left alone with Lorraine, a woman who thought she had every reason to side-eye me. I'd just shown up in her son's life out of nowhere, like a wild storm.

I didn't know how long I could sit here, pretending like I had my life together, when all I really had was a messy past and an urge to jump into something I probably wasn't ready for.

But that was the thing about Tyler. He had a way of pulling me in, and I really didn't want to fight it.

Then, Lorraine's voice broke the silence, slow and deliberate. Her words were slurred and jumbled together, but understandable nonetheless.

"You care for my son. Don't you?"

I stiffened.

She wasn't playing games. She was going straight for the jugular.

For a split second, I almost said something snarky, like, "Oh, no, I just like the free coffee." But I wasn't feeling that brave. Not now. Not with her watching me like I was some kind of experiment.

"Yes," I whispered. "I do. Very much." Ugh. Why did I have to sound so... serious? "But it's complicated."

And it was. Complicated and terrifying.

Lorraine let out a breath, and I could almost see the weight of her words hit her. "Tyler's been through enough heartache to last him a lifetime," she said breathily. "He acts like he's over it, but his scars... they run deep."

Her words lodged in my chest like a splinter. Deep scars? Was that why he was so closed off, so grumpy? Why he couldn't quite let anyone get too close? God, if only I knew the full story. But I couldn't ask him. I felt like he'd tell me when he was ready.

"His heartache... nearly destroyed him."

Her words punched me in the gut, and I felt a weird mix of guilt and empathy for him, like maybe I was about to become another complication in his life that he didn't need.

"I understand, Mrs. Soto," I said. Even though I really didn't. I mean, how could I? But I wasn't about to admit that. "I know I have my own demons to face, and I don't want to hurt Tyler. But... there's something between us that neither of us can ignore. It's intense."

She narrowed her eyes, and I could practically hear the gears turning in her mind, probably calculating how much of a disaster I could potentially cause. "I know about your past, Lena," she said, like she'd been waiting for the right moment to drop that bomb. "I know you left your fiancé at the altar.

Thomas's family told me about it. I can see the pain you're carrying."

My stomach dropped. Everyone knew my business. But, seriously? Was I that much of a disaster that she was bringing that up now? I wasn't even sure how to respond to that.

"Tyler deserves stability," she added, and I felt the pressure of her words slam into me like a freight train. "If you care for him, don't pull him into your chaos."

I opened my mouth, but nothing came out.

She was right. I'd ruined everything stable in my life, and now I was about to drag Tyler into the mess that was me. Wasn't that selfish?

I forced a smile, though it felt more like a grimace. "I'm not here to hurt him, Lorraine. I... I think I care about him more than I wanted to admit."

Her expression softened, just a touch, but it was enough to make me feel like maybe I wasn't completely the villain here. She gave me a tiny nod, approving or maybe just acknowledging that I wasn't a complete disaster.

"Sexual attraction is a powerful force," she said, and I almost wanted to laugh because, seriously, who wouldn't be attracted to Tyler? "But you need to be careful with my son's heart. If you're not ready for something serious, you need to be honest with him."

I nodded, probably looking like a bobblehead on a dashboard, but at least I was keeping it together. "I will be, I promise. I don't want to cause him more pain. I care for him, and I want to be there for him, but I also need to figure out my own stuff first."

Lorraine patted my hand like she was my mom and not a woman whose son I was currently... well, complicated with. "Take your time, Lena. Healing takes time."

That hit me right in the chest. Because maybe I was running from all of my feelings, afraid that if I let myself feel, I'd just get hurt again. But Tyler had shown me something different. Something that made me want to believe in love again, even if it scared the crap out of me.

Lorraine gave me one last look, something almost warm. "Tyler is a good man. He deserves happiness, and so do you."

I felt like someone had just slapped me awake. I deserved happiness? Was I really that far gone? Had I been running from everything good, from everything real in my life?

But then she said the thing that really made my brain short-circuit.

"You both need to heal," she said, her voice quiet but firm. "But you should do it separately. He needs to find his best self. Please. Leave him to heal. Until you can be your best selves, you have to let Tyler go."

The room felt like it was spinning. This wasn't just a "be careful" warning. It was a gut punch.

Tyler came back with coffee and some random comment about how impossible it was to find decent coffee in a hospital, but his words barely registered. Because all I could hear in my head were Lorraine's last words.

I wasn't sure what I was supposed to do now. Ugh, this was all uncomfortable now.

Tyler sat down beside his mom, all sweet and calm like the world wasn't on fire.

I couldn't help but feel like I was intruding on their little family moment.

He smiled at her, gave her a kiss on the forehead, and all I could do was sit there and feel like the third wheel at the world's most awkward party.

"You're doing so much better today, Mom," he said, his voice all warm and soft. "Your speech is clearer and you've got more expression on your face." He leaned in like he was trying to smother her with love.

Which, I mean, I guess was nice. But then I remembered Lorraine's little "talk" from earlier, and suddenly I was the odd one out in this hospital room.

Lorraine had asked me to stay away from Tyler, let him heal. And here I was, in the same room, feeling like my presence was a giant neon sign that read: Look! The girl with the emotional baggage is here!

Then Tyler looked over at me, his brow furrowed. "You okay, Lena?"

You know that feeling when you get caught in a lie, but it's not really a lie, it's more like a well, it's complicated situation? Yeah, that's how I felt right then.

Tyler's eyes flicked back and forth between me and his mom, like he was trying to figure out why the air had gone from warm and fuzzy to I-need-an-exit-now.

"Everything okay here?" he asked, but I could hear the hesitation. He was trying to figure me out, and I didn't know if I was ready to be figured out.

I threw on a smile so fake it could've been made in Hollywood. "Better than okay," I lied, giving him my best "I'm-not-sweating-this" look.

Then I did what I do best—distract. I pulled my phone out like I was some kind of victim of an urgent text message. "Oh, crap. I totally forgot about lunch with my parents," I said, trying not to feel like a complete fraud. "Guess I'll have to miss our next round of ultra-competitive gin rummy. I hear your mom's a beast at that game."

Tyler grinned, and I couldn't help but notice how that small smile of his made my heart do a little flip. "Damn, I was looking forward to that," he teased, tapping his mom's hand playfully. "She plays dirty. No mercy."

I quickly stood up, feeling like I was about to escape some kind of emotional hurricane. "Well, you look great today, Mrs. Soto. I'm sure you'll be out of here in no time." The words tasted like chalk in my mouth, but they were the right thing to say.

I hustled out of that room like it was on fire, my brain spiraling through every word Lorraine had said.

She'd told me and Tyler we needed to heal. On our own. That we were each other's bandages, not cures.

Bandages. Not cures.

What a nice, comforting thought.

I was so wrapped up in my head, I barely noticed the sunlight hitting me like a sledgehammer as I stepped outside. But before I could make it to my car, I spotted Marco leaning against his car like he was waiting for me. Great. Just what I needed.

He raised his hands like he was surrendering. "Lena, seriously. I just want to talk. No agenda. No games. We owe each other at least that, right?"

I stopped in my tracks. Of course, this would happen today. But maybe it was fate. Or whatever. Lorraine's words were still playing in my head, telling me to face what I'd buried. And honestly? If I ever wanted to move forward—whether with Tyler or with my own damn self—I had to do this.

I took a deep breath. "You're right," I said, meeting Marco's eyes. "Let's talk. But somewhere neutral. No hospital room vibes."

His shoulders visibly relaxed. "Of course. How about Woodward Park? I'll grab sandwiches and meet you there in an hour?"

I nodded, watching him climb into his car and drive off. I stood there for a moment, my car keys dangling from my fingers.

Something about the way he said it, something in his tone, made me feel like this conversation was something I needed. A kind of healing that would suck, but it would matter.

And if it helped me make sense of whatever was going on with Tyler, then maybe that was worth it, too.

***

Okay, picture this: Marco and I, sitting next to each other on a park bench like some scene out of a rom-com, except it's not cute or quirky—it's awkward. There's a couple of untouched sandwiches sitting between us, like tiny, sad peace offerings.

Around us, birds are chirping, kids are screaming-laughing in the distance, and there's a guy walking his dog who looks way too smug about life. Meanwhile, I'm over here trying not to implode under the weight of this conversation.

"Lena," Marco started, his voice steady but with just enough raw edge to make me squirm, "I need to understand. You blindsided me that day."

Oh, here we go. *Wedding Day, the Musical: The Unhappy Groom Edition*. I forced myself to meet his gaze, and wow, did he look serious. Like, "about to drop the 'We need to talk' bomb" serious.

"I keep replaying it," he continued, his voice softening, "trying to figure out what happened. Why. I just… I need to know why."

Great. Fantastic. No pressure, right? Just, you know, explain why I nuked his happily-ever-after in broad daylight. Super simple. I swallowed hard and started fidgeting with my sleeve because apparently, my hands didn't get the "stay cool" memo.

"I know," I said quietly, my voice wobbling a little. "And I'm so, so sorry, Marco. You didn't deserve that."

He nodded, not saying a word, just watching me like he was waiting for the rest. So, fine. I took a deep breath and braced myself for the crash landing.

"Three months before the wedding…" Deep breath, Lena. Don't freak out now. "We found out I was pregnant."

His eyes went wide, and for a second, I thought he might actually fall off the bench. But he didn't say anything, just kept staring at me, waiting for the rest of the train wreck.

"We… talked about it," I went on, my voice barely above a whisper now. "And we decided it wasn't the right time for us. It was supposed to be a mutual decision." Supposed to be. Ha. "I thought I could move on. But the guilt… it was like this giant hole that kept getting bigger, and I didn't know how to deal with it."

I crossed my arms, hugging myself like that would somehow make this easier to say. "I buried it. From you, from myself, from everyone. I didn't want to think about it, let alone feel it. But it just kept growing."

Marco let out a breath, his jaw tight. "You never said anything," he said, his voice low, like he was holding back a tidal wave of emotions. "Not a word."

I nodded, biting my lip to keep it together. "I didn't understand it myself," I admitted. "I felt like I'd betrayed you, betrayed myself, betrayed… everything. And the closer we got to the wedding, the heavier it got. By the time I was about to walk down that aisle, I realized I couldn't do it. I couldn't pretend to be okay when I was so not okay. It wasn't fair to either of us."

He was quiet for a long time, staring down at the sandwich wrapper in his hands. Finally, he looked up, and his expression was softer, though still laced with hurt. "So… it wasn't that you didn't love me?"

I shook my head quickly. "No, Marco. It wasn't that. But I couldn't marry you either. I didn't even know why at the time. I just… I couldn't. And I'm so sorry."

He leaned back, running a hand through his hair. "You should've told me," he said, his voice a mix of frustration and something else—understanding, maybe? "I wish you'd warned me. Maybe we could've faced it together."

I reached out, barely touching his hand. "I wish I'd told you too. I've thought about it so much these past five weeks. Wished I'd done everything differently. But the truth is… I didn't even see it coming until it hit me that day. I'm sorry, Marco. Truly."

He gave me this small, sad smile, and for a moment, he looked like the guy I'd fallen in love with all those years ago. "Maybe we were both kidding ourselves," he said softly.

"Holding on to the idea of us instead of what was really there."

Oof. That one hit hard, but it also felt… true. I nodded, feeling a strange sense of relief wash over me. Like for the first time in forever, we were both seeing things clearly.

We sat there for a while in silence, letting the weight of everything settle. The park sounds around us started to feel normal again—birds, kids, smug dog walkers—all of it blending into the background.

Finally, Marco turned to me, his expression gentler than it had been all day. "Lena, I'm grateful to know you're okay," he said, his voice steady. "I don't understand everything, but… I get that you were hurting too. And I hope you can forgive yourself someday."

His words knocked the air right out of me. Forgive myself? That was a tall order. But maybe it wasn't impossible.

"I'll try," I said softly. "Eventually."

He smiled—bittersweet, but real—and then we hugged. It was warm, it was final, and it was what I didn't know I needed.

When he pulled away, he asked if he could text me sometime. I said yes. And then he was gone, walking down the path and out of sight. I sat there for a while, eating my now-slightly-sad sandwich, feeling something I hadn't felt in a long time.

Space. To breathe. To heal. Maybe even to hope.

Chapter 10: Tyler

The next morning, Dr. Feelgood breezed into the room like a sitcom mom ready to deliver life lessons. Her news? My mom was a medical superhero who'd be springing herself from the hospital tomorrow. Okay, maybe not springing—she'd probably shuffle in slow motion with me acting like her backup dancer—but still, it was progress. And the best news ever.

After the last few days, hearing that she'd pulled through felt like hitting the jackpot at the world's least fun casino.

And I knew exactly who I needed to share the news with: Lena. She'd been the real MVP of this hospital saga, a walking, talking guide to "What to Do When Your Mom Has a Stroke." Without her quick thinking, aspirin advice, and general badassery, we might not have gotten here.

Feeling something weirdly close to optimism, I stepped into the hallway and dialed her number. Straight to voicemail.

Fine. No big deal. People have lives. I called again. Same thing.

I left a message, trying not to sound like a droopy golden retriever.

"Hey, Lena. Mom's getting discharged tomorrow. Big deal, right? You're the reason we got her to the hospital so fast, so... thanks. Call me when you can."

Fast-forward to late afternoon: still no Lena. Not a peep. By evening, my phone buzzed, and I had one of those moments where hope flares up like a bad rash.

Lena: Hey, I'm dealing with some family stuff right now. It's a good time for you guys to focus on getting your mom settled at home. Talk soon.

Talk soon. Right. I fought back the thought that that phrase is just fancy packaging for *leave me alone*.

The words hit like a sucker punch, even though they were perfectly reasonable. But reasonable didn't stop the paranoid gremlins in my brain from staging a full-on rave. She'd been my rock for days, and now she was bailing.

The next day, we brought Mom home. Let me tell you, there's no greater high than helping your mom back into her own house after days of cold hospital.

Dad and I flanked her like Secret Service agents, just in case she decided to spontaneously combust.

But she didn't. She made it to the couch, her throne of choice, and took this deep, satisfied breath that could've powered a hot air balloon.

Seeing her smile—really smile—was like flipping the script on the nightmare we'd been living.

But even that didn't distract me for long. My phone practically burned a hole in my pocket all day. Nothing from Lena. Zilch. Nada. Crickets.

I fired off a quick text:

Me: Mom's home. She's doing great. Let me know if you're free to catch up.

Then I waited. Because apparently, I hate myself.

When the silence stretched long enough to make me question my existence, Mom piped up. "Tyler, don't hover." Her voice had this familiar warmth, the kind that could make you believe the world wasn't a complete dumpster fire.

"I'm not hovering," I said, draping her blanket over her like I was tucking in the Queen of England. "I'm just... strategically loitering."

She laughed, kissed my cheek, and told me to go relax. I smiled back, but my brain wasn't anywhere near that couch.

It was with Lena, replaying every moment we'd spent together and wondering what the hell went wrong.

One day turned into two, then four, and still... radio silence from Lena. No texts, no calls, not even a carrier pigeon.

I told myself she was busy, probably drowning in family drama or battling some other Lena-specific chaos.

Her last message said as much, and yet... something felt off. Like milk left in the fridge one day too long.

We'd been through something together. She'd been right there, steady as a rock, when my world was doing its best impression of a demolition derby. And now? Poof. Gone.

I pulled out my phone—again. The last message I sent her stared back at me.

Me: Mom's doing better—do you think we could talk soon?

It was casual. Simple. Non-desperate. The digital equivalent of leaning against a doorframe and pretending you don't care if someone answers. And still, nothing.

Meanwhile, my mom was home and on the mend. I should've been doing cartwheels of relief, but instead, I was stuck in this mental wrestling match over Lena's Houdini act.

The thought that maybe I'd misread everything between us kept creeping in, like an uninvited party guest who wouldn't take the hint.

By day seven, I wasn't even checking my phone anymore. Progress, right? Sure. If progress meant letting the silence settle in like a boulder on your chest.

When Mia and Thomas texted they were back from their honeymoon and wanted to catch up, I jumped at the invite. Because nothing said "I'm totally fine and not emotionally spiraling" like hanging out with your happily married friends.

When I got to their apartment, the door opened, and there she was. Lena. Standing there like nothing had happened.

Her smile was bright, casual, like she wasn't the human equivalent of a ghost emoji for the past week. My pulse kicked into high gear, but my brain was busy playing catch-up, screaming, "What the hell, Lena?"

We settled into the living room. Thomas and Mia looked disgustingly happy, still glowing like they'd been dipped in honeymoon glitter. Lena was perched with them, laughing and chatting like she hadn't just vanished off the face of the earth.

I caught her eye, and for a split second, her smile faltered. Just a blip. Then it was back, plastered on like cheap wallpaper.

"Hey, Tyler," she said, her voice chirpy enough to be a bird.

"Hey, Lena." I forced a smile, ignoring the ache that had taken up permanent residence in my chest. "Good to see you."

Thomas clapped me on the back, snapping me out of my internal spiral. "Man, it's great to be back. How's your mom doing?"

"She's good," I said, keeping my gaze locked on Lena. "She's a trooper. Recovered faster than anyone expected."

Mia smiled, reaching out to squeeze my arm. "That's amazing. Please let us know if there's anything we can do to help."

"Will do," I said, then added, "Lena was a huge help through everything."

That got their attention. Thomas and Mia turned to her in unison, twin looks of surprise plastered across their faces.

"She was?" Thomas asked.

"Oh yeah." My voice was cool, but my insides were a cocktail of hurt and frustration. "She totally stepped up when Mom had the stroke. Took control when the rest of us were freaking out. Got us through it."

Mia's jaw dropped. "Oh my God, Lena, why didn't you say anything?" She turned to her sister, all wide eyes and gratitude. "Thank you!"

Lena looked down, her hands twisting in her lap. "I'm just glad I could help."

"Don't downplay it," Thomas chimed in, pulling Lena into a quick hug. "Thank you so much."

I wanted to grab her by the arm, pull her aside, and demand to know why she'd gone radio silent. But with Thomas and Mia here, I had no choice but to play along.

Before I could even form a plan, Mia was dragging Lena to the kitchen to "whip up some snacks." Lena glanced back at me, her eyes unreadable, but her smile as polished as ever.

Thomas nudged me toward the couch and flipped on the TV. "Game time?"

I nodded, sinking into the cushions like my bones weighed a thousand pounds.

"Everything good?" Thomas asked after a minute, shooting me a sideways glance.

I shrugged. "Just a long week and a half with Mom's recovery." It wasn't a lie, but it wasn't the whole truth either.

The laughter and chatter from the kitchen floated into the living room, but it barely registered. All I could focus on was Lena. How she was sitting just a few feet away, laughing like nothing had happened.

When the food arrived, I played my part, smiling and nodding in all the right places as Mia regaled us with honeymoon stories. But my attention kept wandering back to Lena, wondering how she could be so calm, so... fine.

When the visit wrappd up, I stood and clapped Thomas on the back. "I should get going. Need to check on my mom."

"Sounds good, man," Thomas said with a nod.

Mia hugged me goodbye, and I turned to Lena. "See you later." My voice was steady, but my insides felt like a collapsing circus tent.

"Bye, Tyler," she said, light and easy, like we were strangers.

The drive home was silent, except for the sound of my grip tightening on the steering wheel. Enough was enough. I didn't need this. Didn't need her.

And yet, as much as I told myself to let it go, I couldn't shake Thomas's words from weeks ago, now looping in my head like a bad soundtrack: "She's a mess, Tyler. Don't get dragged into her chaos."

Too late.

I'd brushed it off at the time, convinced myself I was somehow seeing something different, something worthwhile.

But now, as I pulled up to my house, I could feel the weight of it settle in. I'd walked straight into a mess, just like everyone said I would.

The truth was, I'd let myself get carried away with Lena. I saw her in some moment of clarity or vulnerability. I thought maybe I could be the guy to help, to understand her.

But that was just wishful thinking. I was an idiot, plain and simple.

I'd barely killed the engine when the garage door decided to throw a tantrum, jerking back open with an obnoxious *BEEP BEEP BEEP*. And there she was. Lena. Perfect timing, of course.

I turned around, hands still on the door remote like I could will her away with sheer annoyance. She was all brown waves and those big, imploring eyes, standing there like she hadn't ghosted me for a week. Like she wasn't the human embodiment of emotional turbulence.

"Tyler, wait!" Her voice echoed in the cold, cluttered space.

I sighed, loudly, just to make sure she caught every ounce of my reluctance. "What are you doing here?" My voice could've iced over boiling water.

"I need to talk to you," she said, her words edged with desperation as she took a step forward. Her boots scuffed against the concrete like she was here for some dramatic showdown.

"Of course, you do," I muttered under my breath, dropping the remote onto my workbench. "Let me guess—you're here to explain why disappearing for a week without a single text is, in fact, totally normal behavior?"

She winced, which gave me a flicker of satisfaction. A small, petty win for Team Grumpy.

"Please, just hear me out," she said, her voice softer now.

I laughed. Not a cheerful, happy laugh, but the kind of laugh you'd give when the universe decides to play its favorite game: How Much Can We Pile On Before He Snaps?

"Hear you out? Lena, I think I've heard enough. You've got a reputation, and I let myself think—stupidly—that maybe I saw something different. Turns out, I'm just as gullible as the rest."

Her eyes flashed with anger now, a little fire sparking to life. "Warned you about me?" she shot back, her tone cutting. "Oh, let me guess, the peanut gallery has plenty to say about Lena, the runaway bride, right? Because God forbid anyone let me live my life without commentary."

"Maybe if you didn't run from everything, there wouldn't be so much commentary," I snapped, crossing my arms. "You ghosted me, Lena. Not the other way around. Don't act like you're the victim here."

Her hands balled into fists, but then she exhaled sharply and closed the distance between us. She jabbed a finger at my chest. "You think I wanted to ghost you? That I was sitting around, twirling my evil mustache, plotting to screw you over? I was a mess, Tyler. A mess. And maybe I thought you didn't need to deal with all my baggage on top of yours."

"Right," I said, catching her hand and holding it still before she could jab me again. "You're a mess, I'm a mess, so naturally the best solution is for you to vanish without a word. Makes perfect sense."

She tilted her head, her lips twitching like she was biting back a sarcastic retort. "You know what? Fine. I screwed up. Big time. But I'm standing here now, trying to fix it, so maybe get off your high horse for five seconds and let me."

Her words hit me harder than I wanted to admit, and for a second, I just stared at her. This close, I could see the frustration in her eyes, the stubborn set of her jaw, and the faint tremble in her hand where I held it.

"You're asking for something I'm not sure I can give, Lena," I said finally, my voice low. "I don't have the energy for more chaos."

"Then don't see it as chaos," she said softly, her voice dropping a notch. She stepped closer, her other hand brushing lightly against my chest. "See it as a second chance. A chance to let me show you I'm not the person everyone thinks I am."

Her fingers curled slightly against my shirt, right over my heart, and I hated how much my body responded to her. Hated how my brain was screaming "Danger, danger!" While my heart whispered, "But what if…"

"Lena…" I said, my tone full of warning.

"Tyler," she shot back, a flicker of that sass returning to her tone. "Stop thinking. Just… let me in."

And then she leaned in, her breath warm through my shirt, sending a jolt down my spine that I hated almost as much as I craved it.

This was trouble. The kind of trouble I didn't need. The kind of trouble I wasn't sure I could walk away from.

My resolve was weakening, though I thought there was nothing wrong with giving my body what it wanted. Her.

My head had just enough sense to press the button to close the garage door, while my body responded to her touch despite my mind's protests. "And how do you plan to do that, huh? By seducing me into forgetting that you'll just run every time I get close to you??" My tone was laced with desire and skepticism.

Lena's fingers trailed up my arm, her touch sending sparks of pleasure through my veins. "Maybe I just want to remind you of the passion we shared. To show you that I'm worth the risk." Her lips found mine, her kiss demanding and urgent.

I groaned, giving in. Her mouth tasted of temptation, and I devoured her lips, my hands sliding down her back, pulling her closer. I could feel her body pressing against mine, her curves fitting perfectly against my hardness.

"Mmm, Tyler," she moaned, her hands exploring my chest, her touch igniting a fire in my blood. "I've wanted this... I want you."

"You could've had me anytime, Lena," I growled, my lips trailing down her neck, nipping at her sensitive skin. "But you ran, and now you're back, expecting me to just fall into your arms."

She chuckled, a low, sultry sound that sent a jolt straight to my groin. "I'll work for it…"

Her hands tugged at my shirt, pulling it over my head, exposing my bare chest. "Let me show you how much I want this, how much I want *you*."

I let her take control, my body aching for her touch. Her hands roamed freely, her fingers tracing the contours of my muscles, sending shivers of pleasure through me.

I groaned, arching into her touch, my dick straining against my jeans.

"You like that, huh?" she teased, her lips brushing against my ear. "You like it when I touch you, when I make you feel things."

"Fuck, Lena," I breathed, my hands gripping her hips, pulling her against me. "You have no idea how much I wanted you, how much I've thought about you."

She smiled against my neck, her breath hot on my skin. "Oh, I think I have a pretty good idea." Her hands moved to my belt, expertly unbuckling it, her fingers sliding beneath the waistband of my jeans. "I've thought about this too, Tyler. About being with you, like this."

I couldn't resist her anymore, my desire clouding my judgment. I backed her against the hood of my car, my lips crushing hers in a hungry kiss. My hands explored her body, my fingers slipping beneath her shirt, caressing the soft skin of her back.

"Oh, God, Tyler," she moaned, her body arching into my touch. "This feels so good, but it's not enough."

I grinned against her lips, my hands moving to the front of her shirt, deftly unbuttoning it. "You want more, huh? You want me to make you feel everything?"

Lena nodded, her eyes dark with desire. "Yes, please. I want to feel everything with you."

I kissed her again, my hands sliding her shirt off her shoulders, revealing her lace bra and the swell of her breasts. "You're so fucking beautiful," I whispered, my lips trailing down her neck, nipping and sucking on her sensitive skin.

She moaned, her hands tangling in my hair, pulling me closer. "You make me feel things I never thought I'd feel again."

I unhooked her bra, my mouth capturing her nipple, sucking and teasing it with my tongue.

Lena arched against me, her hands gripping my shoulders, her breath coming in short gasps.

I switched to her other breast, lavishing attention on it, while my hands explored her curves, sliding down to cup her ass.

"Oh, yes, there, Tyler," she panted, her head thrown back, her body writhing against mine. "Touch me, please."

I obliged, pushing her skirt up and sliding my fingers between her thighs. "You're so wet, Lena," I growled, my fingers stroking her folds, teasing her bud. "You want this, don't you?"

"Yes, please, Tyler," she begged, her hips thrusting against my hand. "I need you, now."

I couldn't deny her any longer, my own need matching hers.

I lifted her, turning her around so I stood behind her. Her thong was still on, so I held the thin piece of fabric aside and positioned myself at her entrance, teasing her with my tip.

"Please, Tyler, now," she pleaded, looking back at me, her hands on the hood of my car.

I thrust into her, filling her in one smooth motion, groaning at the sensation of her tight heat surrounding me. Lena cried out, her hands on my car trying to find something to grab. I began to move, my hips pumping in a steady rhythm, sliding in and out of her.

"Fuck, yes, Tyler," she panted, her head thrown back, her breasts heaving with each thrust. "Harder, please."

I obliged, one hand gripping her ass, holding her steady as I pounded into her, our bodies slapping together in a frenzied rhythm.

Lena's moans filled the garage, her breath coming in short gasps. She looked back at me, her eyes closed in pure pleasure.

"You feel so good, Lena," I grunted, my body on the brink of release. "I'm gonna come, baby."

"Yes, Tyler, with me," she cried, her hands reaching between us, her fingers finding the hard peak between her legs, rubbing in time with my thrusts.

"Oh baby, I can't." I knew I didn't have a condom on, but she felt so damn good.

As I felt the beginning of her orgasm, she cried out and her walls started to clench around me. I was in danger of being past my point of no control.

I pulled out, spreading my milk all over her beautiful round butt, our bodies trembling, our heartbeats racing.

After a long minute, I slid my emptied member back into her smooth wetness, gripping her hips with slow thrusts. I held her ass against me, our sweat-soaked bodies slick with the evidence of our passion.

"That was so..." I began, searching for words to describe the intensity of what we'd just shared.

"...so fucking hot," Lena finished for me, her eyes sparkling with satisfaction. "It was well worth the wait."

My heart was still pounding. "You've got some nerve coming here, Lena. You know that, right?"

She smiled, her hand reaching up to caress my cheek. "I know, and I'm sorry for the way I handled things. But I'm here now, so let's talk about what happens for us next."

I sighed, my body still buzzing with pleasure. "I can't deny that I wanted this, but I can't trust you. What happened just now doesn't mean I plan to take part in your habit of disappearing on people."

She pulled her ass away, releasing me. Then she turned around and looked into my eyes, her expression serious. "That's fucked up, Tyler."

"Well, it's the truth." I could see that she was displeased with what I was saying, but it had to be said. "I... I still need some time, Lena."

She gathered her clothing and opened the door to my home. Looking back at me, the anger in her eyes was unmistakable. "Take all the time you need," she said, as the door slammed behind her.

Chapter 11: Lena

I stood under Tyler's shower, the hot water cascading over me like a disapproving therapist with no filter. The kind that just lets you marinate in your poor life choices without offering any solutions.

The steam rose around me, thick and suffocating, which, to be fair, matched my current mental state perfectly.

My heart was still racing, and my skin? Well, my skin was betraying me, tingling like it wanted an encore of *him*. Tyler. Mr. Grumpy Pants with a six-pack that had its own fan club. His touch, his kisses…ugh, they were like a drug. And I wasn't talking some over-the-counter, mild-side-effects kind of drug. No, he was the call-your-doctor-immediately variety.

I reached for the shampoo, lathering it into my hair like I could scrub away the last week—or, you know, my entire existence. But no amount of suds was going to erase the fact that I'd hurt him. Disappeared without a word.

Classic Lena move, right? Wild card, unpredictable, human disaster. Pick your favorite adjective. They all apply.

As I rinsed my hair, my mind drifted to the holiday season—the time of year that's supposed to feel like a Hallmark card exploded. My family gathered around, pies in the oven, cookies cooling on the counter, and carolers strolling through the neighborhood like cheerful, well-dressed Spotify playlists.

Instead, I was the Ghost of Terrible Decisions Past, skulking around the edges of everyone else's happiness. And then there was Tyler's mom. Lorraine. Sweet, concerned Lorraine, who had looked me dead in the eyes and basically said, "Girl, you're a train wreck, and my son does not need to be a passenger."

Okay, not in those exact words, but the vibe was there. At the time, I'd nodded and promised to keep my distance because it felt like the noble thing to do. Turns out, nobility sucks.

Now here I was, dripping in Tyler's shower, realizing I'd not only added another layer to the drama sandwich everyone thought I was, but I'd also managed to hurt the one guy who could see past the mess. Maybe.

I sighed, pressing my forehead against the cool tiles. "Nice work, Lena. You've officially hit the trifecta:

heartbreak, self-loathing, and somehow still managing to be naked and stressed at the same time." Alright, that was four things, but I think I should be the one person allowed to overlook my own mistakes.

The thing was, I wasn't messy because I liked it. I was messy because I was scared. Scared of being judged, scared of screwing up, scared of being me. But Tyler? He made me want to try anyway. And that, apparently, was scarier than everything else combined.

"Great," I muttered to no one, blinking up at the showerhead. "Now I'm naked, stressed, and falling for the guy who probably thinks I'm a walking red flag factory."

The shower didn't answer. It just kept pouring water over me, like, *Good luck with that, sweetheart.*

The temperature dropped so fast it felt like the hot water had turned into an arctic slap, snapping me out of my spiraling thoughts. I barely had time to shiver before the shower door slid open, and there he was.

Tyler.

Standing there in all his brooding, grumpy glory, with those ice-blue eyes zeroing in on me like he was about to deliver some soul-crushing monologue. Oh, and let's not forget the whole "filling the shower doorway" thing. Like it was possible I wanted to escape anyway.

He stepped into the shower without a word, closing the door behind him, and suddenly the tiny, steamy space felt a whole lot smaller. My heart did this Olympic-level somersault, a mix of "oh wow" and "oh no."

"Tyler, I..." I started, because someone had to say something before the awkwardness hit critical mass. But my words got drowned out by the water pounding against the tile.

Before I could find my footing—metaphorically and literally—he raised a finger to my lips, silencing me.

Cue full-body jolt. That one simple touch might as well have been a lightning bolt, and now my brain was screaming, "Abort mission! Danger, Will Robinson!" But my body? Oh no, it was saying, "Let's see where this goes."

Powerless to resist him? Yeah, that tracks.

Tyler moved closer, his hard, muscular body pressing against my wet skin. He reached for the bottle of conditioner and took it from my hands, placing it on the shelf.

"You've taken care of me," he whispered, his breath warm against my ear. I shivered again, this time from the intensity of his desire. "Let me take care of you."

His hands slid down my arms, sending a trail of goosebumps, before he gently cupped my breasts. His thumbs teased my nipples, circling and pinching gently, causing me to gasp. He knew exactly how to touch me, how to drive me wild with pleasure.

I arched into his touch, craving his attention, leaning back against the shower wall, giving myself to him completely.

"You have no idea how much I want you," he murmured, his lips trailing kisses down my neck. "I've been dying to taste you," His hands moved lower, gliding over my flat stomach, and I couldn't help but moan in anticipation.

His fingers found the sensitive spot between my legs, and he gently parted me, his touch sending sparks of pleasure through my core. I was already ready for him, my body craving his possession. His skilled fingers brought me to the edge of ecstasy and I bit my lip to stifle my cries, not wanting to disturb the peacefulness of his home.

"Please, Tyler," I begged, my voice hoarse with desire. "I need you inside me."

He chuckled, the sound low and seductive. "I plan on it. But first, I want to taste you."

Before I could respond, Tyler dropped to his knees. He lifted one of my legs and grasped my other thigh, spreading my legs wider and positioning himself between them.

I felt a rush of vulnerability mixed with pure desire. His hands held me firmly, leaving no doubt about his strength and determination.

Even over the shower steam his hot breath caressed my sensitive skin. Then he blew gently, sending cooling air that made me squirm. "So beautiful," he said, his eyes dark with desire. "I want you to come apart for me."

With that, he lowered his head and ran his tongue along my slit, teasing me with the lightest of touches.

I gasped, my hands clutching the shower wall for support.

His tongue was warm and wet, contrasting with the hot water that rained down on us and cooled as it ran down our bodies. He licked and sucked gently, his breath sending shivers through my body.

When his tongue found my sensitive bud, he suckled it gently, sending shockwaves of pleasure through my system. I bucked against his mouth, unable to control my reactions.

He held me firmly, his hands now exploring my hips and thighs, his touch both possessive and adoring. He was a master of pleasure, knowing exactly how to build the tension within me.

"Tyler, oh God!" I cried out, my voice echoing off the tiles. I was close, so close to the edge, and he showed no signs of letting up.

His tongue flicked and swirled, his lips sucking gently, driving me wild. "Come for me," he commanded, his voice thick with desire. "Let me feel you with my tongue."

His words were my undoing. I exploded into a million sensations, my orgasm ripping through me with intense force. I cried out, my hands gripping his hair, holding him to me as my body trembled.

As my tremors subsided, Tyler stood, his eyes smoldering with satisfaction. He pulled me close and I rested my head on his chest, wrapping me in his strong arms.

"I've missed you, Lena," he whispered, his breath warm against my ear.

He held me a few moments longer while I regained strength in my legs and could stand on my own. Then he stepped out of the shower and started drying off.

After I finished showering, I reached for a towel, patting myself dry while attempting to scrub away the emotional whirlwind of the last hour.

Spoiler alert: no amount of fluffy cotton was going to do that.

I wrapped my hair up in a makeshift turban, secured the towel around me, and stared at my reflection in the foggy mirror. "You're a delightfully messy human, Lena," I muttered. "Now go face the guy who's probably rethinking all his life choices because of you."

Downstairs, Tyler was doing his best impression of a brooding statue on the couch. Elbows on his knees, hands clasped tight, eyes boring into the carpet like it held the secrets of the universe—or maybe just answers to the "why me?" energy he was radiating.

I took a deep breath, bracing myself for whatever brand of emotional dodgeball this was about to be, and padded over to him. Dropping onto the cushion beside him, I tried to ignore how my bare skin reacted to the lingering heat between us.

He didn't look at me, but he shifted slightly—just enough to acknowledge I was there. Just enough to remind me of the live wire of tension still humming between us. Subtle, yet effective. Like the guy could brood professionally.

"So," I started, keeping my voice steady even though my stomach was playing hopscotch with my breakfast. "Earlier, in the garage… I told you I wanted to talk about what comes next, but then you said…" I tilted my head back and lowered my voice into a cartoonishly gruff growl. "'I still can't trust you, Lena.'"

His lips twitched, the faintest smirk threatening to break free. "Solid impression," he said, deadpan. "Except for the part where I sound like Batman with a sore throat."

I blinked at him, full of mock indignation. "Those were your exact words!"

He chuckled softly, the sound catching me off guard. "Yeah, but I don't growl like that."

"Oh, you definitely do." I crossed my arms, smirking as a small laugh bubbled out of me before I could stop it. It was unplanned, unexpected, and surprisingly nice.

For a second, the air around us didn't feel like it was holding its breath, waiting to explode.

But then my heart gave a twist—a sharp reminder of why I'd started this conversation in the first place. The laughter was nice, but it wasn't the point. I needed clarity, even if it hurt.

I shifted, forcing myself to look at him. "Seriously, though. I need to know where we stand. I need to say some things... and I need to hear yours, too. No growling required."

Okay, so here's the deal: things were starting to get real. The kind of real where you can't just sweep everything under the rug and pretend it's all fine and dandy. Not after all the mess we'd waded through.

I took a deep breath—because, oh boy, here it came—and turned to Tyler. This was it.

"Where do we go from here, Tyler? What's going on in that brooding head of yours?" I tried to sound casual, but inside I was like a bag of fireworks, waiting to go off.

He let out this long, tortured breath, finally locking eyes with me. And—surprise!—there was a storm in them, like he was battling with himself, deciding if he was going to go full Deadpool or stay on the "grumpy, misunderstood guy" side of things. He stayed grumpy.

"I'm gonna need time, Lena," he muttered, low and raspy, like he was forcing the words out through gritted teeth. "After you ignored my calls and texts for a week, can you blame me for not trusting you?"

Oh. Great. Here we go. Guilt trip time.

"I... I didn't ignore you," I tried to defend myself, but he just turned away. Then, like he was doing some weird mental gymnastics, he forced himself to look me in the eye again. And let me tell you, it wasn't pretty. This wasn't the 'smooth talker' Tyler I'd gotten a glimpse of. This was the raw, honest version that, if I'm being honest, scared the hell out of me.

"It's not as simple as pretending none of it happened. You know that." His words dropped like stones into the pit of my stomach.

I nodded because, honestly, there wasn't much else I could do.

His silence felt like it was wrapping around us, thick and uncomfortable, the tension so heavy I thought it might crush us both. He shifted, leaned in a little—

Seriously, how was he still so close and not bursting into flames from the heat between us?

—and his gaze searched mine like he was trying to find something. Hope? Regret?

Whatever it was, I didn't want to know, but I also kind of did.

"We're attracted to each other. No one can argue that," he said, the faintest hint of a smile softening his features. "You're the most damn captivating woman I've ever met, and I know you know it." He gave me this cocky little smirk. Oh, here we go, the ego trip was back. "In the garage, in the shower… I think we've proven that attraction isn't the issue here."

I fought a smile but lost. "*Issue* is definitely not the word that comes to mind," I shot back, because who was I kidding? This was like a rollercoaster of chaos, and I loved it.

But, as per usual, Tyler couldn't just let the moment ride out without dragging us back into deep, dark, brooding territory. The smile faded from his face, and he got all serious again, like someone who'd just read the manual on *How To Be a Grumpy Genius*.

"But you… you can't just erase everything. All the mess, the wreckage that came before this. I'm not judging you, Lena, I swear."

Ugh. I was already cringing at the thought of all the mess. No one had to tell me about the wreckage. I was the wreckage. I opened my mouth to say something, but he wasn't finished. Of course he wasn't.

"I have to be real with you. I can't do this if we're not honest with each other. And you can't just up and leave. I don't know if I can trust that yet."

Well, shit. This was the part where he basically pulled the rug out from under me and left me dangling like a piñata at a toddler's birthday party, just waiting to be knocked into oblivion. What was I supposed to do with all of this?

I swallowed hard, his words sinking in like a rock to the bottom of my stomach.

Tyler was looking at me like he was about to make *the* decision. *The* one that would shift everything.

And here I was, stuck, dangling in midair with no clue where I'd land.

"At first, I did judge you. The day of Thomas and Mia's wedding rehearsal, I'd already heard about what happened at your wedding, and everyone warned me, 'Avoid her. She's a hot mess.'" He sighed, his voice rough, like he had to peel each word out of himself. "With all the stuff going on with my life, I didn't need more chaos. So, based on all that, I saw you as a problem."

A problem. A *problem*. My heart hit my feet, and for a second, I felt like I might actually choke on it. That's what he thought of me from the start. A problem to be avoided.

I wanted to snap back, to explain, to argue, but my mouth went dry, and my words got tangled up in the pile of emotions that had been brewing ever since the day we first met. Damn it, why was everything so complicated?

And then, as if the universe had decided to throw me a pity party, I couldn't hold it in anymore. Tears started to slip down my cheeks faster than I could blink them away, like my face had become a leaky faucet. I wiped at them desperately, but they kept coming. Great. *Just great*. Way to go, Lena. You're totally winning at this emotional maturity thing.

I hadn't planned on breaking down, but, well, apparently my brain and heart were in a race to see who could make me fall apart first. And right now? Heart was winning.

My tears were coming in hot, a complete meltdown that I couldn't keep in any longer. I looked away, mortified, like I could somehow hide my embarrassment by just staring at the wall.

But then—poof—his hand was on my back, and before I could even blink, Tyler was pulling me onto his lap, holding me tight. Like he was some kind of superhero, except instead of a cape, he had a deep, brooding vibe and a lot of emotional baggage. It felt... grounding.

I needed it, I really did.

There I was, sniffling like a toddler in need of a nap, and Tyler? He was just holding me, like he knew that words weren't going to fix anything. They sure as hell wouldn't fix me.

He didn't say a word—probably knew I'd snap at him if he did—but just his presence was enough. He held me as if he understood exactly what was going on inside my head... or, more likely, that I didn't have a clue what was going on in there myself.

Once the sobs started to quiet down, I sucked in a breath, feeling the ache from all the emotions I'd been bottling up. God, this was a mess. And I had to tell him.

"Tyler..." I said, voice shaky as I wiped my eyes. "I want to tell you something. I need to. The truth about why I left Marco at the altar. You're the only person, other than Mia— and Marco— who will know this."

There. It was out. No turning back now. I paused for a moment, preparing myself for what I was going to say next.

"I... I was pregnant," I said. My voice shook like a leaf in the wind.

Tyler just looked at me, all silent and intense, like he could read every stupid, messed-up thought in my head.

And for some reason, that gave me the courage to keep going. Who knows why? Maybe I was just too tired to keep it in anymore.

"Marco really wanted me to get an abortion. And I convinced myself that it was the 'right' thing to do too. You know, because he didn't want a baby yet and we were supposed to get married in three months. So, I thought, 'Hey, I can handle this.' I thought I could just move on, no big deal. But it was a big deal. It turned out that it wasn't nothing. It felt like a weight I couldn't shake, and instead of dealing with it, I just shoved it down and pretended it didn't matter."

I swallowed hard, and my voice cracked. Of course it did. Everything was coming out in this jumbly mess.

Tyler's grip on me tightened, like he knew I was starting to crumble, but he was right there, steady, keeping me grounded.

"The day of my wedding... I couldn't keep pretending. Everything I'd buried deep inside me just... opened up. Like my insides just exploded and I broke. And it was impossible to try to rein in all those pieces of me that were somehow just floating around. Outside my body," I whispered, the last word barely escaping my lips. I felt my face heat up, shame rushing in, and I tried to hide, but then his hand was there—soft, gentle—wiping away the tears before I could even protest.

We just sat there, the silence stretching between us, thick and comfortable, like we had all the time in the world to just *be*. His arms around me felt like the only thing keeping me from falling apart completely.

"Thank you for trusting me with that," Tyler's voice was soft, almost like it came from the heart of him. "I can't imagine the weight of carrying that alone."

It felt like the first time anyone actually got it. The weight. The guilt. The chaos. I suddenly felt less alone.

Something in his words wrapped around me like a cozy blanket, making me feel safe in a way I hadn't allowed myself to feel in ages. Like maybe I wasn't completely messed up.

It was like he was holding out his hand, offering to catch me before I fell, even if I didn't deserve it.

But then, Bam! Reality smacked me in the face again.

His words replayed in my head like a broken record. *"I still can't trust you."*

And damn it, he was right. I had so much more healing to do than I wanted to admit. And being with him? That wasn't going to magically fix me.

I pulled back from him, bracing myself like I was about to take a punch I couldn't avoid. *But I know what I have to say to him.*

"Tyler, my instinct is to say that what we need—like, for real closure—is to just call it quits right here." I could feel my heart thudding against my chest, like it was trying to make a run for it. "I keep telling myself I'm not ready for a relationship. That it wouldn't be fair to you."

My voice trembled, but I forced myself to keep my ground, even if it felt like I was standing on shaky ground. The words burned, but they needed to come out.

His face went blank, like he was bracing for a punch he wasn't ready to take. And those damn eyes of his... they flashed with disbelief and pain, and for a split second, I regretted saying any of it. But he just nodded, slow and heavy, like the weight of my words hit him harder than I intended.

"If that's what you want…" His voice was thick, like he was swallowing down something he didn't want to say. "I'll respect it."

I didn't hesitate. "Well, it's not what I want," I shot back, a little too fast. But honestly, I wasn't sure I knew what the hell I wanted.

He stared at me, all exasperation and hope, like he'd just been hit with a double whammy. "Then tell me." His voice dropped, like he was afraid he wouldn't like the answer. "What do you want?"

I took a deep breath, bracing myself for the storm that was brewing in my mind. I wasn't sure how much sense any of this was going to make, but damn it, I had to get it out.

"I tried to stay away," I started, my voice surprisingly steady despite the hurricane inside me. "Thought it was better for both of us. But then I came here today, and seeing you—knowing that we're going to keep running into each other because of Mia and Thomas—I couldn't help it. It tore me to pieces, Tyler, because I want to be with you."

I watched him carefully, looking for any sign that my words were hitting home. The flicker of relief and understanding that crossed his face made me pause.

Maybe he thought I was all cool and nonchalant at Mia's place, like I didn't give a damn.

"Being with you…" I swallowed hard, trying to put words to the muddle of emotions I was feeling. "It's incredible. When we're together, the part of me that's been sad or angry or just... broken, it actually feels something real. Something good. And it makes me feel free, like I used to. Like I want to feel again."

I let that hang there for a second, watching him, feeling a connection that was both wonderful and terrifying. But, of course, reality was never far behind, waiting to sucker-punch me when I was least prepared.

"But now that we're out of the moment, with our clothes back on and reality checking in…" I let out a frustrated breath, rolling my eyes as I said it, even though I was definitely not feeling eye-roll-worthy. "It just smacks me in the face. Telling me maybe I'm not ready, or else I wouldn't have all these damn doubts. And then, like clockwork, I start remembering how everyone else thinks this is a bad idea. Maybe they see something I don't. Maybe they're right."

I could feel the words getting heavier. But I couldn't stop now.

"And that brings me back to the biggest truth of all. That I'm just not good for you right now. Not in the way that you deserve. I have to work harder at being able to be around you without, I don't know, making it weird. I need to figure out how to be your friend first, before any of this can even start to make sense. So we can be around Mia, Thomas, our families, and not have it be this... huge drama bomb every time."

I took another breath, looking at him with a vulnerability I wasn't used to showing. "We need to do what's best for everyone, and that means what's best for us too."

There. I'd said it. Everything. All the doubts, all the reasons I thought we were wrong for each other. Every single one of them flying around in my head like a goddamn storm.

Tyler looked at me for a moment, then turned away like he was trying to find the right words. Not that I expected him to go all soft and cuddly on me, but hey, a little less of the brooding might've been nice.

After what felt like an eternity of silence, he exhaled like he'd just run a marathon and finally said, "But Lena, this—" He trailed off.

I could practically see the gears turning in his head, trying to decide if he was about to say something that would make me regret everything or if he was just gonna go with the honesty thing. Which was terrifying in its own right.

"If you're suggesting we can be friends... that's going to be damn near impossible."

I swallowed hard, because, yeah, he had a point. That wasn't exactly the most fun thing to hear, but I wasn't backing down. I had a stubborn streak a mile wide. "I know. But for Mia, for Thomas, we have to try. We have to be civil."

His jaw clenched as if the words left a bad taste in his mouth. "This is your choice," he muttered, meeting my eyes with that intense, unreadable look that made my stomach flip. "Not mine."

A cold shiver ran down my spine, and I could feel the walls I'd worked so hard to put up starting to crumble. It had been absolute hell trying to stay away from him this past week. I'd barely made it through without falling apart, and now here I was, practically giving him permission to shatter everything again.

I fought back the tremor I could feel in my hands and did my best to steady my voice. "Yeah, well, sometimes life gives us choices we don't get to make."

Chapter 12: Tyler

"Can't help but notice you've been a little… off, lately," Thomas said, adjusting his grip on the bar, like he was trying to act casual about it. "Is it your mom? How's she doing?"

I finished my last set with a clang of weights that was probably louder than I intended. The sound echoed through the gym.

Thomas was standing near my head, spotting me like some overly concerned big brother.

I wiped the sweat off my forehead and shook my head, trying to brush it off like it was no big deal. "She's doing alright. Recovery's tough, but she's getting stronger every day. Stubborn as ever, you know her."

He nodded, but I could see the look in his eyes, the one that said he knew I wasn't telling him everything. "Good to hear. But that's not all, is it?"

I stiffened a bit, my jaw tightening as I avoided his gaze.

Talking about the holidays with him these past three years have been like opening a wound that has recently scabbed over.

But Thomas was my best friend. If I couldn't be real with him, then who the hell could I be real with?

I sighed, grabbing the towel to wipe my neck. "Nah, it's… it's just some holiday blues," I muttered, trying to make it sound like it was nothing. "This time of year, you know? All the shit I try to keep buried just decides it wants to come up anyway."

He tilted his head, like he could tell there was more under the surface. "Carrie?"

"Yeah." Her name felt like a punch in the gut, even though I've said and thought it a thousand times a day.

I sat down on the bench beside him, suddenly feeling the weight of it all again. "Feels like another lifetime now, but also like it was yesterday? It's still this… quiet ache."

I stared at my hands, flexing them like I could somehow hold onto a feeling that'd been gone for years.

The holidays used to mean something different. They used to mean family and normal and easy. But now, they just reminded me of everything I'd lost.

"Losing her, my injury, losing the game… it just—back then, I thought I had it all figured out. My family, my future. She was my first love. Then suddenly… everything I knew just slipped through my fingers."

I could feel the weight of those memories pressing in again.

The holidays used to be filled with things I took for granted. Family dinners, picking out the perfect gift for Carrie, watching her light up when she strung the Christmas lights or hung mistletoe above my head.

But now they were just… empty. And that emptiness? It wasn't just about her. It was about me. The guy I used to be. The version of me that was long gone. Lost somewhere in the wreckage of all the shit that happened.

Thomas nodded, watching me like he was waiting for the punchline.

I could tell he was letting me work through my thoughts, not pushing too hard.

"It's hard to snap back from all that," he said , voice quieter than usual, but still sure. "But you've been carrying it alone too long. Ever think maybe you just need a breather?"

I shot him a look, brows furrowing. "You suggesting a therapist or something?"

"Funny, but no," he chuckled, like I was the world's funniest stand-up comedian. "I'm talking about us taking a weekend off. What do you think about getting away to the cabin for the weekend? Just a couple of days to shut out the noise, get back to the basics. Us, a lake, and way too much beer. What do you say?"

The idea hit me like a slow wave, rolling over me, making everything feel... a little quieter. "The cabin..." I muttered, memories creeping in. Long drives, fishing lines tangling, chopping wood like a badass lumberjack, late nights around the fire, mornings so peaceful the only sound was water lazily slapping the dock.

I opened my mouth, but I was already thinking about it. "Sounds equally appealing as sleeping for three days." The words sounded sarcastic, but hell, the thought of it? It was actually starting to settle in as something close to... peace.

Thomas cracked up, slapping me on the shoulder like I wasn't just the world's grumpiest human being but also some kind of joke machine. "Then we're definitely going. A little quiet might be exactly what you need."

I looked at him, feeling the tension start to seep out of me for the first time in weeks. Huh. Yeah, he wasn't wrong. "Yeah. You're right. A weekend at the cabin sounds good."

I could already picture it: fresh air, endless stretches of sky, and for once, maybe a little peace in my head. What a fucking concept.

"Let's make it happen, then," I said, the words coming out before they even formed in my mind.

It had already been late afternoon when we arrived at the cabin. As I stepped inside, the familiar scent of pine and fresh air hit me, but it didn't take long for my peace to get shredded to hell.

The last person I'd expected to see in this secluded spot was Lena, but there she was with her sister. Her presence hit me like a bolt of lightning.

Thomas, my best friend, had organized this trip, promising it'd be a much-needed break from the holiday chaos. He knew I hated this time of year—couldn't stand it. All it did was remind me of everything I'd lost.

"Surprise, buddy!" Thomas exclaimed, grinning like a kid on Christmas morning as he entered the cabin behind me. "You know I'm a newlywed, so I hate being away from my beautiful bride for too long. So I invited Mia. She said she was just going to come up and read a book. But I promise you, this is time away for us guys, too. We'll still go off and do our manly man stuff on our own."

I nodded, trying my best to look enthusiastic, but my brain was already on high alert, running through every possible reason why this was a terrible idea. "Yeah, sounds great, man. I was looking forward to some peace and quiet."

"Well, we are getting peace and quiet, just with a little extra company," he said, motioning toward Lena and Mia by the fireplace.

Mia and Thomas had no clue about the storm Lena had stirred up recently. As the women were chatting away, all smiles and completely oblivious to how much them being here was screwing with me, Lena sat there, her long, brown hair spilling over her shoulders, framing her perfect face. Those brown eyes of hers, the ones that used to burn with desire for me, now had that hint of apprehension. Like she was maybe regretting all the things she'd said to me.

Or maybe regretting being in the same room as me.

Yeah, I wasn't sure I wanted to stick around to find out.

Mia looked up at us with a burst of excitement. "My Tommy!" she yelled, jumping up and wrapping herself around him like a koala on a tree.

"How was the drive, Ty?" she asked, tilting her head in my direction, though she didn't bother pulling herself away from her husband. "Did you have any idea we'd be here?"

I forced a smile, trying to act normal when everything in my head was telling me this wasn't normal at all. "Not a hint. I didn't know you two were coming."

And just as I thought the moment might be quiet for a second—of course, Lena had to open her mouth. Her voice, sharp and unmistakable, sliced through the air like a hot knife through butter. "It seems Mia didn't tell me you two would be up here either."

I glanced at Thomas, who just shrugged with that 'Who me?' look he always had when he was up to something. An innocent little gleam danced in his eyes. "My wife. Already hiding things from me."

Mia, ever the expert in looking guilty while trying to sweet talk her way out of it, pouted. "I'm sorry, baby," she said, pushing out her bottom lip like she'd been practicing it in front of a mirror. "I wanted some quiet time away with my sis too. Don't worry. We'll stay out of your way!"

"You're never in my way!" Thomas pulled her back into his arms, kissing her like a scene from one of those sappy rom-coms that I pretended not to hate.

I shifted on my feet, trying not to roll my eyes. The whole thing was like watching a soap opera that I desperately wanted to turn off. But I couldn't help it—I was already in this mess. Just another family bonding weekend I wasn't sure I'd survive.

As I processed the unexpected turn of events, my mind started replaying the last two weeks.

Lena and I had this electric connection, a kind of forbidden romance that everyone warned us to avoid. But damn, the chemistry between us? Unstoppable. Too bad it was doomed from the start, like one of those terrible movies you started watching while eating pizza and drinking beer just because it was on TV and you were too lazy to reach over for the remote and change the channel.

She was dealing with her own life. Already tangled up in enough. And here I was, trying to toss a new connection on top of it.

To be honest, it was probably the same for me too. I had my own baggage. Stuff I'd rather not unpack in front of anyone.

The guilt, the regret, everything. It created this wall between us, and every time we got close to breaking it down, we pushed each other away. Afraid to let the other person in too deep. Because who the hell wants to get hurt again?

"Tyler, you wanna grab some beers and jump in the hot tub?" Thomas asked, his voice slicing through my thoughts. "It's time to start day one of R and R!"

I shook my head, shaking off the weight of everything, even though it didn't quite leave. "Yeah, let's do it," I muttered, feeling a bit of disappointment that the 'guys only' weekend I was hoping for was officially out the window.

The cabin had always been my escape. A sanctuary in the middle of nowhere where I could just breathe for once. Now, with Lena and Mia popping up like they were the surprise guests on some reality show, it felt like my safe haven had been invaded.

Thomas and I spent the next few hours on the back deck, drinking beers, getting in and out of the hot tub. It wasn't the worst way to kill time. Actually, it was starting to feel like exactly what I needed. Relaxing. No pressure. But I knew it wouldn't last because I'd eventually have to go inside.

When evening hit, we went back inside and settled in. The quiet didn't last long.

Thomas and I threw together a simple dinner, trading light-hearted banter that helped distract me from the awkwardness that lingered in the air. It wasn't exactly a comedy routine, but it worked.

Lena and Mia offered to help, but I shot them down with my go-to excuse. "Let the guys work their magic." Sure, I was technically trying to be a gentleman, but mostly, I just wanted to limit any potential awkwardness with Lena.

Once dinner was done, we all settled around the fireplace. Glasses of wine and whiskey in hand, we basked in the warmth from the flames. I could feel the tension starting to melt, though not nearly as quickly as I would've liked.

Mia suggested a game of *Never Have I Ever*, because, of course, nothing says "relaxing evening" like digging up the deepest, darkest corners of your personal history. I groaned inwardly. The last thing I needed was a game that could trigger awkward conversations about my past. But I wasn't about to be the guy who killed the vibe, so I went along with it.

The game kicked off, and Lena and Mia were already in full-on comedy mode, giggling and teasing each other like they were rehearsing for a stand-up routine. Thomas, the smooth talker he was, jumped in, cracking jokes and lightening the mood with his usual charm.

"Never have I ever... kissed someone on a first date," Lena said, taking a sip of her wine like she was asking about the weather.

Thomas, Mia, and I exchanged a glance, all of us taking a drink at the same time.

"Juicy, juicy," Lena teased, pointing at me and Thomas, narrowing her eyes like she'd uncovered a secret. "I bet there are some wild stories behind those glasses."

My cheeks heated up, but not because my story was wild. Oh no, my secrets weren't the fun kind. More like the kind that made you want to crawl under the couch and never come out. They were painful reminders of the past, and I wasn't ready to share them with anyone. Especially not with Lena in the room.

The game kept rolling, each round peeling back layers of our experiences like an onion, making the air thicker with unspoken tension.

I caught Lena's eye across the fire, and my gut twisted. Great. Just what I needed. A reminder of how messed up things were between us.

"Never have I ever... had sex in a public place," Mia said, her voice low and sultry, making it sound like a scene from one of those raunchy movies that you pretend not to watch but totally do.

Mia's and Lena's glasses stayed where they were. Unraised. Thomas and I exchanged a look, both of us taking a drink, the heat in the room cranking up a notch.

"Oh ho! I saw that look," Lena chimed in, voice dripping with challenge. "You two obviously have some wild stories to share. Come on, spill."

Thomas leaned back in his chair, grinning like he was about to deliver a punchline. "Well, I'll admit, there was this one time in college when I hooked up with a girl in the library stacks..."

As Thomas rambled on, I felt Lena's eyes on me, waiting for my turn to confess. I took a deep breath, trying to decide if I was really ready to let go of my usual stoic bullshit. But, hell, why not? I was on my third glass of whiskey and maybe it was time to get into the game.

"Okay, fine," I said, my voice steady even as my mind raced. "There was this one time in high school, when I snuck out to meet a girl at the park after dark…"

The words came out, almost too easily. My story was harmless enough. Except for the part where it made me think of Carrie. The one woman who would always have a permanent spot in my heart.

The game kept going, each round peeling back a little more of everyone's secrets. Meanwhile, I stayed on the edge, a shadow from my past keeping me from jumping in too deep.

Lena's questions got bolder, like she was daring us all to spill something we'd rather keep locked away. Her eyes were sparkling with curiosity. And let's face it, maybe a little desire too.

I tried to loosen up, but all I was really doing was stirring up the hangups I couldn't seem to shake. Especially now that Carrie was on my mind.

"Never have I ever... had a one-night stand," Lena said, her voice all husky and dripping with something unspoken. She lifted her glass and took a sip, her lips curling just a little.

I froze. My hand hovered over my glass, unsure if I should take a drink or just pretend to be invisible. I thought about it. Hell, I almost had one. But then it hit me. My one-night stand with Lena ended up not being a one-night deal. Nope. It had turned into two, and who knows, maybe it could've been three if I hadn't hit the brakes.

So, yeah, it didn't technically count. Besides, Lena was the only woman I'd been with since Carrie, and Lena and I had already put a stop to what was sure to become a mistake anyway.

My drink stayed in my hand, unmoving. The moment stretched out, thick with tension, like a rubber band about to snap.

Thomas and Mia? They were practically treating the game like foreplay, laughing and egging each other on. The pause in the game? That was their cue to make a stealthy exit.

And they did. Mia and Thomas snuck off, leaving just me and Lena alone.

The firelight flickered across her face, highlighting that mischievous gleam in her beautiful brown eyes.

I should've gotten up. I should've walked away before things got even more complicated. But spending an entire weekend in close quarters with Lena? Yeah, that had clouded my better judgment, and here I was, stuck in this moment.

"So, Tyler," Lena began, her voice soft but playful, like she knew exactly what she was doing. "It seems like we're the only ones left." She took a sip of her wine, her eyes never leaving mine. "What could we possibly do to make the most of it?"

I shifted in my seat, trying not to look too uncomfortable. My gut was already giving me the kind of warning that only a guy like me could recognize—danger, with a capital D.

Lena had this way of pulling me in, making me forget my name, forget my past, and just... forget. Hell, I was trying to leave all that stuff behind, but her? She could make it feel like it didn't even exist.

But my head? My head was still haunted by the ghosts of my past, and now she'd just dropped me into the "friend zone" like a brick in a lake. My brain screamed at me to resist.

"Lena, I..." I trailed off, trying to find the words, but they weren't coming. "We decided to stay away from each other."

"I know what we decided," she shot back, leaning in a little, her voice low. "But we keep ending up together." She paused, then added with a sly grin, "Although, I'll admit, I wanted to come up to the cabin with Mia because... you'd be here. I wanted to see you."

The air between us thickened as she leaned forward, resting her elbows on her knees, locking me in with that intense stare of hers.

I shifted again, uncomfortable, but damn if she wasn't starting to make me second guess every decision I'd made in the past few days. "We agreed we wouldn't have to see each other," I muttered, hoping she'd back off. But no such luck.

"I've been feeling like I want to explore what's really going on between us," she said, her voice soft and almost serious. "Is it just sex? Or is it something more?" She took a breath, letting it hang in the air, then leaned closer. "What I want to find out is... why don't we take things slow and explore what we have, no expectations?"

It was like she'd tossed a match on a dry field and was just waiting to see if I'd burn down with it. And the worst part? I was close to saying yes.

I couldn't help but be drawn into her words, her voice like a siren's song. My body was already betraying me, my dick hardening at the mere thought of her touch.

I wanted to believe there was something between us. But my mind screamed at me to pull back. Trust was a four-letter word, and I wasn't sure I could handle the chaos that came with it.

"Slow is not how I'd describe us, or our last encounter," I said, my voice rough with the desire that I was doing my best to ignore. "And I'm not sure I can trust myself to keep it under control this time."

Lena's lips curved into a smile that could melt steel, and she leaned back, swirling her wine like she was savoring the moment. "Control is overrated, don't you think?" she said, her voice dripping with mischief. "Sometimes you just have to let go and see where the night takes you."

I watched her lips, remembering the way they had felt pressed against mine. Soft, insistent, like they knew things about me I wasn't ready to admit.

My chest tightened, and I wanted to let go. Wanted to just burn up in the fire between us. But I'd promised myself I wouldn't let anyone in, not after losing Carrie. I'd built walls around my heart so thick that not even a wrecking ball could get through.

And Lena? She was the kind of woman who could tear them down with one touch, one look, maybe just by breathing the same air as me.

"It's not that simple, Lena," I said, my voice tight with the weight of it. "I have... demons. I'm not ready to let someone in, not yet. Besides, we both know exactly where the night will take us if we don't keep ourselves in check."

She reached out, placing her hand on mine. And damn it, if that touch didn't feel like a lightning bolt straight to my chest. "Tell me about your past, Tyler. Let me know the pain you've been through. You don't have to face it alone. Maybe we can help each other heal."

I looked down at our hands, the warmth of hers seeping through my skin, and I felt something I hadn't in years—a pulse of hope.

But I couldn't let it in. "I don't want to hurt you," I whispered, my voice barely cutting through the crackle of the fire. "I don't want to get hurt."

"I'm not asking you to give me anything, Tyler," she said softly, her voice carrying a quiet conviction. "Just let me give you something. Let me show you that there's more to life than pain and sorrow."

Her words hit me like a punch to the face. I wanted to believe her. I wanted to let her show me a way out of the misery I'd been living in. But the doubt was still there, a nagging voice whispering that I was just setting myself up for more heartache.

"No," I said, stepping away from her, my heart pounding like a damn drum in my chest. "We're not doing this."

Chapter 13: Lena

The crisp morning air hit my lungs like a slap in the face—oh right, I was still alive and feeling every ounce of last night's bad decisions.

"Please, just push me into some poison oak and let me roll down this mountain into sweet, sweet death," I groaned.

Honestly, I had no business drinking that much, but when you're faced with a bottle of pinot noir that practically whispers your name, you don't just say no.

Mia, the overachiever, was practically dragging me along on our morning hike.

I hated her for it, wanted to rip that perfect little smile off her face, but deep down I knew I needed this.

She was making me sweat out the booze, and as much as it sucked right now, I could appreciate that she was actually doing something useful with her perky little self.

"We're not going far, you big wimp," she teased, clearly enjoying my pain. "Besides, there's too much snow on the ground. We can only walk on the road for an 'out and back.'"

Out and back? What the hell was that? "Oh, look at me, I'm so cool because I know what an 'out and back' is," I mocked, throwing my hands in the air dramatically.

She rolled her eyes and turned around to face me, walking backward like some kind of ultra-healthy, hangover-free superhero. "It just means we'll hike out and then take the same route back."

Oh, how original.

We trudged down the main road, the snowplows having done their job. The winter landscape was actually kind of gorgeous.

Don't tell her, but she was right—being out here in the quiet, with just the trees and the soft crunch of snow underfoot, was helping my headache a little. Almost like the forest was whispering at me to spill my guts or something.

Yeah, no thanks. Not happening.

"So, you and Thomas just vanished last night, huh?" I couldn't resist the jab. They slipped away in the middle of our epic game of *Never Have I Ever*. Must've been nice.

"Well, I am a newlywed, Lena! Can you blame me?" she giggled, her cheeks flushing a light pink.

I couldn't help but smile. She was so damn happy, it was contagious. I was glad for her—truly. But still... I had to give her crap about it. Just because.

It was the least I could do.

As we trudged down the winding road, I couldn't help but notice Mia's eyes practically glittering with curiosity. I knew what was coming.

"But let's talk about those sparks flying between you and Tyler. I can tell there's got to be more to the story."

Oh, Mia. Always digging.

I spotted a long, thick branch lying across the road, and for lack of anything better to do, I picked it up like it was some sort of mystical artifact. "You're right. I won't lie to you. I couldn't even hide an ingrown hair from you, let alone something as explosive as this."

Stabbing the branch into the snow with a little too much enthusiasm, I used it like a walking stick to take out all my excess energy. "Tyler and I... yeah, we hooked up. Twice. Just to be precise. It happened while you and Thomas were off in honeymoonland. Doing whatever it is that newlyweds do. You know, probably eating ice cream in bed and making the rest of us feel bad about our single lives."

I glanced at her, watching her face go through the stages of Mia-discovery: sparkly excitement, followed by the realization.

It was almost like clockwork. Mia had mentioned, right before the wedding, how our families were basically praying I'd stay away from Tyler.

Before she could say anything—and I mean anything—I jumped in, my voice surprisingly steady considering how my brain was running in circles. "But don't worry. It was over before it even really started."

I threw that last part out like I was fine. Totally fine.

But my mind wasn't fine. In fact, it was going wild. I could practically see the memories flashing before me.

Those stolen moments with Tyler. The way he'd held me after my run-in with Marco. I shuddered just thinking about how quickly we went from comforting each other to ripping each other's clothes off.

Was it the emotional rollercoaster after seeing my ex? Was that what set everything in motion?

And then there was the second time... when Tyler came up behind me in the garage and, well, had his way with me.

That—oh, that was hot. I could practically feel it again just thinking about it.

But wait, there was a third encounter. The memory of him going down on me in the shower? Yeah. That one made my knees go weak just now. It was that good.

I cleared my throat, trying to focus, because talking about Tyler was making me all hot and bothered again, and now was not the time for that.

Mia's eyes were wide with curiosity, and I had to put on my best serious face. "It was... intense, Mia. The attraction between us? Electric. Tyler's something else."

I paused for a moment, trying to gather my thoughts—because, let's be real, I was still reeling from the whole thing.

"He's quiet, keeps to himself, but he really cares about his friends and family. But deep down? There's a storm inside him. Wild. Untamed. It's like... he's fighting something, but I can't figure out what. There are just so many layers to him. Like an onion... a very broody, handsome onion."

Okay, I might've lost my serious tone there for a second. But honestly, how do you describe a guy like Tyler?

I thought about his strong arms pulling me closer, his whispered words that sent shivers down my spine. His muscular frame, that tanned skin, and those piercing ice-blue eyes. God, my heart still raced just remembering them. My body practically ached for his touch. I could almost feel his hands roaming over me again, igniting a fire that only he could quench.

Mia, of course, had to ruin my delicious daydream. "So, there's nothing going on between you two?" She waved her hand like I was supposed to stop being all lost in my own head.

I sighed, pulling myself out of my Tyler-induced fog.

"Things are complicated," I said, trying to sound more composed than I felt. My voice betrayed me, though. It was laced with all the regret I had bottled up. "Despite the... intense attraction, we agreed it would be best to stay away from each other. Mutual decision, you know? No one wants to risk getting hurt again."

Mia's eyes went wide, and I could practically see the questions forming in her brain. She was dying to know. "But why? Was it the sex? Was he not good to you?"

Oh, sissy, if only that were the issue.

I shook my head, rolling my eyes at her. "No, the sex was—" I paused, a tiny smile playing on my lips despite myself—"Mind-blowing. Tyler's an incredible lover. Incredible."

I let the words hang in the air like I was suddenly the expert on great sex, which, well, I was. "He's attentive, passionate, makes sure I'm the one having the good time, you know?"

I cleared my throat and kept walking, using the stick like it was my emotional javelin. "But it's not just about that. It's complicated. It's the way he looks at me, Mia. Like he can see right into my soul. Like he understands all the pain and fears I'm carrying around, 'cause I'm pretty sure he's fighting his own demons too. Like, our pasts? Even though I don't know what he's been through, I can tell they're like these shadows that follow us everywhere we go, and no matter how hard we try, we can't shake them off."

I jabbed the stick into the ground with each word. "It's just... too much." I let out an exaggerated sigh, feeling the weight of everything pressing down. Sometimes, it was easier to break a branch than deal with the mess inside my head.

We walked side by side, arms locked together like some cheesy rom-com montage.

I loved that we could talk like this. That I could unload all this mess in my brain, especially the tangle Tyler had somehow tied me into.

"You'd think I was the one who needed fixing," I muttered, rolling my eyes. "But honestly, the more I think about it, Tyler's the one with more baggage than an airport carousel. He's got more to straighten out than I do. And that's why I have to protect myself, Mia. Because if I let him in, I might lose what's left of me."

We paused to catch our breath, mostly because I was about to pass out from the emotional weight of the conversation. Also, my hangover still wasn't fully gone. And the altitude? Let's just say I wasn't made for mountain hiking.

Mia's expression softened. "So, what now then? You both decided to steer clear of each other, and that's that. But you were there when Thomas asked me if I wanted to come up to the cabin, and you knew he'd bring Tyler. Yet, you're the one who volunteered to come keep me company. Before I'd even decided I was coming. Sounds like you wanted to see him."

And just like that, she called me out. I let out a huff and waved a hand in surrender. "Yeah, okay, fine. You caught me. I did want to see him. What can I say? It's the masochist in me, I guess. I enjoy torturing myself."

I rolled my eyes at my own self-pity, then took a deep breath. Time to spill the beans. Great.

"There's something else," I said, my voice dropping to almost a whisper. "Something I didn't tell Tyler. And if I tell you, you have to promise me you won't say anything. No one else can know."

Mia looked at me, brow furrowed, concern creeping into her expression. "This doesn't sound good," she said, worry lines creasing her forehead. "But you can trust me. I won't say anything. I promise."

I bit my lip and let out a shaky breath, trying to hold it together. "When I was at the hospital with Tyler's mom—after her stroke—Tyler stepped out for coffee. Left me alone with Lorraine for about forty-five minutes. She said thank you for being there, for keeping her company. But then… then she made a request that's been haunting me ever since."

Mia's eyes widened, her concern deepening. "What did she want?"

I swallowed hard, my throat tightening. "She asked me to stay away from him," I whispered, barely audible over the thud of my own heart. "She said Tyler was still healing, that I might disrupt his recovery. She begged me to let him move on, whether that meant being alone or finding someone else who could give him the stability he needed."

Mia squeezed my hand, and I felt a little bit of the tension drain out of me. "Oh, Lena. That's a lot to process."

I nodded, feeling a lump rise in my throat. "But what did she mean by 'he's still healing'? What's he recovering from? Do you know?"

Mia gave me this soft, steady look, squeezing my hand a little tighter. It calmed me down more than I wanted to admit.

"When we left the cabin, I didn't realize it was mostly downhill," Mia grunted. "Getting back is really challenging my cardio right now. Sorry, sis, but saving oxygen for this hike back home is more important than your problems. I have to focus on breathing!"

I could've snapped at her for avoiding the conversation, but instead, I found myself laughing, even as the weight of the dilemma pressed down on me.

"I think she has every right to go mama bear on him," I said after a pause, my voice quieter now, more resigned and limited by the altitude. "She probably seized her moment to take control when she had the chance. Can't blame her for wanting what's best for him. At the end of the day, I decided not to tell Tyler about our talk. He could get angry at her, or worse, hurt."

Mia gave me a knowing look, squeezing my hand once more before letting go, probably because she needed to focus on not passing out from the hike.

"I get it," she said softly, but I knew she was still thinking about what I'd said.

As we neared the end of the road, Mia suddenly stopped, her eyes zeroing in on a sad little tree poking out from a mound of snow like it was holding the meaning of life in its tiny, frail branches.

She nudged me with her elbow, and I glanced over at the tree, her finger pointing to a few green pine needles struggling to survive on a handful of sad, dry twigs. "Do you see that? You know what would be perfect?"

I raised an eyebrow. "Is this a trick question?"

"That tree is like the Charlie Brown one. We should totally bring it back and decorate it for the Christmas feast!"

I laughed out loud, shaking my head. "Only you would think of hauling back a sickly tree to commemorate the *best* cabin trip ever."

She shot me a playful look, practically bouncing on her feet. "Oh, come on! The cabin's right there. Go and bring something back to dig it up. It'll be fun!"

Before I could protest, she was already climbing up the little hill toward the tree like a determined elf on a mission. "This could be a tradition! We'll bring our kids up here, pick out the worst tree that looks like it's on its last breath, dig it up, and see if we can bring it back to life!"

I could already picture it: a family of tree-killers, attempting to resuscitate pathetic little saplings every year.

With the kind of dramatic flair that only Mia could pull off, she reached the tree—and then, in a slow-motion sequence that I swear could've been in a movie, her foot slid right out from under her.

I watched her arms flail like she was trying to hold on to air, and then—thud—she hit the ground with all the grace of a sack of potatoes, letting out a loud yelp.

"Mia!" I scrambled up after her, but by the time I got to her, she was already trying to push herself up, wincing like she'd just run a marathon on hot coals.

"It's just a little twist," she said, clearly trying to downplay it, but her face went white as soon as she put weight on her ankle.

"Yeah, and I'm the queen of England. Can you stand at all?"

She winced again. "Not... really."

"Great. Perfect. This day is shaping up to be amazing." I could barely keep the sarcasm from dripping off my tongue as I eyed the tree that had caused all this drama. And yet, somehow, I couldn't stop the smile creeping onto my face.

I glanced back at the cabin, feeling that heavy realization settle over me like the snowflakes that were drifting down. "Alright, you stay here. I'll go get the guys."

"Oh, great. Now I'm a damsel in distress," Mia sighed, leaning dramatically against her little tree, flashing me a smile that was more about hiding pain than anything else.

I raised an eyebrow. "You've officially earned that tree now. I'll see about hauling it back for you," I said, already turning to head back up the road toward Thomas and Tyler.

By the time we got Mia in the car so Thomas could take her to urgent care, I found myself standing in the driveway with Tyler, in a silence so thick I could've cut it with a knife—if only I had one.

"So…" I said, wrapping my arms around myself, looking at everything but him. "It's just us."

"Looks like it." Tyler ran a hand through his hair, then threw a glance at the cabin that was loaded with way more unspoken things than I wanted to deal with right now.

I cleared my throat, trying to sound casual, but let's be real, nothing about this situation screamed "casual." "We have to bring that tree for her. She'll be so bummed if I don't go get it."

Tyler snorted, his dry sense of humor coming through like a punchline I wasn't quite prepared for. "Sure, because it would be a tragedy to leave the 'perfect tree' behind."

I rolled my eyes, but the tension was still there, hovering between us like a third person. "Yeah, well, she has very specific tree-related needs," I said, trying to make light of the situation.

But the way he looked at me then, like he could see straight through me, definitely didn't help matters.

***

Tyler and I stood side by side, staring at the sorry excuse for a tree Mia had somehow decided was worthy of being hauled all the way back here.

It was, in every sense of the word, pathetic. A crooked little pine about three feet tall, with maybe four branches if you squinted real hard. It looked like it had survived some storms, none of them in its favor. But, oddly enough, there was something endearing about it.

"Well," Tyler said, folding his arms and smirking like he was debating whether to punch me in the arm or steal my coffee, "Do we think this little guy has a chance, or are we just wasting our time here?"

I grinned, because, really, how could I resist? "Oh, we're definitely wasting our time. But, you know, what Mia wants, Mia gets. If I don't haul this sorry tree back now, I'll be making a second trip up here tomorrow, and no one needs that kind of nonsense."

Tyler arched an eyebrow, his smirk turning into something more like a challenge. "Alright, but if this thing's not already dead, it might not survive the journey."

I grabbed one of the shovels from the pile we found in the garage, crouching next to the tree like I was about to perform some kind of botanical surgery. "Care to help, or are you just here for the heckling?"

"Fine," he sighed, bending down beside me, his proximity making it way harder to focus on digging than it should've. His coat brushed against mine as he grabbed the second shovel, and I swear, it felt like a heat wave hit me. Or maybe I was just on fire from the inside out. Either way, this was unfair.

I tried to focus on the tree. *The tree, Lena. Focus on the tree.*

"So, Mr. Woodsman, any tips for digging up a tree without, you know, committing tree murder?" I asked, trying to sound casual. But let's be honest—I was doing anything to keep my cool.

He let out a soft chuckle, the kind that went straight to my chest and made my insides do backflips. "You just dig. Like this." He shoved his shovel into the earth, leaning in so his arm brushed against mine. My whole body jolted. Not fair.

I pretended not to notice, but by the way my neck heated up it felt pretty damn obvious. "Seems simple enough," I muttered, shoveling from the other side and sneaking a glance at him.

Of course, he looked completely at ease—like this was just another normal day for him. Meanwhile, I felt like I might burst into flames. Was I the only one sensing this, uh, electric tension?

We worked in silence for a bit, each scoop of dirt coming with a clink of our shovels. And every time our coats brushed or the metal hit rock, it was like a little zap of static shot through me. It was ridiculous, honestly. Why did he have to look so good while digging up a sad little tree?

Finally, I decided I had to break the ice. "So, if you weren't here, what would you be doing? Not digging up a poor, pathetic tree in the snow, I bet."

"Oh, definitely not," he said. "I'd be somewhere warm, probably watching football or catching up on sleep." He shot me a sideways glance, his voice dropping slightly. "But, if you're asking if I regret being here… I don't."

I swallowed hard, my pulse suddenly erratic. "Not even with all the, uh, unexpected company?"

"Nope. Wouldn't change a thing."

His gaze lingered a little longer than necessary, and my heart did a weird flip in my chest. My throat went dry, and I couldn't think of a single clever response, so I just kept digging. But I was all too aware of him so near me. His steady presence was practically buzzing.

We eventually dug deep enough to unearth the little guy, and I pulled back, letting out a frustrated huff. "I know we're so close. But, whew! I just need a second."

Tyler chuckled softly, reaching over to steady the shovel in my hand. His fingers were warm, even through our gloves, and the way his big hand covered mine made my breath catch.

Nope, don't think about it.

"I can finish this," he said, his voice a little huskier than before. "You grab the pot for me." He flashed me that grin of his, the one that had me second-guessing every decision I'd made in the last hour. "I'll be right behind you."

I stood up, my heart still trying to play catch-up. "Right," I managed, holding his gaze for a second before I broke. "You know, this might be the saddest tree I've ever seen."

He didn't seem to mind. He stared up at the bare, wonky branches, his expression softening. "Saddest, maybe. But…" He let his gaze drift over the little tree. "…I'm starting to think Mia's idea of saving it was a really good one. Don't you think?"

I wasn't sure if he meant the tree or something else, but my heart somersaulted either way.

"Okay, I'm just going to lift this up by the roots and you stand here with the pot."

I held the pot as he instructed, trying to keep my hands from shaking.

Tyler knelt down, his hands disappearing into the earth to grab the tree, and the sound of snapping roots was oddly satisfying.

But just as I was about to comment, he accidentally leaned back on the shovel that was lodged next to me in the ground. Trying to avoid it, I tried to move and he did too. Actually, I'm not sure about the physics and probability of it all, but we both tumbled backward, together into the snow.

I landed with a soft "oof," and Tyler ended up next to me, wiping snow off his face and laughing.

"Well," he said, grinning up at the sky like nothing just happened, "wasn't expecting that."

I rolled onto my side, brushing snow off my sleeve and trying not to laugh too loudly. "Neither was I. But hey, the tree's free, right?"

He held up the sapling in his hands, glancing at me, his eyes locking onto mine. I swear, the world stopped for a second. "Guess it is."

We both lay there for a moment, catching our breath. Because the altitude. The quiet was heavy, like it was waiting for something.

I should've said something, cracked a joke or lightened the mood, but I couldn't think of anything. Every thought was being drowned out by the steady rise and fall of his chest beside me.

Then, almost without thinking, he reached over and brushed a stray lock of hair from my forehead. His fingers lingered for just a beat too long, and I felt the warmth spread across my cheeks. I held my breath, waiting.

But just as quickly, he pulled his hand back, standing up with that same cool composure. "Come on," he said, his voice rougher than before. "We've got a tree to pot."

Tyler held out his hand, and I took it, letting him pull me up like I was some kind of Victorian damsel instead of a grown woman who just fell over while trying to rescue a tree.

My heart? Oh, it decided to throw a little rave in my chest, because apparently, it hadn't gotten the memo that this was a bad idea.

We stood there for a second. Or maybe it was a year. Our eyes locked, and the air between us felt so charged you'd think we were in a rom-com trailer with swelling music. Except no one moved. No one spoke. And that right there was the problem. We were just standing in this snow globe of awkward tension, waiting for someone to smash it and let all the messy feelings spill out.

"Mia will appreciate our hard work," he finally muttered, breaking the spell with a sigh that sounded like he'd been carrying it around in a backpack for years. He bent down, scooping up the tree like it was his long-lost child, and helped me wrestle it into the pot.

I forced a smile, because hey, fake it till you make it, right? "So... I guess we should load this thing up and head back before Mia decides to write us off as missing persons?"

"Yep," he said, delivering that single syllable with all the enthusiasm of a man volunteering for jury duty.

And there it was. The full extent of our pending road trip conversation, neatly summed up in one word. Perfect. Could this be more awkward? Probably not. But knowing my luck, I'd find a way.

As he started walking toward the cabin, tree in hand, I followed, trying to focus on literally anything else. Like, I don't know, the snow crunching under my boots. Or how my hair was probably doing its best impersonation of a yeti.

But nope. My brain had decided to hyper-focus on the unfair fact that Tyler, even while lugging a scraggly tree, looked like a freaking lumberjack ad.

And me? I looked like an ad for seasonal allergies. Classic Lena.

Chapter 14

Tyler

The drive back from the cabin was silent. Silent in that tense, teeth-gritting way that made my knuckles clamp a little tighter on the steering wheel.

It wasn't peaceful, though. No, this was the kind of silence that stretched too far, where every unsaid word felt like it was sitting in the backseat, crowding us both.

Lena had her headphones in, her head turned toward the window like she'd just discovered a sudden, burning interest in barren winter landscapes. I'd turned on music, not because I cared about the playlist, but because the quiet was starting to feel like it might swallow me whole.

Every so often, my eyes darted to her. Just quick glances, nothing that required her notice. But she didn't look back. Didn't flinch. Hell, she didn't even shift in her seat. Meanwhile, the tension between us was like static electricity, buzzing, building, waiting to spark.

The miles dragged on, each one stretching the silence until it felt like it might snap. Then, mercifully—or cruelly, depending on your perspective—my phone buzzed with a text.

I tapped Lena's leg, breaking the barrier of her little headphone cocoon. She pulled out one earbud and gave me a questioning look, not quite meeting my eyes. I gestured to my phone. "Your sister wants us to stop by your parents' house," I explained, keeping my voice neutral.

She just nodded, popped out the other earbud, and slouched back into her seat without saying a word.

So much for conversation.

When we pulled into the driveway, something in her posture shifted. Her shoulders loosened a fraction, and I couldn't decide if her relief made me feel the same. Or if it just left me hollow.

Before I could even cut the engine, she was out of the car, moving toward the front door with a speed that made it look like she had something to prove. I followed, slower, every step up those stairs tightening the weird knot of anticipation in my chest.

Inside, her mom greeted us, all smiles and cheer with an energy so out of sync with what we were supposed to be walking into that it made me pause. Wasn't this visit about Mia spraining her ankle?

Then I saw Mia standing in the living room, with an apologetic look that seemed to explain why she wasn't hobbling around in pain.

"What the hell, sis?!" Lena's voice cut through the awkward moment, sharp with confusion and a growing irritation.

I didn't need to look at her to know she'd frozen in place, processing what was happening. The tension rolling off her was practically visible.

Mia shrugged, a smile that could only be described as annoyingly smug tugging at her lips. "Might've been a slight exaggeration," she said, glancing at their mom, who just sighed like this was par for the course.

Lena's jaw tightened. "Wait, you're fine?"

"Perfectly fine," Mia admitted with a sheepish shrug, the smugness dimming slightly under Lena's glare. "But, honestly my ankle and the reason we called you over are not related. Two different things. I promise."

She gestured toward the living room, her expression faltering into something a little more nervous.

That's when I saw him.

Marco.

Perfect. Just what this night needed. A walking reminder that sometimes life doesn't just throw curveballs; it aims for your face.

The guy I'd met once. Briefly. Outside the hospital. When he'd thought putting his hands on Lena was a good idea.

Marco. The guy who'd nearly broken her in two. The one she'd been engaged to until she walked away from him and a wedding that sounded like it could've been on the season finale of *The Bachelorette*.

And now, here he was. Standing smack dab in the middle of her parents' living room, hands stuffed into his coat pockets, wearing the kind of practiced smile that screamed, "I'm the hero in this story."

"Lena. Love." His voice was smooth, cocky. He didn't even flinch at seeing us walk in, though his eyes did a slow once-over of me, like he was deciding if I was worth the effort.

Meanwhile, Lena froze beside me, her face going pale like she'd just seen a ghost—and not the friendly, holiday kind.

"Marco?" she whispered, her voice barely audible, like she couldn't quite believe it herself.

"Lena," he repeated, flashing a smile so full of confidence I half-expected him to pull out a marriage license right then and there. "We need to talk. I've come here, surrounded by your family, because I thought that would help us... reconcile."

Reconciling sounded like the absolute last thing Lena wanted. Her whole body stiffened, and I could feel the tension radiating off her like heat from a furnace.

I didn't like it. Didn't like the way this guy was looking at her, like he thought he still had a claim on her.

Mia cleared her throat, her voice unusually tentative. "He just showed up out of nowhere, but we thought it might be better if you two talked this out with everyone around." Her usual smugness was gone, replaced by a hint of guilt, even though it was obvious she had nothing to do with him being here.

Marco, of course, wasn't fazed. Probably because he knew Mia was the weak link. The one person Lena likely shared her secrets with.

He stepped closer to Lena, ignoring me entirely. "Look, I know things got crazy before. But in the park, I felt we'd come to an understanding. But look, I didn't come here to rehash all that. I came because I realized what I lost. I know I made mistakes and I think we can make it work. We're meant to be together, Lena."

And that's when my fists clenched. Hard. Who did this guy think he was? Showing up uninvited, pulling this

Hallmark movie garbage, like he could just waltz back into her life and everything would magically be fine?

Lena, to her credit, didn't back down. Her voice was steady, even if I could hear the strain underneath. "You don't get to decide whether we give it a shot."

Marco's smile faltered for a split second before he recovered, stepping closer again. "I think you needed time, Lena. We both did. But we can fix this. Just… let's go somewhere and talk."

That's when I stepped in, literally, putting an arm between him and Lena. "You don't get to go anywhere with her," I said, my voice low but firm.

His head tilted slightly, his eyes narrowing as he finally turned his attention to me. "And you are?"

"Tyler," I said, meeting his gaze head-on. "And you don't get to decide what she needs."

His bitter laugh was immediate, his gaze shifting back to Lena. "So, this is how it is now? You just… moved on that fast?"

I caught Charla leaning toward Mia, her expression full of curiosity. Mia whispered back, just loud enough for all of us to hear, "No, Mom, they're not dating. We were all just at the cabin together, remember?"

Lena sucked in a breath, her shoulders tensing. I could see the battle playing out in her eyes—fight or flight. And then, just like that, she shoved my arm aside and stepped forward.

"Who the fuck do either of you think you are deciding anything about what I want, where I go, or what I do?" Her voice was sharp, cutting through the tension in the room like a knife.

Marco blinked, clearly not expecting that.

"And Marco," she continued, looking pointedly at her parents before turning back to him. "The audacity of you showing up here, thinking my family has any sway over my decisions? I'll give you your talk, like you so desperately wanted, but let me save you some suspense—you're not going to like the outcome."

I bit back a grin. Go Lena.

Then she turned on me. "And you, Tyler. This has nothing to do with you."

That one hit like a punch to the gut. Not because she was wrong. She wasn't. We weren't together. We weren't even friends, really. At best, we were acquaintances who kept orbiting each other for Mia and Thomas's sake.

But knowing she was right didn't make it sting any less.

Thomas was giving me that look. The one that said, "We're going to have a talk, and you're not weaseling out of it."

He'd barely let me finish snapping, "I'm outta here," before grabbing my arm and dragging me into the kitchen.

He leaned against the counter, arms crossed. That signature smirk plastered across his face like he'd just stumbled onto a front-row seat to the drama of the year. "All right," he started, keeping his tone light, though his eyes were laser-focused. "What was that all about?"

I shrugged, playing dumb. "What was what all about?"

"Oh, don't pull that with me, man." He chuckled, but there was an edge to it. "You and Marco looked like you were one wrong move away from throwing hands. I thought you didn't even know the guy."

I sighed, dragging a hand down my face. This wasn't a conversation I wanted to have, but Thomas was my best friend. If anyone deserved some insight into why I wanted to punch Marco's perfect teeth in, it was him.

"Alright," I admitted. "Last week, Lena and I were at the hospital visiting my mom. Marco showed up out of nowhere and cornered her outside. When I walked out, he had her by the arm, saying something about 'talking things out.' Let's just say he wasn't thrilled when I interrupted."

Thomas's expression darkened, his smirk evaporating. "He put hands on her?" His voice dropped, all traces of humor gone.

I held up a hand. "Look, I don't know what led up to that moment. All I saw was him holding her arm—" I reached out and tapped Thomas on the bicep to illustrate, "—like this. It wasn't violent or anything, but it didn't sit right with me. Instincts kicked in."

Thomas frowned, processing that, his brows knitting together. "Marco's always seemed like a decent guy. Lena never told me much about why they split, and Mia's been tight-lipped, too. But if he's showing up uninvited and grabbing her, that's not okay."

"Glad we're on the same page," I muttered, crossing my arms. "Now explain this. Wasn't Mia supposed to have sprained her ankle? Because she looked pretty damn spry in there."

Thomas shifted, the corner of his mouth twitching like he was trying not to laugh. "Yeah... about that."

I narrowed my eyes. "Don't tell me—this was all a setup?"

He rubbed the back of his neck, finally letting out a sheepish laugh. "Okay, fine. Yes, it was a setup. Mia thought if you and Lena had some uninterrupted alone time, maybe you'd figure things out."

I barked out a laugh. Short, sharp, and entirely humorless. "So, she faked an injury to trap us in a cabin together? Hmmph. Real high school logic there."

Thomas had the decency to look guilty, but there was still a flicker of amusement in his eyes. "Look, man. When we got back from the honeymoon, the tension between you two was impossible to miss. It felt like... remember when we played Spin the Bottle in middle school, and you had to kiss Jeanie Samson in the closet?"

I groaned. "Don't remind me. I still cringe thinking about it."

"Exactly," he said, pointing at me. "That's how it felt watching you and Lena. Awkward as hell. We figured if we forced you two to talk, you'd at least figure out where you stood—whether you'd end up together or not."

I shook my head, my frustration bubbling over. "You two are unbelievable. You seriously thought a weekend in the woods would solve anything?"

"Not solve, exactly," he hedged. "But at least get you two to figure shit out. We're all going to be together for Christmas in a few days. And, honestly, nobody wants to sit through a holiday where you and Lena act like you just completed your Spin the Bottle dare."

I glared at him, deadpan. "You're an asshole."

"Yeah," he said. "I might be. But honestly, the last thing we expected was for Marco to show up. I think those loose ends trump whatever issues are going on between you and Lena."

I threw my hands up, defensive. "Well, congrats. Your little plan worked. There is no me and Lena. We were trying to keep some distance. Lena's still dealing with all her shit. And your grand idea to shove us in a pressure cooker? Yeah, that just blew the lid off whatever chance we might've had."

The humor drained from Thomas's face completely. He looked genuinely uncomfortable now. "I get it, Tyler. But listen, you're my best friend, and Mia's her sister. She wouldn't have done it if she didn't think it would… help, somehow."

"Help?" My voice came out colder than I meant it to, like a freezer on full blast. "I get you're both invested, but I didn't ask for that kind of help. All I've always needed was for you to trust me to handle shit on my own terms. Now it just feels like you threw me under the bus."

Thomas nodded, his face tense, like he was finally realizing how much their little 'plan' had cost. "Fuck. I'm so sorry, man. I really am."

But the apology was as empty as a soda can after I'd drained it—hollow.

"Well, damage is done." I met his eyes, just long enough to make my point, then I turned and walked out the door.

Chapter 15: Lena

My heart pounded in my chest as Marco and I stepped onto the front porch. The winter air hit my cheeks like a slap, sharp enough to snap me out of my daze.

I glanced back at the door, a small flicker of comfort knowing my family was just inside, ready to witness this disaster that I was about to finally clean up.

As much as I didn't want to be here, it was time to close this damn chapter once and for all.

Marco leaned against the railing, looking every bit as polished as the day we met. Back then, his easy charm was like candy. Sweet. Sticky. And convincing enough to make me think he was the guy I'd grow old with.

Now? I saw right through it. The smooth smile, that perfectly composed expression on his ridiculously handsome face. It was all part of the same act, and honestly? I was over it.

"So," I started, keeping my voice steady, though I wanted to throw something at his perfectly polished face. "What are you doing here, Marco?"

He tilted his head, giving me that look. Like he'd practiced it in front of a mirror until it was as smooth as butter. "I told you. I'm here because I still believe in us, Lena. I know I messed up, but I want to fix things. I can be the guy you need."

Ugh, I had definitely heard that one before. His words were so rehearsed, I half expected him to take a bow after delivering them.

But this time? This time, I wasn't buying it. I saw through him. All I saw was a guy who still didn't have the slightest clue about what he'd done wrong.

"See, Marco? That's just it," I said, tilting my head and giving him the you-can't-be-serious look. "Do you even know how you messed up?"

He blinked, like I'd slapped him with a wet fish, and I could practically hear the gears grinding in his brain as he scrambled to come up with the perfect thing he thought I wanted to hear.

"I... I know you felt pressured, Lena, but I just thought I was helping. I was doing what any partner would, looking out for our future together."

I bit back a laugh, but it slipped out anyway. Sharp and way more biting than I meant. "Helping?" I repeated, disbelief oozing out of my voice. "Marco, you didn't help me. You tried to control me. You wanted me to fit into your perfect little box, live by your rules, your timeline. And when I needed someone to support me, you made me feel like I was the problem."

There. That felt better.

His face tightened, frustration flaring in his eyes. "I can offer you stability, Lena. We could have a real future because we did things responsibly."

Oh, here we go. The same old pitch.

I shook my head, trying to shake off the ache of frustration that had been building for months. "A 'real future,' according to you, meant me giving up everything I wanted and living the life you envisioned," I shot back, crossing my arms. "You didn't care about what was important to me, Marco. You only cared about what fit your plan."

He exhaled, his face softening. Almost like he thought he could win me back with that fake sincerity. But then, in a blink, it morphed into something colder, something menacing. "Well, now you just sound crazy because we were making plans. Together."

Together.

I wasn't even angry that he'd just called me crazy. Whatever. I was too busy hearing that word, *together*, over and over in my head. And it felt like a slap across the face. Like I'd been punched straight in the chest. I couldn't even speak.

Months of silence, of swallowing every damn thing I'd wanted to say, crashed over me in a horrible, suffocating wave.

I stood there, staring at him, totally mute, like I'd forgotten how to breathe.

Finally, I spoke, my voice sharp and unsteady. "After the abortion, I didn't know."

He frowned, brows furrowing like I'd just spoken in a foreign language. "You're not making sense," he muttered, clearly confused and annoyed. "You didn't know about what?"

I exhaled, pushing past the tightness in my chest. "I didn't know how I'd feel, or how it would affect me. I didn't know what would happen to my body, all those hormones and the mess of feelings that just... engulfed me. You don't just walk away from something like that, Marco. It stays with you. You don't get to be a bystander and pretend it doesn't."

He didn't say anything, and for a moment, he looked away. Like he needed a second to pull himself back together. The cracks in his perfect, polished mask were showing.

And, of course, because I'm a sucker, I felt a little bit sorry for him. Ugh.

I folded my arms, letting my back rest against the cold brick of the house. Because clearly, leaning into the wall was the only way I wasn't going to collapse under the weight of all of this.

He shifted, looking like I'd just hit him with a sledgehammer made of truth. "Baby, I'm an idiot," he said, voice thick with regret. "I can see now how I messed up. I was so caught up in the idea that we were getting married. I was marrying you. The woman of my dreams. I didn't stop to think about how the abortion really affected you... how it affected us both."

His words hit me, even though I wanted to pretend they didn't. I glanced at him, and for a second, I saw pain flicker in his eyes.

It was tempting. So tempting to believe him, to let that familiar hope spark in my chest.

There was still a part of me, buried deep—so deep it was practically in the core of the earth—that wanted to believe we could go back to what we had. Or, at the very least, be the people we thought we could be together.

But that part was fighting the overwhelming tide of reality. And reality, my friends, is a cruel, unrelenting beast.

I wrapped my arms around myself, letting the cold of the brick wall seep through my sweater. It grounded me. Not in the warm, fuzzy way, but in the way that reminded me to stay here, right here, in this moment. Because if I let myself feel, if I let myself want what I used to, I'd be back in the same old mess I'd wanted to claw my way out of. And that? Was not happening. Not today.

"Marco…" I hesitated, the words I'd never said to him feeling like bricks in my chest, weighing me down. "I know I left you with no warning, and I know I hurt you. I'm sorry for that. But after. It. I was… different. I couldn't bring myself to tell you how hard it was, and I just…"

He reached out, his hand brushing my shoulder like he was trying to fix something broken, his face twisted in a way that almost looked real. Like maybe he actually felt bad.

"Baby, I'm sorry I was so stupid. I was focused on what I thought was best for us, but I didn't listen to you." His voice cracked then, which was totally unexpected. "I've learned, Lena. I swear I have. I want to be the guy you need me to be."

And there it was, my throat tight, the sting of everything I'd tried to ignore rushing in like a freakin' flood. Before I could stop it, a tear slipped down my cheek, then another, and I totally hated myself for it.

I covered my face with my hands, letting out a shaky breath. "How can I blame you for not noticing my feelings?" I said, my voice almost breaking. "You were probably so focused on our wedding, and I should've told you how I was feeling back then—how… how lost I was. And how much pain I was in."

I swallowed hard, trying to hold myself together. The ache was still there, like a wound that never fully healed. "Afterward… it was like I was walking through this fog I couldn't shake. Every day felt muted, like I was underwater. I couldn't feel… anything, really. It surprised me, how much it hit me, even though it was my choice. I thought I'd bounce back, just keep going, but it wasn't that simple."

I wiped another tear away, my voice trembling, because *Surprise Surprise*, I was actually emotional about all of this.

"It felt like something inside me had cracked, and I couldn't fix it. And instead of letting you see that, I kept trying to patch it up alone. I kept hoping one day I'd just wake up and feel normal again. But it didn't work like that. And you… you were there, but somehow you weren't. I needed you to really be there, Marco. To understand, without me needing to explain every single thing. But it was like… it was like we were speaking different languages."

He pulled me into his arms, his hand rubbing my back as we stood there in this weird, silent truce.

I could feel his shoulders shuddering against me, and when I looked up, I saw that he was crying too. It was raw and real and just too much. And that part of me—the part that had loved him once—felt it, and I hated it.

"Thank you for coming here, Marco," I said, because apparently, I was being the bigger person today. "I'm glad we had this talk. It's been long overdue."

I paused, catching my breath because, surprise, I wasn't exactly thriving in the feels department.

"It makes me happy to finally know what happened that day," Marco said, his voice a little rougher than he probably meant. "To understand why you just left me standing there and—"

But before he could finish, I interrupted, not wanting him to misinterpret my empathy. "I need some time to think." I felt a sudden urge to make sure I wasn't being too nice. That was one of my problems before, right? I wasn't clear enough.

His expression softened, like he was trying to be understanding, but I caught a flicker of something else. Frustration, maybe? It was hard to tell, but whatever it was, he tucked it away quickly, replacing it with a tight little smile.

"Of course. I get it. I'll give you space, but I hope you don't take too long," he said, his voice all sincere and that irritatingly perfect tone. "I love you, Baby. And I'm here. Whenever you're ready."

I nodded, feeling a knot in my stomach. And then, because he wasn't totally horrible, he added, "Please tell your mom and dad I said goodbye."

I watched him turn and leave, his footsteps fading as he walked down the sidewalk, and I stood there on the porch for a while, just watching his car drive away. The weight of everything we'd finally said hung in the air like a bad perfume I couldn't shake. And no matter how much I tried to breathe, it felt like it was sticking to me.

Marco's car was nothing but a speck in the distance when I caught a glimpse of Mia sneaking a peek through the front door. Her eyes were wide as she scanned the porch like a secret agent in training.

"Is the coast clear?" she whispered dramatically, barely holding back a giggle.

I wiped my cheeks with my sleeve and smiled. "Yeah, he's gone."

Mia burst out of the house, pulling me into a hug that felt like warm comfort after a bad day. "Good, because I was fully prepared to throw myself in front of him if he tried to storm back in."

I laughed and leaned into her, amused but also relieved. "Not sure he'd see you as much of a roadblock, Mia."

She gasped, pressing a hand to her chest. "Excuse me, I'm small but mighty."

I shot her a look. "Sure, mighty. Like a chihuahua in a pit bull's body."

She nudged me gently, pulling me down to sit on the porch steps beside her. "Sooo... just so you know, Marco showing up here was not in my plan."

"Yeah, didn't cross my mind that you'd pull something like that," I replied with as much conviction as I could muster, though I was secretly relieved she'd been there to intercept.

Mia looped her arm through mine and gave me the side-eye. "Okay, spill it. That was... quite the scene having Marco here. How do you feel? What did he have to say? What does he want?"

"Whoa, twenty questions? Chill out, Mia." I chuckled, but then I sighed, staring out into the yard, trying to make sense of the mess of emotions Marco had stirred up. "It was... weird. I mean, there he was, standing right in front of me, saying everything I wanted to hear. And, God, the comfort, the familiarity. That hit me like a ton of bricks. It almost felt like we just… slipped back into place."

Mia nodded slowly, like she got it. "Makes sense. When he was 'Mr. Perfect,' he was really Mr. Perfect."

"Exactly," I muttered, feeling a pang in my chest. "And then, I felt… guilty. Like I'd abandoned the life we'd planned together. Like I threw it all away without even trying."

Mia tilted her head and gave me a knowing look. "Is that why you're going all 'Confused But Determined to Reflect' right now?"

I gave her a shove, half-laughing, half-exasperated. "Maybe. It just… threw me off. Before he showed up, I was sure he was out of my life for good. Now? Now, I could see the possibility of us picking up where we left off."

Mia's eyes widened, and I could tell she was both surprised and… maybe a little disappointed? But I knew exactly what was running through her mind.

"I don't mean that I see us getting married tomorrow," I added quickly, my voice laced with uncertainty. "I just mean going back to loving each other, figuring out what we want for the rest of our lives."

Mia's face softened, but she gave me a little smile. "I get it. I could see from his reaction to what you were telling him that he still loves you and that maybe he thought you still felt the same way."

"Nosy Nellie much?!" I pushed her shoulder, trying to change the subject. "You're such a snooper!"

She raised an eyebrow, giving me a sly grin. "Can you blame me? This is the most exciting thing to happen since I got back!" Then, she leaned in, eyes wide with anticipation. "So he said he's sorry and wants you back, right?"

"Well, yeah. More eloquently than that, but yeah." I shrugged, the memory of Marco's apology still fresh. "I explained about not realizing my feelings about the abortion sooner, and he was really sweet about it. I think he got where I was coming from. I told him I needed time, though. Time to figure out what's real and what's just... nostalgia."

Mia's eyes sparkled like she was about to burst. "How much time do you think you're going to need? Because, I mean, cabin season is coming up, and my last trip was cut short because of a severe ankle injury."

I snorted, laughing. "Yeah, that was some stellar acting," I said, fake-punching her in the leg. "Honestly, I don't know if I should be more embarrassed about my love life or the fact that you looked so convincing."

I stood up, brushing off my butt and making my way back inside. "Let's go back in. I'm sure I'm gonna have to give Mom and Dad the full play-by-play of my life."

Mia was right behind me, rushing to get ahead of me, but she stopped in the doorway, turning back with a mischievous gleam in her eye. "Hey, would you mind bringing that tree in for me? My ankle hurts."

"You're such a bitch!" I laughed, pushing her through the door ahead of me.

But before she made it through, she paused, cocked her head, and shot me a curious look. "That reminds me... you and Tyler. What happened back at the cabin?" She glanced at me, clearly waiting for an answer. "I totally forgot to ask with all the Marco drama."

I froze, and for a moment, it felt like my breath had been knocked out of me. Tyler. Just hearing his name brought everything back—the tension, the charged moments, the way he made me feel. And now? It all felt so far away.

I took a deep breath, looking down at my hands before speaking. "Honestly? I don't know what I thought was going to happen with him, Mia. But whatever I did think? It doesn't matter now. Tyler and I were over before we even met."

Chapter 16: Tyler

I had to see Lena. Especially since the last time we'd crossed paths was when Marco showed up at her parents' house.

It was two days before Christmas, and I couldn't stop thinking about how we'd survive being in the same room together at the family Christmas gathering without it being completely awkward.

So, I texted her.

Hey, wanna grab a coffee?

I hit send and waited. Just a few seconds, but long enough to imagine her rolling her eyes at me.

Finally, the three little dots showed up. She was typing.

Tyler, it's the busiest time of the year. I'm at the Christmas Fair, taking photos. If you want to see me, you can come here and help me out.

Of course, she had to throw in the "help me out" part. I couldn't say no to that. We needed to have this conversation, and if that meant helping Lena with her photography, then fine. I'd do it.

Alright, on my way. See you soon.

Navigating through the chaos of the fair, the scent of cinnamon and pine hit me, pulling me into the holiday spirit I hadn't really cared about in years.

I spotted Lena standing near a giant Christmas tree, looking like she belonged there.

Her long brown hair tumbled down her back, and her brown eyes sparkled with that signature excitement of hers. She was rocking a cozy red sweater and black jeans—effortlessly beautiful, of course.

I felt that familiar tug in my chest.

When I walked up to Lena, she was busy photographing a little girl with blonde pigtails, big red bows, and a red velvet dress. The girl was holding a large envelope that read *"Letter to Santa"* in big, bold script.

"Hey, Lena. Wow, this place is hu—"

"Hey, grab this reflector." She held out this big, white, squarish piece of fabric supported by a wire frame. "Like this."

She wasn't even looking at me. Just pointed it at me like I was some kind of prop. I grabbed the reflector, and she angled it so the light bounced onto the girl's face.

Lena snapped a few more pictures, clicking away like she was in her own little world.

"My mom and aunt used to bring me to a place like this in my town when I was young," I said, glancing around. "It feels a lot smaller than I remember, but I can imagine it looking so big as a kid."

She glanced at me briefly, barely acknowledging my sentiment. "I think everyone in town came here during Christmas." Then she handed me a stack of cards, clearly expecting me to do something with them. "Give these to the people we photograph. It has the link where they can download their pictures."

I raised an eyebrow. "You sure you trust me with all this?"

Her response was a half-grin, but it was enough to make me feel like I was doing something important. Even if it was just handing out cards.

We spent the next hour walking around the fair, snapping photos for families and couples. I had to admit, Lena's eye for detail was impressive. She had this knack for making people feel like they were the most important thing in the world, which made it easier for them to relax in front of the camera.

I helped with the poses, mostly by making stupid faces to get the kids to laugh, and I even played assistant with the *"Letter to Santa"* prop for the kids lined up to see the big guy.

As we moved away from Santa's Grotto, I nudged Lena, figuring I might as well try to stir the pot a little. "Remember when all we wanted for Christmas was a BB gun?"

Lena let out a laugh, the kind that made my chest feel way too warm for comfort. "Oh, please, I wanted a Backstreet Boys poster, thank you very much."

I snorted. "Ah, yeah, of course. You and every school girl's boy band fantasies."

We kept strolling, moving from one group to the next, taking in the lights, the decorations, and the general Christmas chaos around us. The fair was a visual overload—colorful lights twinkling like they had a caffeine problem, giant ornaments hanging from trees like they were too big to be real, and a DIY ornament station that was probably a disaster waiting to happen. But somehow, it all worked, even if I wasn't exactly in the holiday spirit.

"Look, they're making snow globes," Lena said, grabbing my arm and pulling me towards the station. "Let's take a break and make one!"

We were supposed to make it together, but of course, it ended up being me watching while she meticulously crafted the globe. Her hands were so damn delicate, like they were made for something way more graceful than dealing with a grumpy guy like me.

She carefully placed a tiny Christmas tree and a sleigh inside, and I couldn't help but think about the old days, back when my family would gather around and do a whole "reason for the season" thing where we'd go around the Christmas table and share why Christmas was important to us. My mom was all about Family, and my dad and I would joke and add, "Food!" as if it was the best part of the whole damn holiday.

Lena didn't look up from her little project, but she asked, "So why did you need to see me?" She placed two little figures, a man and a woman, into the scene like she was arranging some tiny, festive version of herself. "We decided not to see each other. Then we did, which led us to deciding again not to see each other. And now here we are, spending time with each other."

She finally glanced up at me, her eyebrows raised like I was some kind of puzzle she couldn't quite solve. "Is that how this is going to continue? A back and forth of 'No, we're not,' 'Yes, we are,' 'No, we're not,' 'Yes, we are'?"

I couldn't help but chuckle. "Well, when you sum it up like that, I think we sound ridiculous."

I rubbed the back of my neck, trying to find the right words. "But the reason I wanted to see you was because we're gonna be in the same room again at the Christmas gathering, and I don't want things to be... awkward."

Lena let out a little huff, like I'd just announced I wanted to start a fire in the middle of the fair. "Tyler," she sighed, looking like she was ready to pull out her "I'm an adult" card. "It's okay. I think we're going to feel a bit uncomfortable for a while. We're both adults. We can pull up our big girl panties when we're around the families."

I rubbed my neck again, my fingers digging into the muscles there like I was trying to work out the stress. "It's not just that, Lena. I know you're right. But I'm concerned."

I stretched my neck, eyes on the ground as I tried to gather my thoughts. "To be honest, I didn't want to be blindsided if you'd reconciled with Marco and showed up with him. I wanted to know now rather than get to Christmas and be surprised."

She leaned back in her chair, her gaze sharp like she'd just caught me stealing cookies out of the jar. "I don't want you to take this the wrong way, but you have no right to worry about who I do what with and where."

Now, my first instinct was to throw out some sarcastic quip about her ego needing a bowl the size of Lake Tahoe just to fit her, but I didn't. I bit it back, held my tongue like a damn professional. Probably for the best.

Lena smiled softly, her eyes catching the glow of the fairy lights. "You know, when I was a kid, I thought Christmas was all about getting presents."

I gave her some leeway to make her point, figuring I probably shouldn't take her earlier comment too personally. So, I just nodded along. "That, and Christmas dinner."

"True. And dinner." She chuckled, going back to her snow globe project.

"But now, I realize it's about being with the people you care about. The family and friends you want around you to make memories with. And, to celebrate the love and kindness around you so that you can spread all that around the rest of the year."

Yeah, I heard her, but I wasn't really listening. Because, as usual, when she mentioned family, all I could think about was Carrie. The flashback hit me like a fist to the face. I could feel my heart drop like I was diving into cold water. Thoughts of high school, of her, flooded my mind.

Carrie, my high school sweetheart, the one I lost three years ago.

It had been almost ten years since I'd graduated, but thinking about high school always brought her back. Always.

"OK, see? There." Lena turned toward me and put her hand on my forearm. "Where did you go?"

I forced a smile, but I could feel it was shaky. "Nowhere," I said, but even to my own ears, it sounded weak.

Lena's eyes softened, and she didn't move her hand from my arm. Her touch grounded me. She didn't press, just waited, like she knew I'd eventually open up—whether I liked it or not.

"It's just...whenever I think of high school..." My voice trailed off, and I felt a lump form in my throat. "My high school girlfriend, Carrie. We were together since sophomore year. Everyone thought we'd be forever."

I felt Lena's grip on my arm tighten just a little. "What happened, Tyler? You can tell me." Her voice was soft, patient—way too patient, like she could sense the storm I was trying to keep locked up.

"I don't know if I'm ready..." I swallowed, my voice growing hoarse.

"Then you don't need to tell me," she said, her tone reassuring.

But there was something about her that made the words spill out before I could stop them.

"She never left my side. High school, college, when I played for the Falcons. One second, we're talking about our future...then the car crash. Christmas Eve. And next..." My throat closed up, and that hollow ache settled in my chest. "I lost her. And my life just...stopped."

The silence between us stretched, but it didn't feel heavy. If anything, Lena's presence made the weight of it all feel a little less crushing. Like, for once, I wasn't carrying it alone.

She spoke, her voice almost a whisper, but somehow it sliced through the darkness. "I'm so sorry, Tyler. I can't imagine what you've been through."

I nodded, letting out a shaky breath. "It's just...weird, right? How we have these moments and people who shape us, and then one day they're just gone. But their absence...it never really leaves." I let out a humorless laugh, shaking my head. "Sorry. That's a bit heavy for Christmas."

"Tyler..." She looked up at me, and in her gaze, there was no pity, just understanding. "You don't have to apologize. Not for that. Ever. Look, you and I. We're here, right now, and that means something. Christmas or not."

Her words hit me harder than I expected. I felt something warm spread through me, something I hadn't felt in a long time. It was like she saw every broken piece of me, the ones I'd buried so deep, and still, somehow, she wasn't turned off by any of it.

"Yeah, it does mean something," I said, my voice finally steady. "But, uh, can we change the subject?"

She quickly picked up on my discomfort, which I had to admit, was impressive. "Here, help me get this tiny snow globe figure glued onto the man's hand," she said, handing me the tweezers. "It's the last piece before we're done."

I appreciated her for this—she was giving me a way out. I'd always found it hard to talk about the accident, like it was a wound that shouldn't be poked at.

Telling Lena a little bit of my story felt like opening up a door I'd locked the day Carrie died, and I wasn't sure why I was letting her in.

While I carefully glued the tiny man's hand, she picked up the conversation like we hadn't just waded through something heavy.

"Before, when I said you have no right to worry about who I do what with and where," she continued, "and how I used to think Christmas was all about getting presents...what I was trying to say is, with all this 'are we friends or are we lovers?' back and forth between us, we need to make a decision, either way."

"I know," I muttered. "We need to figure something out before Christmas."

She nodded like she had been expecting that answer. "We do, because I still think Christmas is about presents. So I need to know whether I should get my list to you so you can get me the perfect gift." She didn't even crack a smile. Not a single hint of a chuckle. The woman was stone cold serious.

"So, if I tell you we're not friends, I don't have to get you a gift?" I asked, raising an eyebrow.

"Well, since we'll be at the same Christmas gathering, you're contractually obligated to get me a gift," she replied, deadpan. "It just depends on whether you get me something from my A list or my B list. Although, I am open to receiving a gift from both lists."

"Great," I said, nodding, trying to mask the anxiety creeping up on me. "You'd better get that list to me now, so I know whether I need to take out a second mortgage."

"Or," she said, glancing up with that sly grin of hers, "you can just get me a house. That's on the A list." She threw her head back slightly, letting out that easy laugh of hers.

A million sparks shot down my spine, reminding me of exactly how impossible it was to just be her friend.

I finished the snow globe scene and pushed it toward her. She took a look at my masterpiece, and after a moment, nodded approvingly and jokingly added, "You've got quite the talent. This snow globe will provide you and your family with years of enjoyment."

I smirked. "Next Christmas, it'll be my second stream of income."

Lena waved over the snow globe station artist to finish the job, like we'd just crafted a little piece of holiday history or something.

Then, with all the subtlety of a sledgehammer, she leaned toward me and said, "It's time we meet this thing head-on and figure out whether there's something between us that's worth pursuing. Or if we're destined to keep running into each other around Thomas, Mia, and the family, and constantly figuring out how not to act like weirdos."

I raised an eyebrow. "I mean, the second option sounds like an absolute blast, right?"

She gave me one of those looks, the kind that told me she was serious about this. And that only made me want to joke around even more. But I shut my mouth, because Lena was right.

The artist walked up, cutting through the tension with her cheerful demeanor. "This looks great," she said, looking at the snow globe. "I'll fill and seal it. Should take about an hour. You can pick it up then."

"Thank you!" Lena chirped, flashing her trademark smile that could probably sell a refrigerator to an Eskimo.

Then, without skipping a beat, she grabbed my hand and pulled me into the heart of the Christmas fair like I was some kind of oversized teddy bear. "Let's go get something to eat."

My brain was still stuck on the whole "figuring us out" thing, but my body was perfectly content following her. Because, of course, it was.

We stood in line at a food truck serving Christmas-themed soup and sandwiches. The menu items were gems—Roasted Red-nose Pepper Soup and Brrrisket on Rye. Yeah, clever.

Nearby, two statues of Mr. and Mrs. Claus stood, looming over the crowd like they were on a mission to judge everyone's holiday spirit.

"That's a bit creepy," Lena remarked, looking up at the Clauses like they were about to come to life and drag her off to some North Pole dungeon. "When I was really young, I saw the Clauses as these nice, happy grandparents in those Christmas cartoons, but up close? I was terrified. Felt like I was never gonna get presents because I was on their naughty list."

I raised an eyebrow, not sure if she was kidding or just reliving childhood trauma. "Santa sees everything. So, I'm sure you had to constantly think of ways to distract his elf spies from all your naughty ways."

Her laugh bubbled up, making me feel like I'd just won a prize. "It was a constant battle. Always having to make up for something bad I did."

I squeezed her hand, my thumb grazing her skin, and yeah, that connection we had—whatever it was—flared up like a damn firecracker. I wasn't stupid enough to ignore it. "So, let's do this. Today and tomorrow, we'll work on figuring out what's between us."

She turned to me, her expression serious, but there was that spark again. "Agreed," she said, leaning in just a bit. "On Christmas, we're gonna be in the same house. And I don't want it to be awkward. Let's see if we can figure this out before that happens."

She had me there. The idea of spending a day under the same roof with her, of all people, was already making me rethink my whole "grumpy, brooding loner" routine.

But what else was I supposed to do? Let the awkwardness simmer? Hell no.

Chapter 17: Lena

The crisp winter air buzzed with holiday magic, and for the first time in what felt like forever, I didn't feel like I was trudging through life.

We'd just finished lunch, and as we walked back into the Christmas fair, everything seemed... brighter. Like someone had cranked up the color saturation. The laughter of kids, the swirl of lights and music, the smell of pine and roasting chestnuts—everything had this electric life to it.

Hell, even I felt alive.

"You know," Tyler said, snapping me out of my head with that easy grin of his, "we could call it a day, maybe grab some snowflake funnel cakes instead of another photo shoot?"

"Oh no, Mr. Assistant," I teased, nudging him with my elbow. "Your shift is not over yet. We've still got work to do."

His smile widened as he held up the reflector, putting on his best mock-serious face. "Lead the way, boss."

And just like that, we were off again. We stopped every so often to snap photos of families bundled up in scarves, mittens, and the occasional bad Christmas sweater.

Tyler had this magical ability to pull out goofy smiles from even the shyest kids. He'd crouch down, make faces, and next thing you knew, there were giggles all around. It was like he had an invisible magic wand that made kids forget they were freezing and start acting like it was the happiest day of their lives.

I stood back for a moment, watching him work his charm, and something in my chest fluttered. I couldn't quite place it, but it felt warm. And complicated.

That's when I heard a voice calling my name.

I whipped around, startled, and saw Julia and Brad, friends who'd dated in high school, walking hand-in-hand. Their two kids, Cara and Chase, were bouncing around them like mini pinballs in their puffy coats and mittens.

"Oh my gosh, Julia!" I rushed over, throwing my arms around her.

We laughed, exchanged hellos, and after a few quick introductions, Julia and Brad got their kids into position for a photo shoot. Tyler, being Tyler, was in his element. Bending down, cracking jokes, and getting those kids to laugh like they'd known him forever. It was like he was made for moments like this.

"Let's see your best silly face," he said, grinning at Chase, who immediately crossed his eyes and stuck out his tongue. Everyone burst into laughter.

Julia leaned in, giving me a wink. "Lena, he's a keeper."

The words hit me like a sledgehammer, but I forced out a laugh. "Yeah, well, he's a great assistant."

When I looked back at Tyler, he was helping Cara adjust her scarf, looking so natural doing it that something in my chest tightened. There was an ease to him with kids. Something I hadn't expected, but couldn't deny that I liked.

After the last photo, I gave Julia a final squeeze before stepping back. She was glowing. Rosy cheeks from the cold and laughter, Brad's arm slung casually around her shoulder.

It felt strange, seeing her like this. She was settled. Happy. With two kids who called her "Mom." She had this perfect little family, and there I was, standing beside Tyler, wondering what my life was supposed to look like.

"Oh my gosh, don't be a stranger," Julia said, pulling me from my thoughts. "We have to do lunch soon. It's been way too long."

I waved as they walked off, Cara skipping at Julia's side, Chase perched on Brad's shoulders. "Definitely! I'll text you," I called, but the words felt like they were hanging in the air as a tightness knotted in my stomach.

Tyler leaned in, his voice low. "You went to high school with them?"

"Yeah." I swallowed the lump in my throat. "I remember when they started dating. They were that couple, you know? The ones everyone figured would make it."

He laughed, his eyes softening. "Yeah, every high school has one of those. Guess they proved everyone right."

I watched them weave through the crowd, laughing, a real family. One that belonged to each other. And for a second, a pang hit me in the chest. It was one thing to imagine people having the picture-perfect lives you always thought you'd want. But it was something else to see it in person.

To see Julia as a mom and Brad as a dad, with their little humans tugging at their sleeves and calling them "Mom" and

"Dad." It was everything I thought I might have had with Marco.

But here I was, standing with Tyler, feeling something shift inside me. It felt... different.

As they disappeared into the crowd, Tyler's voice cut through my thoughts. "You okay?"

I shrugged, trying to sound casual, but my voice was soft. "Yeah. Just... weird, seeing old friends who've settled down like that. It's a different kind of life."

He nodded. "I get it. One day, you think you have this vision of what your future's gonna look like. And then, out of nowhere, it's not there anymore."

His words hit too close to home, but he added quickly, "But that doesn't mean it's gone for good."

I smiled up at him, trying to push the heaviness away. Then, on impulse, I grabbed his arm and yanked him toward the Christmas tree. "Let's take a selfie."

He looked surprised, but after a beat, he laughed, leaning in as I snapped a picture. His arm slid around my shoulders, and for a second, everything felt easy. Simple. Like the Christmas lights twinkling around us were wrapping us up in this moment.

Tyler's voice brought me back to reality, his gaze searching mine. "Lena?"

I forced a smile, trying to keep it light. "Come on, Mr. Assistant. We've got more photos to take."

But as we moved on to the next family, my mind was still lingering on what I'd just seen. Julia, Brad, and their kids—it reminded me of what I'd almost had with Marco. What I thought I wanted. And now... well, I wasn't so sure anymore. I could still slip into the fantasy of it, but something about it felt off.

As Tyler guided a group of kids into position, joking with them until they burst into giggles, I felt a warmth that had nothing to do with the holiday magic around us. Maybe the life I thought I wanted wasn't the life I was meant to have.

By the time the sun dipped below the horizon, casting a soft, rosy glow over the snow, I was starting to believe that maybe this wasn't such a bad place to be.

"You must be famished. How does dinner at Smoke's Pub sound?" I asked, glancing over at him.

He flashed that smile of his, and my heart did an annoying little flip. "Carrying this reflector is surprisingly a lot of hard work. That sounds great!"

As we walked toward the pub, the evening felt... calm. Easy. Like something I could get used to.

We slid into a booth, and I met his gaze. For the first time in forever, I didn't feel like I had to be on. Like I didn't need to hide behind my sarcasm or make light of everything.

After we ordered, the moment stretched out, and I finally spoke. "I don't talk about this often, but I think... I know I'm finally ready to."

He leaned in, eyes soft and focused on me.

"I went through a lot this past year," I started slowly. "The wedding, leaving Marco... but what I never talk about, even to myself sometimes, is the abortion."

I took a breath, trying to steady myself. "The pregnancy wasn't planned, and Marco—he didn't handle it well. He pressured me, and I wasn't ready to fight him on it. So, I didn't handle it well either. But afterward... I was hollowed out."

Tyler didn't look away, didn't flinch. He just listened. "That's... heavy, Lena. I'm so sorry you went through that."

I nodded, swallowing down the ache. "It took me by surprise, how much it affected me. It was like I lost something I didn't know I wanted until it was gone. And now, I think...

I know I want kids. Someday. With the right person. Someone who wants to build that life with me."

I looked up, suddenly feeling exposed. "Sorry, that got real heavy."

He shook his head, his hand warm over mine. "Don't apologize. That's honest. That's life."

And for the first time in a long time, I let myself believe it might actually be okay.

The words slipped out before I could stop them, and I instantly regretted it, but the moment was too perfect to ignore. "What about you?" I asked. "Do you… ever think about having a family?"

He sighed, deep and long, like he'd just pulled that emotion out of a place he hadn't visited in a while. My curiosity couldn't stay quiet, even though I probably should've known better. He stared at our hands for a moment, as if weighing the words he was about to say.

"I did, once. With Carrie. We had plans. Well, not really plans, but we had ideas. Then… the car accident." He paused, and I swear the rawness in his eyes almost knocked me out. "She didn't make it. And somehow, I did."

I felt a tug in my chest. "Oh, Tyler…" I couldn't help it. I reached for him, instinctively, like I was supposed to make it better.

He gave me a weak smile that was more of a sad, defeated twitch. "It took me a while to realize it wasn't my fault. For a long time, I felt like I lost more than just her. I lost my shot at a normal life. But, you know... Now I've started to rebuild. New house, new job... I'm finding my footing."

I swallowed, feeling the weight of his words. "You've been through so much," I whispered, honestly not knowing how he made it this far. "But you're here. You made it through all of it."

"Barely," he muttered, a bitter half-smile on his face. "But yeah, I'm here. And hearing you talk about wanting a family... I get it. I really do. I thought I wanted it, but now I'm still figuring out what that means for me."

I nodded, letting the silence stretch between us. It was the kind of silence that wasn't awkward. Just comfortable, full of a strange kind of understanding. Both of us, two hot messes trying to figure out what the hell came next.

After dinner, he walked me to my car. It was like we weren't quite ready to let go of whatever quiet, unspoken connection had bloomed between us tonight. Snowflakes were drifting down, lazily spinning through the air like the universe was trying to tell us something important.

Tyler opened the door for me, his smile warm enough to melt every inch of ice around me. "Thank you, Lena," he said, his voice low and genuine. "For tonight. For opening up. I know it wasn't easy."

"No. Thank you." My voice was quieter than I intended, barely a whisper. "I don't think I've felt this close to anyone in a long time."

We stood there, neither of us ready to break the spell. Then, without warning, like I had no choice, I found myself leaning in. His breath brushed against my skin, warm and steady, and he closed the distance between us, his hand cupping my face so softly it was like my heart might just melt right out of my chest.

When his lips met mine, it was everything and nothing like I expected—soft, careful, and somehow... like it had always been meant to happen. Time slowed, the world around us faded, and all I could focus on was him.

I braced myself on his shoulder, leaning just a little closer, not even realizing I wanted it so much until it was happening.

Eventually, we broke apart, but he didn't move his hand from my cheek. I felt his thumb brush lightly over my skin, and when I looked up at him, I saw it in his eyes. The same thing I was feeling—something new, something quiet and beautiful, unfolding between us.

"You should get inside," he murmured, voice reluctant. "It's cold."

"Yeah…" I whispered, but I didn't move. I wasn't ready to end it yet.

His smile deepened, and there was something in the look he gave me that made my heart race and my head spin all at once. It was like he was telling me everything without a single word. And yet, nothing made sense at all.

"I wouldn't mind talking more at my place," I said, somehow bold in that moment. I didn't even surprise myself with the suggestion, but I did kind of surprise myself by how sure I was about it. "Would you like to do that?"

He didn't even hesitate. "Absolutely."

***

As I locked my front door behind us, Tyler's gaze never left my face. His eyes, those intense ice-blue orbs, seemed to see right through me, stirring emotions I hadn't felt in a long time. I felt my cheeks flush under his scrutiny, a mixture of desire and vulnerability washing over me.

"Lena," he whispered, his voice deep and raspy, sending shivers down my spine. "I want you." His words were a confession, a release of the unspoken tension that had built up over the weeks.

I took a step towards him, my heart pounding in my chest. "Me too, Tyler. But I... I need to know..." I paused, searching for the right words. "Are we doing this? Are we finally giving in to what's been between us?"

He closed the distance in a heartbeat, his hands cupping my face with a gentleness that belied his muscular frame. "We are, Lena. I'm not letting you go again and I want to show you now how you make me feel." His thumbs brushed my cheeks, sending sparks of desire coursing through my body.

I leaned into his touch, my eyes fluttering closed as I savored the sensation.

His lips brushed mine softly, a gentle exploration that sent a jolt of electricity through my veins. His kiss was a perfect blend of hunger and tenderness, leaving me breathless and wanting more.

I responded eagerly, opening my mouth to invite him in, and our tongues danced in a passionate embrace.

Withdrawing from the kiss, Tyler trailed his lips and tongue along my jawline, down my neck, his breath hot against my sensitive skin. His hands roamed over my body, his touch both reverent and possessive, as if he couldn't get enough of me.

I arched into him, my skin on fire, my hands threading through his dark hair, urging him closer.

He untucked my sweater from my jeans, his fingers skimming the bare skin of my waist, making me shiver. "You're so beautiful, Lena. I want to touch every inch of you." His voice was hoarse with desire, sending a thrill through me.

I giggled, a nervous release of the tension building within me. "We don't have to rush. We have all the time in the world." But even as I said the words, I knew I wanted him, needed him, with an urgency.

He chuckled softly, his breath tickling my ear. "I don't want to rush, but I also don't want to waste a single moment.

I've been dreaming of this, of you." His hands found the hem of my sweater and lifted it over my head, leaving me standing before him in just my lace bra and jeans. I blushed.

He grabbed the hem of his shirt and pulled it up over his head, dropping it somewhere near my sofa as I took his hand and pulled him in the direction of my bedroom.

His eyes roamed over my body, taking in every curve, his expression a mixture of awe and raw desire. "You're stunning," he breathed, his voice thick with admiration.

His hands returned to my waist, fingers sliding beneath the waistband of my jeans, his touch sending tingles down my legs as we walked to my room.

I gasped as he hooked his thumbs into the sides of my jeans, slowly drawing them down my legs, his eyes never leaving mine.

I stepped out of my jeans, stranding them in the hallway. I stood before him in just my bra and panties, feeling both bold and vulnerable.

His eyes darkened with desire as he took in the sight of my bare legs and hint of lace panties. "You're killing me, Lena," he growled, his voice strained. "I want to taste you, touch you everywhere." He dropped to his knees before me, his hands gliding up my thighs, pushing the crotch of my panties aside.

I gripped his shoulders, my breath coming in short gasps as his warm breath caressed my inner thighs.

His hands continued their exploration, squeezing my buttocks, and causing me to moan with pleasure. Tyler's fingers danced along the edges of my lace panties, teasing me, before slowly sliding them down my legs.

I was now completely exposed to his hungry gaze.

We made it to my bedroom where he was able to quickly remove the rest of his clothing.

His eyes locked with mine, a silent communication of the raw desire we shared.

I laid back on my bed and his hands returned to my legs, gently parting them. He kissed the skin on the inside of my ankle, then moved up my calf, knee, and thighs until I felt his warm breath on the sensitive skin between my legs.

"You smell so good," he whispered, his voice hoarse. His tongue traced a path along the inside of my thighs to the warm wetness between my legs, sending shockwaves of pleasure through my body. I arched my back, gripping his hair as he teased my bud with the tip of his tongue, bringing me to the brink of ecstasy.

"Tyler, please..." I pleaded, my voice a breathless whisper. I was on the edge, desperate for release, but he seemed intent on drawing out my pleasure.

He chuckled against my sensitive flesh, the vibrations sending me into a frenzy. "Not yet. I want to savor every moment." His tongue delved deeper, exploring me, his fingers joining in to tease.

I was on fire, my body trembling with the effort to both reach my climax and at the same time hold it so that I could enjoy it at the same time as him.

Just as I thought I couldn't take it any more, he moved up my torso, blazing a trail up to my mouth, his tongue never leaving my body. When he finally reached my lips, I tasted myself on his tongue, a heady mix of desire and satisfaction.

As we tumbled together on the bed, our kisses grew more feverish, our hands frantically working to rid each other of our remaining clothes. Tyler's strong body pressed against mine, his erection hard and insistent against my thigh.

"I need to be inside you, Lena," he groaned, his voice raw with need. His hand found my core, his fingers slipping inside me with ease.

I arched into his touch, my body on the brink of explosion. "Tyler..." I moaned, my voice thick with desire.

He positioned himself at my entrance, his eyes seeking mine. "You are mine."

"Yes. I want to feel you inside," I begged, my hands pulling him closer.

Just as Tyler began to thrust into me, a loud knock on the door startled us both. We froze, our eyes locked in confusion and desire.

"Lena, it's me, Marco! Please open the door, we need to talk!"

Tyler's eyes widened in recognition, and before I could process what was happening, he pulled out of me, getting up to grab his clothes.

"I'll... I'll leave you to it. We can... talk later." He rushed into the bathroom, leaving me lying on the bed, my body throbbing with unfulfilled desire.

I heard the front door open and close. *Damn it! His key!*

Then, Marco's voice filled my house. "Lena, I know you're hurting, but let's talk so we can make it right. Please, give me a chance."

My heart sank, knowing that Tyler must have overheard Marco's plea. I wanted to call out to him, to explain that Marco was my past and he was my present, but the words stuck in my throat. I was torn between the man who had ignited a fire within me and the one who was pleading for a second chance.

As Marco's voice continued to echo through the apartment, I'd stumbled out of bed and picked up the articles of clothing that trailed from my bedroom to my front door, getting dressed along the way.

When I entered my living room, I saw Marco and then looked down at my sweater on the floor.

"You can't just walk into my house anymore Marco," I said, picking up my sweater and pulling it over my head. "Please leave my key."

"I want us to talk and work things out," he said again. "Please. Talk to me."

I was about to answer him when Tyler walked into the room from behind me.

"I'll leave you two alone," he said as he passed me. He was finishing pulling his shirt down and brought a hand up to smooth his hair.

Tyler approached the front door. When he passed Marco and reached for the doorknob, he looked back at me. He opened his mouth to speak, but closed it instead.

I walked over to Tyler at the door and as he was about to close the door behind him, I stopped him.

"Tyler. Please stay."

Chapter 18: Tyler

I stood in Lena's doorway, Marco just a few feet away, and felt like I was holding my breath, like I was in the middle of a traffic jam and couldn't get out.

My pulse was hammering in my chest, the emotions coming at me in a rush. Frustration, confusion, and more than anything, the overwhelming need to figure out what the hell was going on and why she'd asked me to stay.

Part of me wanted to turn around, bolt for the door, and avoid the impending trainwreck that was watching her give him another shot.

But her eyes kept me rooted to the spot. Hell, I couldn't look away, even though my gut was screaming at me to do exactly that. There was a small part of me—tiny, maybe even ridiculous—that held onto the hope that maybe she'd asked me to stay because she was choosing me.

Lena took a breath, glancing back and forth between Marco and me, her shoulders straightening like she was gearing up to say something important.

I braced myself, arms crossed, leaning against the door.

"Marco..." She paused, her eyes flicking to mine before going back to him. "I need to say this. It's long overdue."

I had a bad feeling about this. I could tell she was about to rip open some old wounds, and I wasn't sure I was ready to bleed out in front of both of them. But I kept my mouth shut and let her talk.

"Marco, I'm sorry... for everything." Her voice was steady, but there was a weight to it, like she really meant it. "Leaving you standing at the altar was the biggest mistake of my life. The foundation of our relationship was our friendship. And doing what I did was shitty. It's something I'll always regret putting you through."

I could see it. Marco's face lit up like a goddamn Christmas tree, and I swear, the sight of it made my stomach twist into knots. It didn't sit right with me. I was pissed. She was apologizing for something they'd both screwed up, but the way she was saying it? It felt like she was dumping the entire blame on herself, and I couldn't stand it.

And it was starting to sound like she was going to forgive him. Was that what this was? Was I just an unwilling witness to their happy reunion?

"For a long time, I thought you were my future, Marco. I thought you were everything I needed." She let out a breath, tucking a strand of hair behind her ear. "We had good times. Great ones, even. And believe me, I loved you. I loved you so much."

I hated hearing her say that. Hated how my chest tightened at the thought of them. I couldn't even tell if she was being real or just trying to soften the blow.

Marco's jaw clenched, fists tightening at his sides. "You loved me? So that's it?" His voice was raw, like he was on the edge of begging. "You're just ready to give up on us because of... one mistake? I mean, we both went through that loss, Lena. We both did."

Lena nodded slowly, her expression softening. But she didn't back down. "It wasn't just one mistake, Marco. It was everything after. Being pressured to move on before I was ready, to act like it was no big deal. But it was a big deal for me. It changed how I see myself and what I want. I want a family, Marco. I want that more than anything. And I'm ready for that life that I want to start."

Her eyes finally found mine. There was something there, something that made my chest tighten, and I felt the air in my lungs disappear.

"And I won't settle for less than that, not anymore."

Her words hit me like a ton of bricks. She was serious. She was done with him, with whatever they'd had. There was no turning back from this.

Then she looked at me again.

"Tyler…" Her voice was softer now, almost hesitant, but her gaze held mine.

I swear my stomach flipped.

"I don't know what we'll be or where we're going, but I want you in my life. I can't promise what that'll look like, or that it'll be easy, but I know this is something we need to explore, whatever happens."

Shit. She was really saying it. She was putting herself out there. And I wanted to pull back, tell her it was too soon, that this was too much. But I couldn't. Her eyes—the way she looked at me—stopped me cold. She was serious.

Marco's expression went from hope to something darker, harder. He was pissed. I could see it building, but there was a strange calmness in his eyes too. Maybe he was finally getting it.

"So that's it then?" His voice was tight, bitter. "After everything we've been through, you're just done with us? Lena, I thought you were still figuring things out. I thought..." He shook his head, looking between her and me. "I thought we were giving ourselves some time so we could find our way back to each other. I know I hurt you, but haven't we both?"

Lena's eyes softened, but she didn't back down. "Marco, I know that what happened with us must have changed you too. But this isn't just about what we went through together. This is about what I want for my future, what I need in a relationship. And I know now that I don't want to be the person I was when we were together."

She glanced at me again, and the air felt thick with everything unsaid. Then she turned back to him. "I can't be the partner you want me to be, not anymore. I know that now."

Marco ran a hand through his hair, looking away, letting out a hollow laugh. "So, you're just going to throw everything away... for what? Him?" He glared at me, his face twisted with anger and disbelief. "This isn't real, Lena. You can't expect to build a life with someone you just met, someone who doesn't know you like I do."

That stung. He was right about one thing. I didn't know her like he did. But there was something in me that told me that was a good thing. I wasn't her past. I wasn't the guy who hurt her. And I sure as hell wasn't going to be the guy who let her down.

Lena's voice was quiet, but her resolve was unshakable. "It's not about knowing every piece of someone's past. It's about believing in what's possible." She took a step closer to Marco. "And right now, the future I see—the one I want to try to build—it's not with you."

Marco's face fell. He let out a long breath, defeated. Then he looked back at me, his expression unreadable, before turning back to Lena. "Fine. It's your loss. Don't come crawling back when you change your mind."

He grabbed his keys, and for a second, I thought he might say something else, but instead, he dropped her spare key on the table. With one last, bitter look, he gave me a nod. "Good luck with this train wreck."

And then he was gone, leaving us standing in the silence that hung between us. It was freeing, but it was heavy too.

The weight of everything—everything that had been said, everything that was left unsaid.

As soon as Marco was gone, I felt a mixture of relief and anticipation. Relief that the tension and drama of the interrupted moment had passed, and anticipation for what would come next with Lena.

She must have seen the uncertainty on my face because she took a step toward me and placed her hand on my chest, just over my heart. "Tyler, stay," she said softly, her brown eyes searching mine. "Let's not worry about the timing or what our families will think. Tonight is about us and what we want. We can't keep denying this connection between us. I know I can't. We can save the talking for tomorrow."

Her touch sent shivers through my body, and I nodded, unable to form a coherent sentence in that instant. I wanted her, and I knew that waiting any longer would only torture us both. This was our chance to explore what could be, and I wasn't about to let it slip away.

She stepped closer, and I wrapped my arms around her waist, pulling her gently against me. Her soft curves fit perfectly against my body, and I breathed in the sweet scent of her hair, a mixture of vanilla and something uniquely hers.

My hands moved down to cup her firm ass, lifting her slightly so that our hips pressed together, and I could feel the heat between us.

Lena's eyes closed as she leaned into me, a soft moan escaping her lips. "I've wanted this since the day I met you," she whispered.

"Me too," I murmured, my mouth finding hers in a hungry kiss. Our tongues danced together, and I tasted her sweetness. My hands explored her body, sliding up her back to tangle in her long, wavy hair, pulling her closer as if I could absorb her into me.

Breaking the kiss, she trailed her lips along my jawline, nipping at my ear, sending shivers down my spine. Her hands moved to my chest, slowly unbuttoning my shirt, her touch sending sparks of desire through me.

I helped her remove it, breaking away briefly to let it fall to the floor, before pulling her back into my embrace.

Her hands roamed over my chest, sending waves of pleasure through me.

I tilted her head up to capture her mouth again, our kiss hungry and desperate. I backed her toward the bedroom, never breaking our lip-lock, our need for each other taking over.

As we reached the bed, I lowered her down, following her, never wanting to break our connection. Our kisses grew more intense, and I felt her hands tugging at my belt, eager to explore more of me. The feel of her soft skin against mine as she slid her hands under my shirt was almost too much to bear.

I pulled away slightly, looking into her passionate eyes, and slowly removed her sweater, reveling in the reveal of her lacy black bra and the smooth skin beneath. I traced my fingers along the straps, enjoying the way her breath hitched as I did so. Then, I lowered my head to capture a tight peak between my lips, earning a sharp intake of breath from her.

Her hands pushed me back playfully, and she sat up, a mischievous glint in her eye. "My turn," she said, her voice husky with desire. With quick movements, she undid my belt, sliding the leather from the loops with a soft swish. Then, her hands moved to the button and zipper of my pants, her fingers brushing against my already hardening cock through the fabric.

I groaned at her touch, and she smiled, slowly lowering the zipper, revealing the boxer briefs beneath. Her eyes filled with desire as she took in the bulge that strained against the fabric.

With a swift movement, she hooked her thumbs into the waistband and I helped her pull my boxers and pants down in one go, leaving me completely exposed to her hungry gaze. My dick twitched with anticipation, and I felt a bead of sweat trickle down my spine as she took me in, her eyes flicking up to meet mine.

"You're so hard," she whispered with pleasure, reaching out to gently stroke my length.

I hissed at her touch, my eyes flapping closed as I enjoyed the sensation. "Lena—" I started, my voice hoarse with need.

"Shhh," she said, placing a finger on my lips. "Let me enjoy the view for a moment."

I opened my eyes to see her biting her lip, a look of pure lust on her face. She leaned down, her long hair tickling my thighs as she kissed the inside of my knee, teasingly avoiding my aching cock.

"Tease," I growled playfully, reaching down to tangle my fingers in her hair.

She looked up at me, her eyes sparkling with mischief. "You have no idea," she said, a wicked smile playing on her lips. With that, she leaned forward and took the tip of my cock into her warm mouth, swirling her tongue around the sensitive ridge.

I groaned loudly, as sensations exploded through me. Her mouth was hot and wet, and she took her time, exploring every inch of me with her tongue and lips. Her hands cupped my balls, massaging them gently as she bobbed her head up and down, taking more of me into her mouth with each stroke.

"Fuck," I gasped, my hands tightening in her hair. I could feel the pleasure building within me, my entire body tensing as she expertly worked me with her mouth. I wanted to last, to prolong this feeling, but her skills were too much for my restraint.

She hummed in response, sending vibrations through my shaft, and that was all it took for me. "You have to stop or else…" I warned, my hips bucking slightly as I felt the climax rising within me.

She didn't slow down; instead, she took me deeper, sucking hard as her hand pumped the base of my cock. I felt the explosion rock through me, my eyes rolling back as I cried out her name.

She continued to milk me through my orgasm, her mouth and hand working in tandem to draw out every last drop.

Finally, I was spent, and she released me with a soft pop, looking up at me with a satisfied smile. "That was just the beginning," she promised, her breath hot on my sensitive skin.

I pulled her up to straddle me, needing to taste her, to return the favor. My hands explored her body, sliding down to cup her ass.

She moaned into my mouth, her hips rocking against me as she ground herself on my erection. I could feel her heat through the thin lace of her panties, and I wanted nothing more than to be inside her.

With a quick movement, I rolled us over so that I was hovering over her. I hooked my fingers into the sides of her panties, slowly sliding them down her legs, my eyes never leaving hers. When she was completely bare beneath me, I took a moment to appreciate the view, her breasts heaving with each breath, her hard nipples begging for attention.

Leaning down, I took one tight peak into my mouth, sucking gently as my hand slid down her flat stomach to the soft and warm world between her thighs. I teased her, tracing light patterns on her skin, enjoying the way she gasped as I got closer to her core.

"Tyler, please," she begged, her hands threading through my hair. "I need you."

I wanted to give her what she needed, what we both needed. With gentle fingers, I found her bud and stroked it slowly, feeling her wetness coat my fingers. Her hips bucked against my hand, and I inserted one finger into her tight heat, loving the way she moaned and gripped my hair.

"Oh yes!" she panted, and I obliged, adding a second finger, stretching and pumping her as I kissed a trail down her body, my tongue leaving a wet trail on her skin.

I inhaled her musky scent, before placing a soft kiss on her inner thigh. She tasted even better than she smelled, and I savored her flavor as I continued to finger her, building a fast, hard rhythm.

Lena's breath quickened, and I knew she was close. Her hips bucked against my hand, and her juices coated my fingers. "Tyler, taste me," she stammered, her eyes fluttering closed as she gave in to the pleasure.

Hearing her say that sent me over the edge, and I lowered my mouth to her, sucking her into my mouth as my fingers continued to thrust inside her. She cried out, her body shaking as her orgasm washed over her. I didn't stop, wanting to draw out her pleasure as long as I could.

She bucked her hips, riding out the waves of bliss, before finally collapsing back on the bed, a satisfied smile on her face.

"Oh my—" she started, but I cut her off with a deep, passionate kiss.

We lay there, tangled together, our hearts pounding and our breaths coming in ragged gasps. I wanted to stay like this forever, wrapped in her arms, feeling her soft skin against mine.

As my lids became heavy, questions flooded my mind as I drifted off to sleep. *What now? Do we tell our families about this new development before Christmas Day? Or do we keep this secret a little longer, giving us time to figure out what we truly wanted from each other?*

Chapter 19: Tyler

"Good morning," I whispered, my voice all raspy from sleep and the previous night's… activities. Yeah, I wasn't winning any awards for smoothness.

Lena stirred, her brown eyes fluttering open. She smiled at me, her lips still swollen from the kind of kissing that'd have made a priest pray for forgiveness. "Morning," she purred, all low and sultry, like she had a secret. "Did you sleep well?"

I chuckled, leaning in to kiss her. Because, you know, I didn't have enough reasons to want her closer. "I think you know I didn't get much sleep." Not with that distraction.

Her smile widened, like she was proud of herself. Then she playfully bit my lower lip. "That was the idea."

And, well, yeah. It was a good idea. We definitely spent all night proving how much we were into each other.

After Marco's little interruption, we'd been eager to pick up where we left off. And we didn't just pick it up. We ran with it.

The chemistry between us? It was the kind that set off fireworks and made me forget how to breathe for a few seconds. The desire between us was ridiculous. It burned away every ounce of doubt I had about this, whatever this was.

Lena's hands roamed over my body, tracing the muscles on my chest and abs, and man, it made me shiver like I was hooked up to a live wire.

I couldn't keep my hands off her either. Everywhere I touched, she responded, and it was a hell of a lot more than just physical.

Our passion built, and we made love with such intensity I swear it left us both gasping for air and—let's be honest—probably a little bit proud of ourselves.

Now, as we lay tangled up in sheets, I felt something that hadn't been there within me in a while. Peace.

Christmas was always this mixed bag for me. Like it came with a side of guilt. And not the fun kind. But next to Lena, in her bed? Yeah, there was joy, maybe even a little hope.

"You know," I said, breaking the silence and running my fingers down her bare arm, "I never thought I'd say this, but I'm actually looking forward to Christmas this year."

Lena raised an eyebrow. "Really? Mr. Grinch has rediscovered the holiday spirit?"

I laughed. "Something like that. I guess you could say you've brought some reason back into my season."

Her cheeks turned that soft pink, the kind that made her look like she wasn't used to being complimented, but damn, did I like seeing it. "Glad I could help..." She trailed off, her voice fading a little.

"We're making new traditions now," I said. "And I have a feeling this Christmas is gonna be one to remember."

Of course, Lena's phone buzzed on the nightstand and ruined the moment. She groaned and grabbed it. "It's Mia. She and my mom need my help with some last-minute stuff for tomorrow's family feast."

I sighed. "Guess that means you've got to go."

"Yeah, but don't worry," she said, leaning in for a quick, hot kiss. "I'll make it up to you. If I don't see you later, we'll catch up tomorrow at the family feast."

I nodded, already feeling that empty space in the bed where she used to be. She slipped out of bed, and I watched her get dressed, graceful like she had somewhere important to be.

"I'll see you later, Tyler," she called out, grabbing her coat and heading for the door.

"Yeah, later," I mumbled. My voice felt like sandpaper, still raw with desire. I wanted to pull her back into bed, but I knew she had stuff to do.

The door clicked shut, and I was alone again, my mind already replaying last night like some old, scratched-up record.

Lena's lavender lotion still clung to her pillow, like a reminder that I wasn't just some guy she hooked up with. We shared something, and it wasn't just physical. It was deeper. More real. Hell, I couldn't explain it, but it felt like we were supposed to find each other. Like maybe we could actually heal together.

I got up, dressed, and made my way home.

My place was quiet, like it always was. The fridge hummed in the background as I made my coffee, staring out at the backyard like it had answers to the things I couldn't explain.

I ran a hand through my hair, looking around the room, feeling... something. Sighing, I set my cup down and glanced at the framed photo on the shelf. The one with Carrie and me.

She'd hated the idea of a couple's photo. Thought it was cheesy. But I talked her into it. Because, hell, how could I resist that smile of hers? The way her eyes sparkled? It still felt so real. Like she was right here with me, smiling at me.

And just like that, the weight of Christmas Eve came rushing back. The accident. Her loss. It hit me like a punch to the gut.

The grief was like an old friend. I let it settle in, letting my eyes close as my hand pressed against my chest, feeling the tightness.

Three years. Three years without her laugh, the way she'd brush her fingers against mine when no one was looking, the life we'd planned… and then it was gone.

Guilt punched me in the gut. I survived. But I didn't deserve to.

I forced myself to get up, keeping busy with the stupid little tasks around the house—tightening door handles, changing light bulbs—anything to distract myself. But no matter what I did, every damn thought came back to Carrie.

Even here, in this house she'd never seen, I could feel her. She'd loved Christmas, loved everything about it. The lights. The carols.

I straightened a throw on the couch, and I remembered how she used to tuck the blankets just right. "Snug as a bug in a rug," she'd say, laughing as she made sure the corners were perfect. She'd have loved this place.

In the kitchen, I opened the cupboard to grab a coffee pod and next to it was a half-empty box of tea bags. Carrie always had to have tea before bed, no matter how late we were.

"Helps me unwind," she'd say, pulling out the kettle and smiling at me. "You should try it, too." I did, because it wasn't about the tea. It was about her voice in the quiet. The warmth of her hand on mine.

My mom drank tea, too, so that's why it was in my cupboard. But staring at that box, the weight in my chest got heavier. Three years, and the memories still felt like they happened yesterday.

I could recall every detail of that night. The jokes. The plans. Up until the car slid, the crunch of metal, the smell of smoke…

I shook my head, closing the cupboard. I wasn't ready to go there again—not yet. But it would always be there, lurking.

I went to the window, staring out at the frost-covered backyard. Somewhere in the distance, a dog was barking, a reminder that life was still moving outside this house. People were going through their Christmas Eves with their families, laughter, and plans. And then there was me. Alone. With my guilt.

Carrie was the kind of person who made you feel like you were living, not just existing. She pushed me to go further, try harder, be braver. "Life's too short to sit on the sidelines," she'd say, nudging me when I was too cautious.

Her laugh was contagious. Her smile was like a damn sunbeam that couldn't be stopped. And maybe that's what I missed most. How fearless she was.

Even when life threw curveballs, she took them like a champ. She would've told me to get my shit together tonight, to be strong, to keep moving forward. She'd ask, "Why are you so busy feeling sorry for yourself when there's so much to be happy about?"

But here I was, standing alone in a house she'd never even set foot in, wishing I could hear her voice just one more time.

I moved into the living room, feeling the weight of her absence settle in my chest like an old friend.

I thought about the last gift I'd given her. A travel book wrapped in blue paper with a silver bow. She'd have laughed, jumped on me, and hugged the life out of me. And we would've gone on a trip that summer. But instead, all I had were plans that vanished in a heartbeat.

I dropped down on the couch, my head in my hands, thinking about all the trips we never took, all the things we never did.

But then there was something else creeping in this morning. Something I hadn't allowed myself to feel in a long time. Peace. Or at least the beginning of it.

I couldn't change what happened. I couldn't bring her back, no matter how many days and nights I spent torturing myself with memories.

But the strangest thing was, it didn't feel like she was haunting me. It felt like she was here, urging me forward.

"Be happy," she'd probably say, if she could. Not because she was forgotten, but because life's too short to keep looking backward.

I stood up from the couch and walked to the kitchen, needing to shake the past off, if just for a moment. I wasn't ready to dwell on the old shit. I was ready to focus on the present.

And suddenly, my mind jumped to Lena.

Lena. Somehow, in the last few weeks, she'd done what no one else had managed to do in years. She'd slipped past all my defenses. She'd started pulling parts of me out that I thought were dead and buried.

I didn't even see it coming. Not at first.

She was a damn hurricane of honesty and chaos, and she had this look. Like she could see straight through all my walls, straight into my soul. It was terrifying. And thrilling.

I washed my coffee mug, staring at the running water, my brain flicking back to that night at the Christmas fair.

Lena, snapping pictures of families, laughing, pulling me into all that warmth. I hadn't had fun like that in... ever. And she had this way of making everything feel a little lighter, a little brighter. Maybe even better.

And then last night—God, last night—when she said she wanted to feel something real. She pulled me closer, said the words like she was daring me to believe it. To believe in her.

I wanted to, more than I could admit. Even to myself.

I leaned back against the counter, taking a deep breath.

For years, I'd thought I'd be shut off forever. That part of me was gone. But then Lena came along, all messy and honest, and suddenly I was starting to hope again. Hope for things I'd stopped wanting.

When I realized I was smiling, I stopped, surprised. But damn it, it felt good.

Lena didn't come without baggage. Marco being Exhibit A. But there was something about her. Something that made me want to take on all that mess, wade through it, and come out better on the other side.

Hell, maybe I wasn't as dead inside as I'd thought. Because being around Lena made me want to try.

My thoughts drifted back to last night, and I felt that familiar rush of excitement building in my chest.

I thought about our first kiss, the one revealed everything. The spark between us. It had been pure, unfiltered desire. And it had set the tone for everything after that.

As I stood there with my mug, I felt that same rush of anticipation about what came next.

I glanced at my phone on the counter, my thumb grazing over the screen. I knew she was probably busy with Christmas prep, and I didn't want to interrupt, but damn it, I wanted to hear her voice. I wanted that connection again, that spark between us.

But a knock at the door yanked me out of my thoughts.

When I opened it, my parents were standing there. Mom in her coat, that familiar quiet understanding on her face, like she could sense exactly how I was feeling. Dad in his button-up shirt, khakis, and a burgundy sweater (thanks to Mom, of course), holding two grocery bags.

"I thought I'd check on you, sweetheart," she said, pulling me into one of those big, grounding hugs that I didn't know I needed until I was in it.

"Mom wanted me to bring you some food," Dad muttered, walking past us toward the kitchen, clearly already planning to watch the Iowa game.

My mom was a force of nature. She'd been my rock after the accident, sticking by me when I didn't know if I could keep going. These past few weeks, I wanted to be there for her, especially after the stroke. I wanted to share in the holiday stuff and make new memories. Not just live in the past.

We followed her into the kitchen, and she paused, glancing around at the photo on the counter. "How are you doing today?"

I really thought about it for a second before shrugging. "Better. I think."

I watched as she started emptying the shopping bags, totally unaware she was about to whip up a joyous Christmas Eve dinner. Not exactly a full-out holiday celebration, but hey, the woman had her charm. It was hard not to admire her determination, even if it made my gut twist a little.

I swallowed hard, thinking about Carrie. God, the thought of her still hurt like hell, even three years later.

"I mean, it still feels like it happened yesterday. Wish none of it ever went down, but... I'm learning to carry it differently, I guess."

I paused, searching for the right words that weren't just self-pity. "The guilt, it's not holding me down the way it used to. I know I didn't cause that accident. I know it wasn't my fault."

She nodded, her hand resting on my shoulder like a weight I actually didn't mind carrying. "Carrie loved you so much, Tyler. She wouldn't want you to carry that guilt around. Not for something you couldn't control."

A small smile crept up, but it felt like it didn't quite belong on my face. "Yeah, I know that now." I turned my attention back to the photo on the wall, the ache still there but not as suffocating. "Carrie would want me to be happy. To actually live."

"Ty, can you preheat the oven? 350 please." She handed me a small ham, like this was supposed to be some cozy family moment. "It's enough for the three of us."

We spent the next hour chopping, stirring, setting the table. Basically creating the kind of Christmas vibe that made my chest feel a little warmer than usual. It was a routine. One that felt familiar. Like I'd been doing it for years with her. And, oddly enough, it felt good. Comforting, even.

As I grabbed a potato and started peeling it, Mom turned to me, a glint in her eye. "So," she said, way too casually, "How are things with Lena?"

I froze for a second. The woman was relentless. I glanced over at her, but she didn't look away. She knew exactly what she was doing. I couldn't just ignore it, so I kept my eyes down, focused on peeling the potato. Damn thing wasn't cooperating.

Before the wedding, Mom had been extremely vocal about Lena. She made it crystal clear that she didn't trust her after the whole "left-her-fiancé-at-the-altar" drama.

But, well, things had changed. She'd proven herself to me when I couldn't even be there for my own mom after the stroke. So yeah, things were different now.

I set the peeler down, grabbed a knife to cube the potatoes, and sighed, deciding to just get this over with. "Honestly, Mom?" I looked her dead in the eye. "I've been thinking a lot about her. Lena's been more of a support than I ever expected."

I paused. God, this felt like the worst time to dive into this. But screw it, I was already halfway in. "She makes me feel... different."

Her face softened. And by softened, I mean she probably saw right through me. She put a hand on my arm, like she was trying to ground me. "I see the change in you, sweetheart. I can tell."

I shrugged, like I wasn't about to let the emotional thing hit me. "Being with her... it's like she brought a light back into my life. She's helped me let go of some of this... constant guilt. And the way she was there for you, that meant everything. I know it's still new, but I'm... happy. Actually happy, for the first time in a while."

Her eyes got all misty, and I swear, if she squeezed my hand any harder, she'd have crushed my fingers. "Hearing that, honey... it's the best Christmas gift I could ask for. Just seeing you happy again." She chuckled, sniffled, and then added, "That and my health, of course."

I laughed with her, but there was a flicker of something on her face—something worried. She hesitated, looking down at the table before meeting my eyes again.

"Something's been bugging me, Tyler." She fidgeted with her apron like it was somehow going to help her get through this. "I didn't tell you this before, but after my stroke, Lena came by to see me. And... I told her to stay away from you."

I blinked, trying to process. "Wait, what?"

She nodded, her face full of guilt. "Honestly, I know it was right after my stroke, so I was out of it. But I also thought I was protecting you. I didn't think you needed someone with her... complications. So I told her if she really cared about you, she'd keep her distance."

I stared down at the pile of potato peels, my brain trying to make sense of it. Lena had never mentioned it—not once. She'd been the one to hold it all together when things were falling apart. And my mom had told her to stay away?

I looked up at her, trying to process this new pile of guilt my mom just dropped on me. "What the hell, Mom?"

Chapter 20: Lena

The morning came slowly. Like my brain was trying to drag itself out of a fog of cinnamon-scented, Christmas chaos.

I blinked a few times, trying to shake off the sleep, and was met with Justin's sweet smile.

My childhood bedroom. The walls were a mess of nostalgia: high school photos, boy band posters that my mom had kept up for "reasons" (we don't talk about the reasons), and all the other clutter that screamed, "Hey, look, you're still my baby!"

"Good morning, Lance, Chris, Joey, and JC," I said to the posters, giving them an over-dramatic wave. "I've missed you. Even though, let's be real, Justin you will always have my heart." I blew him a kiss and smiled back at him, my favorite band member that I had a crush on for like 95% of my adolescence.

Then my phone buzzed from the nightstand, and oh, hello, reality. Two missed calls. Three unread texts. All from Tyler.

Excitement shot through me, but then, of course, my inner over-thinker kicked in.

Crap. I had been so wrapped up in baking and pretending to be a perfect, normal person around family last night that I didn't even notice my phone going off.

I opened his last message from late last night.

Tyler: I'll try you tomorrow. Merry Christmas Eve.

A small smile crept across my face, warmth pooling in my chest. Nice. It felt nice.

But then, the second wave of doubt rolled in. What the heck did he think when I didn't respond? Was he sitting there, phone in hand, thinking, "Well, this is it, Lena's finally done with me"?

Ha! Don't be ridiculous. He's not waiting around for me to call him. That would be absurd.

Tyler had been patient, supportive, and open since day one, and I hadn't exactly been the easiest person to deal with. Although I did hope he wasn't wondering if I was ghosting him again.

I quickly typed back.

Me: Good morning! Sorry I missed you last night. Things got a little crazy with family, but I'll see you soon!

I stared at the text, biting my lip. It felt a little rushed. Okay, it was rushed. But I wasn't trying to come off like a flake. I hoped he wouldn't read too much into it. Or worse, think I was brushing him off.

The second I hit Send, there was a knock at the door. Sharp, perky, way too excited for this time of morning.

Mia.

Before I could even think about responding, the door creaked open like she was on a secret mission to invade my privacy. Her head popped in, eyes wide like she'd just discovered the meaning of life.

"Are you up yet?" she whispered, her voice so full of energy it was like she'd snorted a line of Christmas cheer.

I pulled the blankets up to my chin, playing the "I'm so cozy, don't even try it" card. "Does it look like I'm up, Mia?"

But, of course, she wasn't having it. She barged in and launched herself onto my bed with the enthusiasm of a caffeinated squirrel. She hugged me so tight I thought I might actually suffocate, but I couldn't help laughing. It felt like we were ten years old again, and nothing had changed.

"Isn't this just like old times?" she squealed, wiggling her shoulders in a ridiculous, over-the-top way. "It felt like every day was a slumber party back then!"

I raised an eyebrow, fighting a grin. "Your memory's a little foggy, sis. We didn't exactly spend every day in perfect harmony." I nudged her with a playful shove. "And if you'd woken me up this early back then, you'd probably be nursing a bruise on your arm right now."

She laughed and pushed me back gently, and we both collapsed into a fit of giggles. I swear, we were like two kids who forgot they were supposed to grow up.

"Okay, maybe it wasn't all rainbows and butterflies," Mia admitted, shifting around on the bed like she was setting up camp. "But I still say it was the best. And, you know, you're kind of the best sister ever."

I nudged her affectionately. "Aw, you're only saying that because I haven't kicked you out of my bed yet." I paused, softening a little. "But I do miss those days… minus the hair-pulling fights and the six a.m. wake-up calls."

We could hear Mom's familiar clatter coming from the kitchen. The sound of pots and pans, the fridge opening and closing, and Christmas music humming in the background. The scent of coffee and cinnamon wafted up, and I knew for sure she was already knee-deep in holiday prep. Like, mom-level Christmas prep that could probably feed an army and still have leftovers for next week.

Mia's eyes went wide. She sat up like she'd just had an epiphany. "We'd better get down there to help Mom before she recruits Dad to chop onions again. You know he'll be useless the rest of the day if he does."

I threw the covers off with a dramatic sigh, feeling that weird mix of warmth and holiday excitement bubble up inside me. "Alright, let's go rescue Christmas dinner."

Later, the doorbell rang, and my heart did this weird little flip in my chest. Like it was trying to be all dramatic. As if I was in some rom-com.

I quickly shuffled through the chaos of the house, dodging the furniture and trying not to trip over the mountain of presents that overflowed from under the tree.

I was hoping—praying—that it was Tyler.

But no. It wasn't. It was Thomas and his family.

Mia practically tackled him when she saw him, jumping into his arms like she hadn't seen him in a month instead of, like, one day.

The whole gang started exchanging hugs and "Merry Christmas"es, and I was half-heartedly ready to head into the family room when—ding dong—the bell rang again.

This time, Thomas opened the door, and Tyler was standing there, framed against the wintry sky like he just walked out of some holiday ad.

A genuine smile lit up his face. Warm, familiar, Tyler. And of course, right behind him were his parents. Laughter spilled in like the sound of a perfectly edited holiday movie as everyone shared hugs and holiday cheer.

Meanwhile, I stood there, tugging at the hem of my sweater and trying to not look like a total nervous wreck. I felt like I was getting ready to take a pop quiz, except the quiz was about my feelings for a guy who the last person most people in this house wanted me to be getting all fluttery over.

Mia shot past me like a rocket, swinging the door open with a grin that could have lit up the entire street. "Merry Christmas!" she chirped, pulling Tyler's mom, Lorraine, into a bear hug. Meanwhile, Thomas was shaking hands with Tyler's dad, looking all nice and grown-up.

I hung back for a moment, letting the warmth of the scene wash over me. And then Tyler stepped through the door, his tall frame filling the space like it was custom-made for him.

His smile was the same polite one he always wore. Polite, but slightly distant. In his eyes there was a little hesitation, like he wasn't quite sure what to do with me. And, naturally, that just added to the weird, messy swirl of feelings in my chest.

"Hey, Merry Christmas," he said softly, his voice cutting through the noise of the crowd. Which, of course, made my heart do that weird flip thing again.

"Merry Christmas to you too," I managed, my voice feeling a little more breathless than I'd have liked. I wanted to say something else. Something like, I'm sorry I didn't call you back last night, I didn't mean to leave you hanging. But before I could get my act together, my mom swooped in, arms open wide.

"Oh, Lorraine! You look wonderful!" Mom exclaimed, wrapping Tyler's mom in a hug that could've been heard across the room.

Lorraine did look great, considering she'd had a stroke less than two weeks ago. She was already up and moving around with a cane, looking like she was on her way to the "holiday recovery poster child" award.

Then Mom shifted her attention to me and Mia. "Girls, come on. We've got work to do before we can even think about sitting down to eat," she said, like she was about to call in the full cavalry.

"Right," I muttered, shooting a glance back at Tyler. He gave me a tiny nod. But his expression? Still guarded. Like he wasn't sure if we were on the "just friends" page or the "oh, I'm a little bit into you but I'm pretending I'm not" page.

Mia groaned dramatically from beside me. "It's Christmas, Mom! Can't we just relax for five seconds?"

"You can relax after dinner's on the table," Mom shot back with a grin, already ushering us toward the kitchen like we were on some sort of culinary assembly line.

I followed, feeling the weight of obligation settle in like an unwelcome guest. But I couldn't help it. I glanced over my shoulder, trying to catch another glimpse of Tyler.

He was talking to my dad now, nodding politely while Dad launched into his spiel about all the sports on TV today.

So, yeah, Tyler was still being polite. And still acting like he wasn't quietly wrecking my insides with that damn look of his.

"You can obsess about Tyler later," Mia teased, giving me a shoulder bump like she thought she was so clever. Well, I thought she wasn't.

I turned to glare at her, feeling my cheeks heat up like I'd just been caught Googling *How to tell if a guy secretly likes you* for the third time this week. "Says the girl who married the guy she stalked," I shot back, because two can play the sass game, thank you very much.

Mia grinned, completely unbothered, and without missing a beat. "Stalking is a survival of the fittest trait that runs in our family. Ensures our line continues!"

She wiggled her eyebrows dramatically, like this was some kind of Darwinian mic drop.

"Ah, yes," I deadpanned, gesturing vaguely at her like I was introducing her to an audience. "Mia Sheridan, evolutionary biologist and pioneer of modern stalking-as-mating-strategy theory. Proudly carrying the torch for creeps everywhere."

"Exactly," she chirped, completely unfazed. "You're welcome."

I rolled my eyes, but a laugh slipped out anyway. God help me, she had a point.

As I poked at the green bean casserole like it owed me money, the nerves from earlier made a dramatic comeback. Like that one ex who always "forgets" their Netflix login is still yours.

Something was definitely off with Tyler. He hadn't seemed mad, exactly, but there was this...distance in his eyes. And not the romantic, "gazing off into the sunset" kind. More like the "don't come any closer, I'm building an emotional moat" kind.

I shook my head, determined to focus on the casserole. Green beans, cream of mushroom, crispy onions. Easy. Not brain surgery, Lena. I slid the dish into the second oven and gave myself a mental pep talk. *Stop overthinking. He's probably just grumpy. Or tired. Or both. Or—oh God, he hates me now, doesn't he?*

Of course, every time I tried to focus, my eyes kept wandering to the doorway. I'd stir the filling, glance up. Arrange the onions, glance up. Is this what dogs feel like waiting for their owners to come home? Because if so, I owe every golden retriever an apology.

There wasn't exactly time to pull Tyler aside for a heartfelt, "Hey, are we good, or did I do something unforgivable like microwave fish in a shared office space?" The kitchen was a tornado of last-minute prep, and before I knew it, people were setting the table and jockeying for the best seats.

Plates clattered, silverware jangled, and I stood there clutching a spatula like it was a security blanket.

Guess I'm waiting until after dinner to figure this out, I thought, as the knot in my stomach tightened.

Perfect. Just what I needed to pair with green bean casserole—crippling anxiety as a side dish.

***

Christmas warmth filled the house. Or, at least, it was supposed to.

I was sitting at the dinner table surrounded by family and pretending to be part of a Hallmark card, but diagonally across from me, Tyler was serving full-on Polar Express vibes. Cold, distant, and maybe a little haunted.

Last night and this morning had been a disaster of missed calls and rushed texts. Now, he couldn't even look at me without the kind of energy that screamed "I'm totally fine, except I'm not, but let's just ignore it and die slowly inside."

And yet... I kept catching him sneaking glances when he thought I wasn't looking. Except his smile didn't quite hit the "warm and fuzzy" mark. It was more "smiling for a driver's license photo after three hours at the DMV."

Great, Lena, I thought, stabbing my knife into a napkin like it owed me money. *This is exactly what you wanted: a holiday full of awkward tension and cryptic stares. Merry freaking Christmas.*

To my left, from the end of the table, Mom clinked her glass to get everyone's attention. Her official "Mom Smile" lit up the room.

"Before we dive into this feast, let's share our 'reason for the season.' I'll start, and then we'll go to my left."

Oh, good. An emotional icebreaker. Perfect for awkward eye contact and revealing deeply personal truths.

And, I get to be last. A stroke of luck, because I'd get to hear all the reasons and just pick a piece of what everyone else said and make it my own.

Mom raised her glass of sparkling cider like it was champagne at the Oscars. "New traditions, new faces, but the same love that binds us. My reason for the season is simple. Being surrounded by all of you. Cheers to family, love, and many more Christmases like this."

It was sweet, and yes, I did tear up a little, but I blamed the overly aggressive cinnamon floating in the air.

Mia went next, grinning like she'd been waiting for this moment her entire life. "I'm thankful for my wonderful mother- and father-in-law for raising Thomas to be the amazing man he is."

Cue Thomas, looking as smug as a guy who'd just scored the game-winning touchdown. He raised his glass to my parents. "Ditto!"

Wow, I thought, side-eyeing Mia. *She gives a heartfelt speech, and he throws out a rom-com one-liner. Couple goals.*

Christmas dinner had officially turned into a live episode of *This Is Us*, and I wasn't emotionally prepared.

Lorraine, Tyler's mom, took her turn in the whole "reason for the season" speech circle. She started slow, her hands folded neatly in her lap, her gaze flicking between Tyler and me. My palms were already sweating. Not a great sign.

"I remember, from the day he could walk, that Tyler had a light in his eyes," she began, her voice slow, soft, and steady, like she was telling a bedtime story. Her lisp was barely noticeable.

"As a little boy, he lit up my world. He was curious and kind, always bringing the people he loved closer together. I think all of us here have felt that light from him, one way or another."

Cue Tyler, who leaned back in his chair and smirked. "This is not meant to be an hour-long speech about 'your wonderful baby boy" and how you think I'm the 'best son ever.' You're supposed to say something short about your 'reason for the season. Keep it snappy."

She patted his arm like a queen indulging her court jester. "Hush, sweetheart. I'm getting there."

Everyone laughed, because of course we did. Lorraine and Tyler's banter was pure Christmas card material.

"And when he met Carrie, that light only got brighter."

Oh no.

The air shifted. Like, Black Friday at Walmart shifted.

The table went silent, and Tyler stiffened beside her. She didn't say the rest, but we all felt the weight of what wasn't spoken. The accident. The grief. The unbearable loss. Lorraine's hand found Tyler's, giving it a squeeze.

"But," she continued, her voice catching just a little, "these past few weeks, I've seen something change. The light is back. You're finding your way back to yourself, and it's been such a blessing to see."

Her eyes flicked to me.

Wait, what?

I glanced to my mom to my left. Then to Thomas's dad to my right. I thought maybe she was looking at one of them.

Then my eyes went back at Lorraine, who was still looking directly at me.

She smiled softly. "The day I had my stroke, quick thinking saved me from something far worse. There was a calm, steady presence, and I know I wouldn't be as healthy as I am today if that person hadn't been there."

The room filled with murmurs of "so glad you're okay" and "Lena, you're amazing," but my brain was stuck on whether this was real life right now.

Then Lorraine dropped the bomb.

"I have to admit something terrible," she said, her expression shifting to serious. "I had a bad opinion of you before I met you."

Oh. No.

"I'd heard about what happened at your wedding, and I didn't want you anywhere near Tyler. I judged you without knowing the details, which, I now realize, were none of my business." She gave a tiny, sheepish smile.

"And when I was recovering in the hospital? What's the first thing I told you as soon as I could speak?" Her gaze softened, but her words hit like a freight train. "'Stay away from my son.'"

The collective gasp around the table was so loud it could've powered a small city.

"I know," Lorraine said, shaking her head. "Terrible of me. But I see now how wrong I was. That light in Tyler's eyes is because of the hope and joy he's found again. And I'm pretty sure that's because of you."

The words hit me like a snowball to the face. She *was* talking about me.

"I'll never apologize for wanting to protect my son," Lorraine added, her voice unwavering, "but I was wrong to stand in the way of his happiness. So, Lena, I want you—and everyone here—to know that you are my reason for this season."

The table burst into applause, glasses raised in cheers, and before I could fully process what was happening, Lorraine stood and started walking toward me.

Oh, God. She was coming in for a hug.

I scrambled out of my chair, fumbling like I'd forgotten how hugs worked. She wrapped her arms around me, her graying hair tickling my face as she whispered, "Thank you, Lena."

I managed to whisper back, "Thank you, Lorraine," while trying not to ugly cry in front of the entire family.

She pulled back, holding my arms as her smile grew even warmer. "I want you both to be happy. Truly happy. If you can find that in each other, then I couldn't wish for anything more."

I glanced at Tyler, who was watching us with an expression that was somewhere between disbelief and something softer, something... hopeful.

The applause and chatter swirled around me, but all I could hear was Lorraine's words echoing in my head.

When Lorraine let me go, I sat back down, feeling a little like I'd just survived a surprise pop quiz on emotional vulnerability.

But before I could even reach for my glass of wine to recover, her voice cut through the holiday hum like a record scratch.

"Lena, what are you doing?!"

Cue my internal panic button.

My chest tightened as my brain went into overdrive. *What did I do? Did I accidentally offend her during the hug? Am I sitting wrong? Did I inadvertently destroy Christmas?*

A million self-deprecating insults whizzed through my head. *Thoughtless. Messy. Self-indulgent. You can't even sit in a chair properly, Lena? Nice job.*

I swiveled around in my seat, fully prepared to apologize for...whatever. But Lorraine's face broke into a good-natured grin, and she pointed at me.

"What are you doing in my chair?" she asked, like she was scolding a toddler caught stealing cookies. "Get up and sit in your own!"

Oh. OHHH.

The relief hit me like a wave, and I felt my shoulders drop a full inch. *Crisis averted. We're not canceling Christmas after all.*

Everyone burst into laughter as I stood up, muttering a quick, "Well, guess that's my cue," and made the walk back to my new seat next to Tyler, grabbing my wine glass along the way.

As I sat down, my mom chimed in, her voice carrying that unmistakable "Mom's about to put you on the spot" energy. "Okay, Lena, it's your turn. What's your reason for the season?"

Oh, no. No, no, no.

Suddenly, the whole table felt like a spotlighted stage, and I was the unlucky understudy shoved on at the last second. Every pair of eyes zeroed in on me like I was about to deliver a keynote speech at the UN.

I cleared my throat, stalling as I grabbed Lorraine's wine glass to have it passed back to her.

"First, uh, let's make sure this gets to its rightful owner. Can't have wine-stealing and chair-stealing on my holiday rap sheet."

Everyone chuckled politely, but now all I'd done was buy myself approximately seven seconds of breathing room. *Great job, Lena. Time's up. Now say something profound and seasonal before the crowd turns on you.*

I set my wine glass down with a dramatic flair, clasping my hands in front of me like I was about to reveal the cure for a broken heart. "Well," I started, leaning into the moment, "first, I'd like to thank everyone here for coming to my TED Talk."

The table broke into light chuckles, and I took it as my cue to keep rolling. "But seriously, my reason for the season? It's kind of... all of you."

I glanced at Mia, who gave me one of those supportive nods that sisters are contractually obligated to provide in times of public speaking-induced panic.

Then my eyes flicked to Tyler. He wasn't laughing like the others, but there was a faint smile teasing at the corners of his mouth, and—oh God—was my heart doing a tap dance right now? Cool. Totally cool.

"This year has been a ride," I continued, gripping the edge of the table for dramatic effect. "And not the fun kind, like a Ferris wheel where you're all "Ooh, look at the view!"

No. It's been the kind where you say, "Yeah, I can handle this!" And then it spins you upside down, and suddenly you're begging strangers for Dramamine."

That got a bigger laugh, and I smiled, warming up now. "My life has been utter chaos. I know that. But through it all, my family, and apparently my extended family now—"

I gestured toward the Smiths and Sotos with my wine glass.

"—have shown me what it really means to have a safety net. The kind of people who catch you even when you're free-falling. And screaming in an ugly cry voice, mind you."

I paused for effect and locked eyes with Lorraine, the woman who had just dropped a truth bomb big enough to shake the table centerpiece. "And speaking of catching people. Lorraine. Wow. That was... Let's call it a Hallmark mic drop, shall we? Thank you for saying what you said. You didn't have to, but you did. And honestly? I'm still processing the fact that you just called me your reason for the season. I mean, I didn't see that plot twist coming, but here we are!"

The table fell quiet, and I could feel my throat tightening up. Oh, no. No tears, Lena. We're not doing this. "So, yeah. My reason for the season is love. Not just the mushy and sappy kind, though hey, I'm not knocking it. But the messy, complicated, 'we-don't-always-get-it-right' kind of love. The kind that keeps showing up even when it's hard. That's what this year has been for me. And sitting here, surrounded by all of you, I realize just how lucky I am to have it. So... thank you."

I ended with a quick, self-deprecating bow and sat down to applause. Mia was wiping her eyes, my dad looked like he was auditioning for a toothpaste commercial, and when I glanced at Tyler, he was looking at me like I'd just invented Christmas.

I leaned toward him, muttering under my breath, "Wow. How do I follow that? Oh, wait. I don't have to. Phew!"

Tyler smirked, his voice low and teasing. "I'm not sweating it. I'm surprising everyone with the all-encompassing, 'Ditto!'"

When Tyler stood up, I just knew that we were about to get a show.

The way he adjusted his sweater like he was channeling a presidential candidate before a debate? Already killing me. Add the smirk? He was in full Tyler-mode. Equal parts smartass and surprisingly deep. And damn it, I was here for it.

"My fellow Americans—and Worley-Soto-Sheridans—it's an honor to be here tonight," he started, his voice mock-serious.

I bit my lip so hard I was in danger of drawing blood.

"I know what you're all thinking," he went on, holding up his hands like he was preemptively calming the crowd. "'Tyler, how do you look this good in a sweater? Is it genetics? Witchcraft?' The answer is yes."

Mia snorted so loudly I had to shoot her a "pull it together, woman" look. Which, let's be honest, was ironic because I was barely holding it together myself.

"But seriously," Tyler continued, his tone shifting into deadpan territory, "When it comes to the whole 'reason for the season' thing, I've been thinking long and hard. Like, 'skip leg day for it' hard. And I've decided my reason for the season is… carbs."

The table lost it, and yeah, okay, I did too. I mean, how could I not? This man just turned the most sentimental moment of the night into comedy hour.

"Yeah, carbs," he said, warming up now like he had a whole audience to entertain. "Rolls, mashed potatoes, stuffing, sweet potatoes covered in so much marshmallow it could qualify as a dessert. Oh, and pie. Lots and lots of pie. Carbs are the glue that holds this holiday together. You think we're here for gifts? Nah. We're here for stretchy pants and the sweet embrace of a food coma."

Mia's laugh turned into this wild cackle, and I had to fake an unimpressed head shake. But inside? Fully impressed. I mean, who could make carbs sound this profound?

Then Tyler held up a finger, pausing like he was about to drop the wisdom of the ages. "But here's the thing about carbs. They're not just food. Oh no. They're comfort. They're warmth. They're what you reach for when life sucker-punches you, and you need something solid. Preferably smothered in gravy."

Okay. So that hit me. Like, in the feels.

And yeah, I know he was technically talking about mashed potatoes, but the way he said it? Pretty sure he wasn't just talking about mashed potatoes.

He let his gaze sweep around the table before landing on me, and suddenly I felt like the only person in the room. "And you know what? That's what you all are. You're the carbs of my life. The warm, comforting, stretchy-pants-worthy people who've reminded me what it feels like to laugh. To feel something other than guilt or pain. To let the light back in."

Oh, great. Now my chest was doing this fluttery thing, like it couldn't decide if it wanted to cry or spontaneously combust. I caught Lorraine wiping her eyes, which, honestly? Same.

"These past three years have been… a lot," Tyler said, his voice quieter now, softer. "But sitting here tonight, I know I've got more than enough reasons to keep showing up. To keep trying. So yeah, my reason for the season is carbs… and the people I'm eating them with."

And with that, he sat down, casually dabbing at his cheek with a napkin like he'd just delivered the Gettysburg Address. "Thank you all for coming to my TED Talk. Now pass the sweet potatoes. I've got a metaphor to eat."

I laughed so hard I almost knocked over my wine glass. Leave it to Tyler to take something as ridiculous as carbs and turn it into a speech that was hilarious, heartfelt, and way real.

As the applause and chatter died down, I caught his eye. And just like that, it hit me. Carbs might be Tyler's reason for the season, but he was quickly becoming mine.

THE END

Sofie Daves

About the Author

Sofie Daves

My life used to circle around my three kids' schools, sports, and activities. Now that they're older and don't need me to bring snacks after the game, I've decided to take the next logical step … write steamy romance novels.

I love game nights, Happy Hour, book club, golf, paddle boarding, and hiking near home in the Sierra Nevada foothills, California. I probably drink more than I should, enjoy too much time with girlfriends, and over-indulge in "ME" time. But, I'm lucky that the LOVE of my life for over 30 years sticks around and my kids still call me Momma. Oh, and my dogs love me!

Learn more at SofieDaves.com

Sofie Daves

Books By Sofie Daves

Love, the Enemy Series

Love, the Enemy, Prequel

Tell Me the Truth, Book One

Take Me Away, Book Two

Capitol Avenue Series

This Time, the One, Book One

This Time, Together, Book Two

Holiday Series

The Twelve Days of Ex-Mas

Messy Little Christmas

Sofie Daves

https://www.SofieDaves.com

https://www.facebook.com/SofieDaves

https://www.amazon.com/author/sofiedaves

https://www.goodreads.com/SofieDaves

Printed in Great Britain
by Amazon